NO FEIGN NO GAIN

A Sonic Sleuths Series Mystery

CARRIE ANN KNOX

NO FEIGN NO GAIN

Published by Xotolithic Press 2020
Suffolk, VA, U.S.

Cover Design by James T. Egan
of Bookfly Design

ISBN: 978-0-9990032-3-7

ONE

It was just . . . sitting there. Looking at me.

My eyes focused and refocused on the tiny black box, trying to make sense of what I was seeing. But the comprehension just wasn't coming.

Then I heard the shrill scream from behind me. A scream to make your heart stop for an instant. A scream of holy terror.

And that was the moment I was certain that the bloody, sawed-off finger snuggled innocently in velvet was not, in fact, my mind playing tricks on me.

I leaped away from my desk, heart pounding.

My coworker Grant, the apparent source of the abnormally high-pitched shriek, stood in the doorway. He gaped at me, manicured hands up in a defensive pose. "Quinn. What *is* that?"

"I . . . I don't know."

"You *don't know*?" His face told me he was equal parts incredulous and horrified. "Well, how did it get here?"

I shook my head, beginning to feel a strange sense of numbness. "No idea. It was just . . . here." My voice was weak. *Am I in shock?*

Grant inched toward the box and leaned in carefully, as if it might bite him. "Is it real?"

I waited with baited breath as his face lowered toward the desk.

Suddenly he gagged and jumped back to safety again. "I *smell* it. Oh my god, it's real."

And then he promptly collapsed.

***

"*Very* exciting," Sloan said, her piercing blue eyes wide with interest. "So, did you touch it?"

Her reaction to my traumatic story wasn't going quite as expected.

I leaned back in my seat, my fingers scratching anxiously at the cracks in the vinyl booth at our usual hangout, Joe's Diner. "Of course not." I narrowed my own blue eyes back at her. "It's evidence."

"True." She pursed her full lips. "But evidence of *what*, exactly?"

I shrugged. "Your guess is as good as mine. Just a normal workday . . . and then there it was, just sitting there." I grimaced picturing it. "Waiting for me."

"Fascinating." She flipped her long, dark hair over her shoulder and propped her chin in her hand. Her delicate features clashed with her fierce intensity as she gazed back.

"That's one way of looking at it," I muttered.

"The only way." She leaned in further. "So let's figure this out, shall we? Where could it come from? An angry patient?"

My eyes widened further at the thought. I shook my head. "Doesn't seem likely with my patient base. No crazies I can think of."

2

"Well, I know they complain hearing aids cost an arm and a leg." Her grin was sly. "Maybe one of them got confused?"

"Very. Funny." *Not.*

She ignored my unamused response and turned serious. "Twisted secret admirer?"

I recoiled. "Jeez. I sure hope not." I instinctively reached for my hair, pulled back in a long, loose braid. I fidgeted nervously with the dark end.

"You're right. Let's just put that one aside for now." Her eyes narrowed as she considered. "How about some kind of I-Know-What-You-Did-Last-Summer situation? The beginning of some kind of sick blackmail for all your past misdeeds. I mean, how well do I *really* know you?"

"*Such* a comedian." Clearly she wasn't taking this as seriously as I was. "Actually," I continued, giving her the side-eye, "how do I know it wasn't you, starting some new little scavenger hunt? If this is your sick way of getting me back into investigating, I'm warning you. It's *not* going to work."

My first and only case assisting in Sloan's private investigating work had resulted in a few quiet arrests and a profound sense of satisfaction. Turned out, I loved the PI game. But my involvement almost jeopardized my internship, and thus my future career as an audiologist. So I had resolved to stay out of the sleuthing game for good.

Or . . . at least until graduation.

Sloan shook her head. "Severed digits are definitely not my style. Promise. But I bet your butt it *would* work. I know you're dying to know the story here."

Excruciatingly so. I sighed. "Well if it's not from you, then I want nothing to do with it. Maybe it wasn't even *for* me. Just left in the office randomly, on what happened to be my desk."

Her sarcasm was biting. "Right. Just one of those chopped-off-finger-left-behind situations. Nothing to see here."

I sighed again. *Hate it when she's right.*

"Anyway, let's get back to the details." Sloan looked waaay too into this. "I wonder, was it fresh and squishy, or hard as a rock?" She mock-squeezed the air with her fingers. "Could be stiff from rigor mortis. Or maybe even frozen. I *really* wish you'd touched it."

I rolled my eyes. "Not trying to implicate myself in whatever this is, thanks."

Sloan waved her hand dismissively. "Oh, please. There are ways. I'll have to teach you how to poke a dead body correctly. Or in this case, a body fragment. Didn't think we'd be up to *that* lesson quite so soon."

I cringed. "Maybe we skip that lesson altogether." I quickly realized my mistake when Sloan's face brightened just a tad. "*When* we're having lessons," I blurted. "Which we're most definitely not."

"Fine." She shrugged, flippant. "So what about Grant?"

"You're not going anywhere near my coworker with spy-craft lessons. He's nosy enough as it is."

"No, the little surprise on your desk. Do you think it could've been him, trying to scare you off? You *are* about to take the job he wanted."

After revealing my awareness of his fraudulent history, my co-intern Grant had pretty badly flubbed his shot at a coveted permanent audiologist position in our medical center. It hadn't been pretty. I liked to think I would've landed the job regardless of his humiliation, though.

"Pretty bizarre way to get across that message, don't you think?" I shook my head. "And you didn't see him faint. He turned pretty green. Not very likely he could've handled it." I smiled just a little picturing his reaction. That had almost been worth the terror. "And where would he possibly get a dismembered finger, anyway?"

For that matter, where does anyone get such a thing?

"Good point. But I still don't trust that guy."

I shook my head, trying to let it go. "I'm sure it's just some sick prank. Maybe it's not even real." I attempted to convince myself of my own words.

"Probably right." Sloan sat back in her seat and raised an eyebrow at me. "But I assume it *looked* pretty real?"

I hesitated, then nodded reluctantly.

"Good." Sloan leaned in, her face lighting up again. "Then let's talk specifics. Was it skinny like a woman's finger, or a thick, meaty sausage?"

"Definitely not thin and delicate. Likely a man's, I'd say."

"Hairy?"

"Mmm. Couldn't tell. It was face-up."

"So you saw a fingerprint, then?"

I shuddered at the image burned in my brain. "Definitely."

Sloan seemed pleased. "At least we can find out pretty fast who it's from, then. There are worse body parts to receive."

Gross. "So then there's no need to play the guessing game. We'll find out soon enough." I sat back, satisfied. Then froze, rethinking. "Wait, will they even tell me?"

"Likely not." Sloan shrugged. "But I don't know when *that* would ever stop us."

A male voice intruded. "I honestly don't know when *anything* would stop you."

We both looked up to realize a passerby had stopped next to the table. The early-thirties man gazed down at Sloan with a boyish grin, brown eyes twinkling.

Sloan returned a surprised smile. "Christopher?"

His grin widened. "Funny running into you here."

She narrowed her eyes at him playfully. "Is it, though?"

He gave a hearty laugh. "No comment. So how are you? Still playing your spy games?"

"What else would I be doing?" Her smile was devilish. "How's the accounting world?"

"Just as stimulating, I'm sure."

Sloan laughed back. "Right." She motioned toward me. "This is my friend Quinn."

He moved quickly to offer his hand, oozing well-bred charm. "Very nice to meet you."

"Likewise." I immediately felt like an intruder when his eyes quickly returned to Sloan. "Think I'll run to the restroom." I scooted out of the booth and hurried away.

I took my time in the back, hoping to run out the clock on their chat. But upon emerging, I rounded the corner and I saw it had apparently not been long enough. Christopher hopped out of his seat across from Sloan as I approached.

"Alright, I won't keep you guys." He focused intently on Sloan, one eyebrow raised hopefully. "Any chance you want to continue this conversation later? Over dinner, perhaps?"

She studied him for a brief moment. "You know what? Sure."

Christopher's eyes lit up. He watched as she dug a business card from her bag and scribbled on the back.

"Just call me," Sloan said as she handed it to him.

He tried to contain his grin, but failed miserably. "You got it." He gave me a little wave and turned away. We watched him stroll out of the diner.

"Sorry that sort of hijacked things," Sloan said.

I waved it off. "No problem. Old friend?"

6

She thought for a second. "Sort of. I worked for him on a case a while back. Pretty nice guy."

"Seems like it. Did you date or something?"

She shook her head. "Turned him down. I was newly single. After Joel. He was alright, but I wasn't really into dating anyone like him at the time."

I knew the sudden death of her fiancé Joel a couple years before had left her uninterested in relationships, leaving her dating interest solely focused on macho guys she knew deep down were only of short-term potential for her. "Well he does look pretty clean-cut, so that would rule him out. At least no suit and tie, though."

Sloan looked mock-serious. "Now that's where I draw the line."

I laughed. "So does that mean you're interested in dating someone like him now? Like you said, he's a nice guy. Seems maybe stable and reliable, even."

"Who knows? I guess dinner with a stable, reliable guy doesn't sound so terrible these days." Sloan shrugged. "Gotta start somewhere."

TWO

I knew I shouldn't have agreed to it.

Lunch with Grant was sure to be a non-stop pop quiz regarding the, err . . . mysterious package from the day before. He was such a busybody. And I had really been trying to get my mind off it.

But in the spirit of continuing improved relations, I had accepted the meal invite from my hypercritical coworker. Ever since I had stood up to him several months before, revealing I was in on his little secret, he had changed his tune considerably.

Not that his little jabs in the guise of compliments had stopped entirely. But they had definitely lessened. He had evolved to become almost pleasant.

Almost.

Clearly, he didn't want me to spill the beans about his real background I had uncovered. All of his lies about growing up poor and on the streets, when he really came from wealth. Or maybe it was that he actually respected me for standing up to him. Either way, I would take whatever niceties I could get.

When a break in our schedules came, we rushed to a small deli known for quick service only a few doors down from our downtown Norfolk office. He held the door politely, his refined upbringing finally starting to show through a bit. But the change began as soon as the hostess left the table.

"I heard they searched the whole building last night. To make sure no one was *murdered*." Grant's excitement was palpable.

My eyes widened. "Murdered? Did they find anything?"

He slumped back, disappointed. "No. Nothing yet. But could you imagine, the rest of the body stuffed in there somewhere? Like, behind a wall or something? How *scandalous*."

I did not share his enthusiasm for such gory possibilities. I gave a weak nod. "That would be pretty crazy."

"To put it mildly." He leaned forward and lowered his voice. "But I have to wonder . . . why you? Why did they leave a body part on *your* desk? Whoever they are."

Definitely been wondering the same thing. I shrugged. "I'm sure it's just some random prank. Maybe someone dug it up in the graveyard or something."

"Right. Exactly." Grant tried to wave it off, as if he had no interest. "Probably doesn't mean anything, really."

I nodded and tried to come up with a quick subject change. "So what do you think—"

"*But*," Grant interrupted suddenly, index finger stabbing the air, "what about the note?" His eyes glowed with interest. "You *have* to tell me what it said."

I hesitated. "Note?"

"Yeah." He studied the confusion on my face, narrowing his eyes. "Well, surely there was a note, right? I mean, who leaves something like that with not even a note?"

I shrugged. "Beats me. But there was definitely no note, I promise."

Grant looked visibly disappointed. *Crushed, even.*

His overeager interest in what he perceived as the delicious drama of it all was really starting to grate on my nerves. I made a show of opening my menu and studying intently, ready to finally move on from this confusing, disturbing subject. "So what are you going to get?"

It was as if he hadn't heard me at all. "You know, they could've just as easily left the finger on *my* desk." He seemed to be shaking off his disappointment just fine now. "Actually, it was left in our shared office, so it makes sense it could really be for both of us. Don't you think?"

I sighed. *This is going to be a long lunch.*

***

Thirty minutes and a million what-ifs later, we handed our credit cards to the young red-haired server to settle our bills. The afternoon would be beginning back at the office soon. And I had successfully made it through my first voluntary tete-a-tete with my former adversary. It hadn't been *so* bad, really.

But when the waitress returned to the table, she had a funny look on her face. "I'm really sorry. But do you happen to have . . . another card you could use?" Gingerly, she laid the little bill tray in front of Grant and kept her eyes on the floor.

He glanced to double-check the credit card and gazed back skeptically. "Is there a problem?"

"Declined," she whispered, her voice barely audible.

"That's weird. But I'm sure it was just an error." He shoved the tray back toward her. "Why don't you just try it again."

The girl's face flushed meekly as she slid it back. "I tried three times. I'm sorry."

Grant pulled out his wallet and fumbled, his downturned face hiding his own reddening cheeks. "Um. Fine. Hang on."

Former enemy or not, I wanted to put him out of his misery. I swiped the bill from his tray and handed it to the waitress. "No problem. Just add it to mine."

Grateful for an ending to the awkwardness, she hustled away with the tickets.

Grant forced himself to look up at me. "Well, I'm sure you're used to this sort of thing." He scowled. "But I'm not."

I opened my mouth to retort, then thought better of it. I settled for a shrug instead. "I'm sure it's just a mistake."

"You're darn right it is," he said bitterly. "But don't worry, I'll call the company. Somebody's head will roll."

I started gathering my things. "I'm sure it will. But it's fine." I smirked at him playfully. "I'm the one that knows you're definitely good for it, remember?"

"Right." He studied my face for a second before standing. "I'll just get you next time, then."

Next time? *Who knows . . . maybe we could actually end up as friends after all.*

***

"Ummm, Quinn?" Grant poked his head around the doorway to our office, just as I was shutting everything down for the day. "There's . . . something you need to see."

It had been a long afternoon, and I was more than ready to get home. My Grant-drama tolerance had pretty much reached its limit for the day. I continued packing without looking up. "I'm headed out. Can we see it tomorrow?"

"I . . . don't think you'll be able to miss it. Just wanted to give you a heads up."

I straightened quickly, stomach sinking. "Heads up on what?"

He avoided my eyes, looking everywhere but at me. "You should just come with me."

What now? I grabbed my bag and followed him down the hall. He seemed agitated, if not excited. I offered a nervous laugh when we arrived at the front of the practice. "What, you find the owner of the finger or something?"

"No." Grant's return look was strange. "But maybe they did?"

We swung open the heavy double doors to reveal a large swarm of reporters surrounding the entrance. They turned at the movement and pounced immediately, crowding closer. They were all shouting at once.

Bizarrely, they seemed to be shouting *my* name.

Surprised, I let go of the door and it clicked behind me. I immediately felt trapped. Microphones were shoved in my face from every direction, with cameras creeping in behind. I was quickly surrounded, and all the voices blurred together in my confusion.

After my initial shock, I was able to tune into a few of the excited questions.

"Was the takedown part of your plan the whole time?"

"How did you know what they were up to?"

"Were you involved with the crime ring before you assisted the police?"

Takedown? Police assistance? I was clueless. I hadn't been involved in anything in months. My one and only foray into investigating was long over. I had been staying clear of the game. Completely.

I gazed uncomprehendingly at the reporters, all vying for the first response. "I . . . I don't understand."

My meek reply only seemed to encourage them. The

shouts became louder, but no more coherent. More questions. Alarm bells were sounding in my head.

No one was explaining what was happening. But I knew it couldn't be good.

I turned to catch sight of Grant, left behind by the press of bodies encircling me. Our widened eyes met over the crowd. He gave me a shrug, looking just as confused as I was. He watched silently with fascination.

Just as tears of panic began to prick my eyes, the crowd was jolted by a deafening honk. A car horn from just behind the horde, blaring continuously. Everyone turned en masse toward the sound, parting the crowd just enough for me to recognize the dark sports car making all the racket. And the smiling girl in the driver's seat. *Sloan*.

Everyone quieted for a moment, processing. Then someone in the crowd yelled out.

"It's the other one!"

The tangle of bodies stumbled over one another in their rush toward the vehicle, leaving behind their clearly uncooperative subject. Sloan appeared utterly unfazed by the excitement as they surrounded the car.

"Ms. McKenzie! Ms. McKenzie!"

She kept her eyes on me. "Get in," she yelled.

I hustled to the passenger side and elbowed my way into the car.

Once I was buckled in Sloan leaned her head out her window, throwing some chum to the throng. "Sorry, guys. We have somewhere to be."

Her radiant smile was captured by dozens of clicking cameras. Then she gently stepped on the gas, sending reporters leaping out of our way.

I sighed into my seat as we escaped, relieved by the solace of the car. *People actually like this sort of thing?*

The appeal of celebrity was definitely lost on me. But Sloan had handled the situation with poise and grace, as usual.

I checked behind us to be sure we weren't being followed. Satisfied, I turned to Sloan for answers. "What in the world was that? What's happening?"

Her characteristic confidence fell away. She glanced over, concern edging into her eyes. "I'm actually not sure. All I know is a pack of them bombarded me at the office out of nowhere. I didn't stick around to find out why. Standing in front of rolling cameras is *not* the time to ask questions."

"But you knew they'd come for me, too?"

"Your name was being thrown around, so I snuck out the back and came to find you. Apparently, we've made the news in some way. And I don't like not knowing why."

I grimaced. "I don't like any of it, period. Do you think it's about the finger?"

Sloan paused. "Maybe. But there has to be more."

"Have you been into something lately I should know about? Are you in trouble?"

Sloan smirked. "Nothing more than usual."

I sighed. "That's not exactly reassuring."

She glanced over and saw the uneasy look on my face. "Really. Nothing that I know of. And definitely not anything that would bring you into it. Hard as I've tried, you've stayed away. So I'm as baffled as you are."

That's never good. "So then, where to?"

"My apartment will be safe. They shouldn't be able to find it. I keep my home address extremely private."

I perked up a little at the thought. *Private, indeed.* So private even I hadn't seen it.

THREE

"Now, don't get too excited," Sloan said as she pulled out her keys. "It's all boxed up for my move."

Move? It was the first I'd heard.

Sloan swung open the oversized metal door to reveal a high-ceilinged open space with weathered hardwood floors and giant paned windows. It reminded me of an expanded version of her office. She clearly had a thing for lofts.

I eyed the stacks of boxes littering the otherwise hiply furnished great room. "Going somewhere?"

She took in the room with me, then shrugged. "Just time for a change, I guess."

"More changes, huh?" I swallowed to loosen my tightening throat. "Somewhere close by, I hope."

Sloan threw her bag on the concrete counter in the small but modern open kitchen. "I don't know. One day I just started packing, ready to get out. I'm looking around, seeing what might pop up. Just want to go where the wind blows."

"Well, the wind better be blowing somewhere here in town. 'Cause you can't leave."

She laughed. "Don't worry, I'm not going anywhere. It's

only boys and living spaces I can't settle down with these days. I'm otherwise very grounded at the moment. And I'm sure you're partly to blame for that."

"Glad to hear it." I felt my shoulders relax a little as I took another look at the space. The dark woods and leathers were a little masculine but right up my alley. I felt a twinge of envy picturing my own spare little student apartment.

"Make yourself at home," she called, her head deep in the stainless steel refrigerator. "You know, I was thinking you could maybe move in here when I go. Gotta be a lot better than that postage stamp you call an apartment."

I let myself mentally drool over the idea only for a moment, then shook it off. No way I could ever afford it. "I have a postage stamp for a reason. And a lease. I'm fine where I am."

"I'm sure we could work something out. And I happen to know you have a short-term lease, up for renewal soon."

I shot Sloan a knowing look. I had definitely never told her that information. *Why doesn't it surprise me anymore?*

She returned a sly smile, fully understanding. "Besides, you'll be making the big bucks soon, right?"

"Ha!" I blurted. "That's a good one." I hadn't meant to sound quite that sarcastic. *Touchy subject.* "Next comes the student loans, until about . . . Oh, retirement, most likely. And that's if I'll even still *have* a job."

I paused, realizing the truth of my initially-joking words. I actually had no idea what was going on, or what it would mean. Dread stabbed at my gut.

Sloan ignored my dark musings completely. "Well, I'd hate to have to let some stranger in here." She placed two bottles on the counter and turned to sweep the room with her eyes. "Lot of memories here, that's for sure." Her eyes were soft and wistful, for just the briefest of moments.

Then she shrugged and dug noisily in a drawer, retrieving a bottle opener. "But I guess the search is on hold anyway, until whatever *this* is dies down."

I sighed. "Right." I collapsed onto the closest rich leather sofa, my mood continuing to sink. "Should we check the news, then?"

"Hudson's headed over. Says he has the scoop." She held up an enticing glass. "A little wine in the meantime?"

"Definitely."

Sloan busied herself with cocktails while I pondered her business partner. Hudson was still fairly a mystery to me. I knew he was dark-skinned, handsome in a buff, macho sort of way, and handled the security side of their business. And he had been in on the deception that kept me out of the loop during my first investigation showdown.

A reminder of that situation derailed my pity spiral. *A clue.* "You think this . . . whatever is happening . . . has anything to do with our little sting operation a few months back?"

Sloan headed into the room, drinks in hand. "Afraid so. If you weren't involved, it could really be anything. But your connection certainly narrows things down quite a bit."

Great. I took the offered glass and watched her pace around the room, my growing curiosity and anxiety fighting for control. If *she* was nervous, I knew I should probably be verging on terrified.

A loud pounding sound shook the door and made both of us jump.

"I know *that* bang." Sloan's expression lightened as she strode across the room.

She opened the door and Hudson waltzed in without a word, headed straight for the kitchen. His tight red athletic shirt hugged his enormous biceps and was soaked with what I assumed was profuse sweat.

Sloan closed the door and followed him. "You know you knock like a gorilla, don't you?"

"Take that as a compliment." He reached into the fridge and pulled out a bottle of water. "Gorillas are magnificent creatures."

We watched as he tossed the cap on the counter and began chugging, quickly draining the entire bottle in one long pull. He was out of breath when he slammed the empty bottle on the counter. "Whew," he exclaimed.

Sloan grabbed the debris and threw it in a nearby bin. "Good workout?"

He grinned back at her. "Nothing like it."

"Glad to hear it. But you can't come into the den like that. Why don't you pull up a stool?"

"No need to sit on my butt. I'm good." Hudson seemed to notice me for the first time and moved closer. "Quinn. Good to see you."

I gave a little wave, my mind racing with anxiety about his news.

Sloan jumped in anxiously. "So what do you have? The media just now find out about our run-in with Little Miss Overdose months ago? Is that why they're going crazy?"

Our one and only joint spy venture thus far had, some-what incidentally, uncovered a plot to facilitate a CEO's overdose in order to push through an underhanded com-pany takeover. Tragically, the man ended up dead—and it became our mission to expose those responsible, despite the risk to my career getting involved presented. The late CEO's wife was still awaiting trial for her misdeeds and thus far there had been no public knowledge of our par-ticipation. My education had been blissfully unaffected, with completion of my Doctor of Audiology degree only weeks away.

Hudson shook his head in slow motion as he stared at us, open-mouthed. "You really have no idea the shit-storm you two have created, do you? They did find out about that, yes. But only in the context of all the *other* arrests."

Sloan sank to the sofa next to me. Her voice was now smaller, distant. "Other arrests?"

"Yeah, from today. Dozens. Of most of the local mafia organization. A huge takedown of the whole network."

My eyes widened. There was that word again. *Take-down.* "But what does it have to do with us?"

"Are you kidding? You guys lit the match that started the whole thing burning. You're going to be heroes."

Heroes. My head was swimming. "Come again?"

"Look, when you two played your little game and got the president of Quandom to confess to conspiracy to murder her husband, there were ramifications. Big ones. They just took time to percolate."

I glanced at Sloan, wariness rising. "So this is about Carolyn Evans? The CEO?"

"That's where it starts, but definitely not ends." Hudson took another step toward the couch, looking excited. "Once you got her arrested, she made a deal to testify against the drug dealer she hired, in exchange for going easy on her."

"Of course," Sloan said.

"Right. That didn't surprise anyone." He raised his eye-brows. "But what people didn't expect is that then that punk dealer would squeal like a pig."

"On who, his boss? Salvatore?" The Italian restauran-teur's icy glare popped into my head and I shuddered.

"Sal, his buddies, underlings. You name it. He was look-ing at capital murder. I hear he rolled over every warm body he could think of in order to save his scrawny butt and get a lesser charge. He talked their ears off."

My eyes widened. "And that was enough? They arrested the whole operation on the word of that kid?"

"Not a chance." He shook his head. "But it *was* just enough to get the ball rolling. Once they had one inside man telling all his tales, it just kept moving up the chain."

Sloan looked skeptical. "How's that?"

"They've been working on these guys a long time. Deep-cover investigations. So in addition to the slinger's testimony, they had tons of evidence all lined up and ready to go. Years worth. Just waiting for the right time.

I glanced to Sloan. "And this was it?"

Hudson shrugged. "Guess it lit just the right fuse. Nobody had paid any attention to that little pipsqueak. He was in the room for all kinds of illicit activity." His chuckled. "But they sure noticed him once he started talking."

It was my turn to be skeptical. "So he starts naming people, and then the named guys just willingly hand over all their information?"

"Not exactly." He flinched. "But when the cops did their first quiet round of interrogations, the guys he fingered did start to get scared. They were sweating long prison stints, some of them life. And with the years of evidence piling up already, pretty quickly the whole organization started looking like it was going down one way or another. So the idea that it was better to do the time than face the 'family' didn't look quite so wise anymore."

Sloan finished his thought. "And so the cards started tumbling down. Every man for himself."

Hudson grinned. "That's right."

I was feeling overwhelmed. "So they got them *all*?"

"Not everyone. Many, assuming the charges stick. But that's just the opening act. I'm sure there's plenty of deals still to be had. Especially once some of the elected officials start talking. They're certainly not going to take one for the team."

I gulped. "Elected officials?"

"It's widening beyond just the actual mobsters at this point." He nodded, into it. "They're rounding up quite a few low-level government employees, hoping to go from there. Probably right about now, from what I hear. Even have a mayor's office in the mix."

"Which one?"

"Haven't heard yet. But corruption charges are coming down. People'll be singing from every direction." His face darkened as he gave us a direct look. "Which is why you two need to lay low. This isn't finished yet."

Sloan and I exchanged a glance. "Are we in danger?"

"Hopefully it'll just be the media hounding you for a few days, wanting to get your story. And then things can settle back down. But there's no telling for sure."

"What does *that* mean, exactly?" I said.

He sighed. "This wasn't supposed to happen. I was assured your names would be left out of this."

"Assured by *who*?" Sloan said.

"I have a source in the investigation." He shook his head. "Can't say any more right now. But I've been getting updates on this for a while now. I really thought you guys wouldn't get hit when it all blew up. But now that you are, I need you to be careful."

Sloan's eyes shot daggers at Hudson. "Getting updates for a while? Appreciate the heads up on this. *Partner.*"

He returned an apologetic shrug. "Wasn't my secret to

tell. Source won't trust me if I'm spreading it around. But I had your back. Or at least I tried."

Sloan crossed her arms and avoided his eyes.

Hudson continued. "I think you need to lie low for a few days. Both of you. Stay home, preferably in the same place. I'd feel a whole lot better if you did."

"Can't." I shook my head. "I have to work. If I don't get my final experience hours in, I won't graduate."

He was unmoved. "Just for a few days. I'm sure it won't last long."

I stood up, ready to fight if necessary. "I *have* to go. I can handle a bunch of reporters."

"It's not just reporters I'm concerned about." He looked me directly in the eye. "If *they* know who you are, other people will too. People that are not locked up yet. But should be."

My stomach sank. "So we *could* be in danger."

Hudson sighed. "There's no immediate threat that we know of. But I'm not taking any chances. No way around it, your names are out there."

Sloan leaned in. "Look, I know you mean well. But I certainly don't want to be responsible for Quinn not finishing her internship in time. I can't do it."

"I'm not trying to cause trouble. I'm trying to keep you *out* of it."

"But you said yourself there's no immediate threat," she pleaded. "We can just have some of our guys escort her to work. Both of us. No big deal."

Silence hung in the air as we waited for an objection. When Hudson didn't immediately argue, she quickly continued, her voice playful. "We'll even let you be in charge of security."

Hudson studied both of us for a moment before sighing,

exasperated. "Fine. I'll at least think about it. But do me a favor and stay in through the weekend. Call in sick a couple days. Let it blow over. We'll see how things look on Monday."

FOUR

I just couldn't stop checking. Every time I passed a window, I had to pull the curtain back and confirm the horde was still out there. It was utterly fascinating. And I was addicted.

Apparently our role in the bust of the century was important enough to keep a small team of reporters outside my apartment building day and night. Standing around chatting, just waiting for me to step out the door. Or for something juicy to happen. Whatever that could possibly be.

But despite my intense impulse to check on them, I was not relishing the attention. My mood sank lower and lower the more I paced around the apartment, as I considered the possibilities for my work situation on Monday. They were all sure to know everything by then.

What would my bosses think about my participation in such a scheme? No, I hadn't been one of the criminals. But I had been around them. Cavorting with them. *Spying* on them. Perhaps that would make *me* suspect in their eyes.

No. *Hudson said we would be heroes.* Those reporters want the story of our selfless actions that helped bring down a conspiracy. Surely my superiors would forgive a one-time dalliance in the covert arts?

One-time? Hmmm.

I tried to distract myself from the activity outside with some online shopping. With graduation only weeks away, and my new grown-up job lined up with my current employer, I was all set to begin improving my living situation. I would soon be able to afford a non-postage-stamp-sized apartment for the first time. And so some actual, adult-like decorating would finally be attainable.

I was just beginning to get lost in the eternal question of shades versus drapes when a quick rap on my door broke my reverie. I froze. The reporters had been pushy and aggressive when I arrived home, but none so far had ventured all the way to my door. They had kept their respectful distance. *Do I open it?*

A sing-song voice came from behind the door. "Oh, Quiiiiinnn."

That was no reporter. *Grant.*

I hesitated only a moment, considering my options.

"I know you're heeeere," he called out.

There goes option one. I sucked it up and opened the door, my eyes wide. "How do you know where I live?"

Grant breezed past me into the room, waving his hand. "I asked the boss when all the reporters showed up. Told her I needed to check on my buddy, of course."

I raised an eyebrow. *Buddy?* We'd had one quasi-friendly lunch so far. That he still owed me for.

He ignored my skeptical expression. "It was crazy out there. We didn't know *what* was going on."

I took a deep breath, steeling myself. "So does everyone know now?"

He shrugged. "There were some rumors. But I wanted to hear straight from you." His gaze intensified. "So you have some secret double-life thing? And you didn't *tell* me?"

"Well, it wouldn't be a secret if I had, now would it?" I tried to play it off, but knew I couldn't keep it up. He stared back, impassive.

I sighed and flopped to the sofa. "Actually, it was just a one-time thing. Sort of. I got caught up in helping with this investigation. And it turned out to be more than I bargained for."

"I'd say." Grant made himself at home, stretching out on the loveseat. "You single-handedly brought down the mob, or something like that?"

"*Something* like that. I guess. And it certainly wasn't single-handed. If anything, I was just along for the ride."

"Now, don't be all modest on me." Grant used a finger to peek out the window and glanced back at me over his shoulder, coy. "Clearly those reporters outside don't believe that. For real, what went down?"

I shrugged. "One minute I was helping a private investigator check out possible scandals between business-partner brothers. And the next I was listening to the confession of a murder-for-hire scheme from a prominent businesswoman. Apparently it just took off from there."

"Investigating scandals. Sounds so . . . scandalous." His eyes glowed with excitement. "So you weren't recruited to do some big setup? I heard they were working on a case against those guys for years and years, or something."

I shook my head. "Just stumbled onto it. I had no idea our simple case would be connected. Or have such huge implications. Although now in hindsight, I guess I should've seen it coming. These are powerful people, after all."

"Hmmm," Grant mused. "But what about this private investigator you were helping? Her name's Sloan?"

"What about her?"

"Was she in on all this? Did she trick you into helping set them up?"

I narrowed my eyes, unsure where this line of questioning was coming from. "There was no setup. I told you, it was an inquiry that got out of control."

He held his hands up in surrender. "Okay. Just asking. So you 'accidentally' got mixed up with the wrong people."

I sensed skepticism. Was everyone going to be so suspicious of us? Of me? "We honestly had no way of knowing it would lead where it did."

"Which is where, exactly?"

"I'm not . . . completely sure. I just know the confession we taped lead to other confessions. And then more and more. Resulting in this huge case against the whole lot of 'em."

He narrowed his eyes. "You lucky dog then, you."

"One way to look at it, I guess." I shook my head. "But I'm not sure all this attention is my cup of tea. I just want my old, quiet life back."

"So your secret-investigating days are over, then?"

Ummm. I didn't like that question. I wasn't ready to face up to an answer. I shrugged, trying for nonchalant. "Think so. And Sloan certainly didn't trick me, by the way. I had a blast playing spy for a while. It just doesn't fit in with the rest of my life." I rolled my eyes. "Especially now that I see what can come of it."

Grant nodded sagely. "Good thinking. Better to focus on your real career. I doubt you can afford not to, really."

I sighed, letting that one go. He really had been doing better.

Suddenly Grant winced and put his fingers to his head. "Ack. All this drama is giving me *such* a headache. Do you have anything I could take, dear?"

I'm pretty sure you live for the drama. "Of course." I hopped up and pulled a small bottle from the kitchen cupboard. "This work?"

He sneered in response. "Got anything stronger?"

"Um." I dug around the limited selection of over-the-counter drugs. "Nothing prescription, if that's what you mean."

"You're sure that's all you have?" He held his head with both hands as if in serious pain. "Nothing in the bathroom?"

"Ummm. I can check." I turned and scurried into the bedroom. "Be just a minute," I called over my shoulder.

The journey was primarily for goodwill. I knew there was nothing any more powerful in my apartment. But I rummaged through the cabinets anyway, making plenty of noise. And then made sure to put everything carefully back in its place, labels facing out, before heading back. No reason to leave chaos.

"Sorry, I don't—" I stopped short as I rounded the corner, unsure what I was seeing.

Grant startled at the sound of my voice, sending his phone flying out of his hands. I was certain he had been holding them outstretched, snapping a picture. Of my family photos hanging on the wall.

What I didn't know was *why*.

We both looked at the phone lying face-up on the floor between us, camera app still open. Then at each other.

"Whatcha doin'?" I tried to sound unconcerned.

He did the same, exaggeratedly pressing his hand to his chest. " Give me a heart attack, why don't you." He snatched the phone off the floor and shoved it in his pocket.

"Didn't mean to scare you." I watched Grant, trying to feel out the situation. He avoided my eyes. I conjured up a little chuckle. "Pretty sure it's not my decorating you would want to take a picture of."

He eyed the wall of frames momentarily before taking in the rest of the room with a dramatic eye of disdain. "You might say that." He echoed my fake laugh. "No, I was trying to take a selfie. This apartment is just so *basic*. That always makes me look extra good, you know?"

I blinked back at him.

He's been doing better. He's been doing better.

"But I can never get that little reverse-camera button to work," he continued. "Think it's this headache, I just can't think right. I take it you're fresh out of the good stuff?"

"Something like that."

"Figures. Well, I better get home, then." He practically bounded the few feet to the door and flung the door open, then turned back to me. "But listen, your celebrity-status excuse is really wearing thin around the office. You'll be back to work on Monday?"

I studied his face one last time, but found no clues in his mask of shallow impertinence. "That's the plan."

"See ya thennn," he called over his shoulder as he yanked the door closed. I stared at his vacated spot in the doorway. Then at the wall in question. *What exactly am I missing here?*

FIVE

My return to work was fairly uneventful. My non-intern coworkers, fully-fledged audiologists who generally only socialized amongst themselves, continued their pattern of indifference toward me. Only now with their eyes askance. And a deeper sense of hush whenever I was around.

Being shuffled past reporters and into the building by armed escorts probably didn't help my popularity in the office. But the one person I was looking forward to seeing was nowhere to be found. I was ready to ask questions. And Grant must have been cowering at home, afraid or embarrassed to answer those questions after his strange episode.

I kept my head down and focused on my patient schedule, which was now extra-full from doing double the work to cover for him. But having just taken two sick days, highly discouraged as a student, I really couldn't complain. And it would only be a couple more weeks before I would no longer be the underling in the office.

On day two of his disappearance, however, a brief conversation with my boss left me a little concerned about that prospect. Dr. Seymore seemed to be a little wary of my predicament, with all the media attention and talk of spying and criminals. She didn't say much. But she definitely had the same suspicious look in her eyes as the rest.

And the conversation also left me concerned about Grant. Something wasn't right.

Sloan answered on the first ring as I left the parking lot at the end of the day. I got right to it. "I know you did your secret research on my coworker Grant. Can you get me his address?"

"Only if you tell me what it's for. Did you confront that weasel about his little photo incident?"

"He never showed to work. Apparently didn't even call out sick or anything. They haven't heard from him, for two days now. He's going to get fired."

"Eh," Sloan replied. "Wouldn't be the worst thing."

I couldn't *totally* disagree. But I still felt compelled. "I just want to check on him. Can you give me the address?"

"Pick me up and you got it."

***

"I'm pretty shocked you've never been to Grant's place before." Sloan took a break from her navigation duties to play comedian again. "He's like your best friend, right?"

"Right." I smirked back at her. "Certainly didn't picture myself trying to hunt him down in my free time, I know that. But something feels strange. Especially after I talked to my boss."

"So she hasn't heard from him?"

I shook my head. "I had to cover for him. Said he texted me that he was home sick."

Sloan gaped at me. "Why in the world would you do that?"

Good question. "Maybe because we had just had lunch, and he seemed to be trying to be friendly? He's really been much more pleasant lately."

"Until he showed up at your place acting all sketchy."

"True. Although I could be over-reading that whole thing. But what's really weirding me out now is that Grant told me he got my address from the director at work. So he could come check on me."

"And . . . they shouldn't have done that?"

I shook my head. "Today I asked her for Grant's address, for the same reason." I pulled to a stop at a red light and turned to face Sloan. "And she said it was against office policy to give out personal information."

Her eyebrows flicked up. "Interesting."

"When I mentioned her giving my address to Grant, stupidly arguing with her, she got pretty angry. Didn't appreciate the accusation that she had broken the rules. I apologized and got out of there quickly."

"So now you don't know *how* Grant got the information."

I sighed and leaned back in my seat. "And I'm not really on my boss's good side at the moment, either. I'm really batting a thousand right now."

***

"Not bad for a richie-rich pretending to be a poor student," Sloan said as we approached the door to a cute, well-tended bungalow-style house in light blue. "So what do you think, he's hiding out in shame after being found out once again?"

I shrugged and knocked on the door. "I just want to make sure he's okay. Then we can lay into him."

We waited for signs of life. There was no movement.

"Could be just avoiding you," Sloan said, easing off the porch. "I wouldn't blame him. Let's go poke around."

I followed her around the side of the house, where she crept up to an eye-level window. We both pushed our faces to the glass. Just a normal living room, modern and neat with a beachy feel. A rack of towering surfboards stood next to the front door.

Sloan turned to me, quizzical. "He surfs? I'm not sure that fits, in my head."

I shrugged. "Probably just for show. Wouldn't surprise me now."

We moved on to the next set of windows, but they were too high.

"Lemme give you a boost." Sloan leaned over and laced her hands together, waiting.

I glanced to make sure no one was watching us. "Why me?"

"He's *your* frenemy." She shrugged. "You want to leave him potentially bleeding out on the floor, it's your call."

She knows just how to get me. "Okay, fine." I stepped a foot into her outstretched hands and immediately flew up to the window. She must've been a cheerleader in a previous life.

I gripped the window ledge for dear life. Balance regained, I pressed closer to the window, my hands blocking the light. I couldn't make out much through the half-closed blinds.

"So, anybody dead?" Sloan sounded almost cheery about it.

A male voice responded before I could. "Bloody hope not."

I spun at the sound, forgetting I was several feet in the air. The movement knocked me quickly out of balance. My left foot stepped out of Sloan's grasp and into a nearby bush. The rest of my body followed. I found myself splayed on top of the greenery, branches poking me painfully all over. Luckily it hadn't been recently trimmed.

I groaned in agony and Sloan leaped over to help, dragging me off the plant. I quickly brushed myself off before looking up to the wide-eyed stranger.

"Didn't mean to scare you there." There was a distinctive Australian accent to match his Aussie good looks. His longish dirty blond hair was perfectly messy, framing his tanned blue-eyed face. We stared back for a moment, unsure how to proceed.

He returned the gaze. "Ya know, if you want to look in on me, all you have to do is ask. I don't bite."

Sloan and I exchanged a glance, confused but amused.

He looked us over carefully. "But I could always make an exception. If you're into that sort of thing."

We both laughed, despite ourselves.

"Sorry, playboy," Sloan said. "But we're not here for you. Is Grant around?"

His face fell. "What do you want with that good-for-nothing liar?"

I loved the way his accent pronounced 'lie-uh'. "Sounds like we're definitely in the right place," I said. "So he lives here?"

"My flatmate. Or was. Not really sure anymore, tell you the truth."

Uh oh. "What makes you say that? He move out?"

"Nah, his stuff's all here, but I haven't seen him in days." He raised a bare muscular arm and wiped at his forehead. "Think we could take this inside? I'm kinda wiped."

We nodded and followed him back to the front door. The air conditioning inside was cool against the unusually warm spring day outside. He moved quickly to the adjoining kitchen. "Can I get you ladies anything?"

"We're good."

I took in the room while he retrieved a bottle of water. Everything was neat and tidy, not exactly what I would expect from a pair of mid-twenties men. He took a quick gulp and moved back toward us, extending his hand. "Jackson, by the way."

I returned the offer. "Quinn. I work with Grant. This is my friend Sloan."

"And to what does my disappearing arse of a roommate owe the pleasure?"

"That's why we're here," I said. "He hasn't shown up to work, either."

"We just wanted to make sure he wasn't lying here dead or something," Sloan added with a shrug, clearly not genuinely concerned.

"And thus the peeking in my bedroom window, I guess." Jackson grinned. "That excuse is not nearly as interesting as I'd hoped it'd be."

I chuckled. "Sorry to disappoint. So he didn't tell you where he was going?"

"Wasn't here for him to tell. I've been down south with my mates for the last week or so. Getting an early start on the season."

I glanced at the rack near the door and took a shot. "Surfing season?"

"That's it. No year-rounding it here, so I have to hit the road. Thought you guys might be groupies, wanting to peek in on me."

Is he famous or something? I tried to hide my skepticism. "That typical for you?"

"They've never followed me home before, that I know

of." He flashed a goofy half-smile that was sure to charm surfing fans. "But out on the beach, I am kind of a big deal."

Sloan and I just glanced at each other. I could imagine the truth to his words.

He quickly dropped the smile. "But anyway, I got back the other day and Grant was nowhere to be found. *And* all the lights were out. He never paid the power bill. Stingy bugger."

His accent was adorable. But I had to stay focused. "Any idea where else he could be? Does he have any family or significant others around here?"

"Couldn't say, really. Personal stuff is not part of our arrangement."

"Arrangement?" Sloan said.

Jackson shrugged. "He's got the money, so he pays the bills. Rent, power, stuff like that. And I have a bit of a talent for cooking, so I keep us stocked and make the meals. Plus a little housekeeping. I don't mind staying neat."

"Sounds like a pretty good deal," she said.

"Has been, until now. I earn my keep, but we aren't exactly friends. He pretty much keeps to himself. Don't have a clue what he does out there."

"Is there anyone he might talk to?" My optimism was fading quickly. "*Anything* you can think of? "

"Well, I did try to track him down. Seeing how I don't want to get thrown out on my arse. But his parents were no bloody help at all."

I perked up. "You talked to them? Do they live around here?"

"Don't think so. I get the feeling they're far away. But I don't know for sure."

"So then you called?" Sloan asked.

He nodded. "Talked to his mum. And trust me, I regret it. Told her I hadn't seen Grant in a while, and found out the bills weren't getting paid for weeks now. Just checking in to see if they knew where to find him."

"And had they heard from him?" I encouraged.

"She just laughed at me, real mean-like. Said they weren't surprised by any of it. That he's always been irresponsible and reckless, and is just good at faking otherwise when he needs to. That I shouldn't be worried. He would turn up when he wants something."

My eyes widened. "Yikes."

"And then she accused me of trying to get the rent money out of them, like it was some kinda scheme. I got off the phone pretty fast after that."

"Wow." Sloan looked as stunned as I was. "Guess we can rule out visiting the fam, then."

Jackson shrugged. "Don't know anything else, where to look. Or if I should just give up and take off. Really don't want to move, but I don't see much choice if he doesn't turn up soon."

"That really stinks." I gave him a sympathetic look and considered. "So how did you know his parent's phone number? Does he have an address book we can see?"

He shook his head. "Just remembered the phone calls. Only a few. But it's hard to forget when someone lists their mum as 'Hag' on their phone."

We all cringed.

"Always makes me feel bad when that shows up on the screen," he continued. "But I figured it was worth a shot. So I just dialed it back."

"Wait." I met Sloan's wary eyes. "Grant's phone is here?"

"Left it in the kitchen." Jackson shrugged and pointed to a cell phone in the corner.

It was, undeniably, the phone I had seen Grant carry every day. "So he's been missing for a few days *and* he left his phone behind." I picked it up and stared, gently touching the dark screen as though it would give me answers. It didn't seem right. I knew Grant. It was like him leaving behind his arm.

Then my eyes alighted on a pencil holder on the counter nearby. Sticking out of the top were not pencils, but syringe plungers. The container was full of needles.

I turned back, eyes wide. "Any chance he has a drug problem?"

Sloan met my gaze, understanding. "That could certainly explain his disappearance."

Jackson shook his head, unconcerned. "Nah. Those aren't his."

Sloan and I exchanged another glance.

"Maybe we should go," she said.

"I mean, they're mine" Jackson continued quickly, "but it's not what you think."

He rushed forward, brushing past me to reach into the cabinet above. His face reddened a little as he emerged with a small glass vial. He held it up gingerly.

"Insulin." Jackson's cocky gaze now held steady on the floor. "I'm diabetic."

"Oh." I glanced at the bottle and shrugged back at him. "Okay. Nevermind, then."

He looked up, seeming relieved at our reaction. "Yeah, whatever." He threw it hastily back into the cabinet. "But you think we could keep that kinda quiet? It would sorta ruin my rep and all."

Who would we tell? I gave him a reassuring smile. "Our little secret." I glanced down at the phone still in my hand, concern reasserting itself. "But would he really leave his phone behind, if something else weren't wrong?"

"Unless he has another one," Sloan offered. "The guy already has a double life. Why not more than one phone?"

SIX

Armed with the new insight that my coworker was notoriously irresponsible and inconsiderate, in addition to being a profuse liar, I returned to work the next day mentally washing my hands of his situation. I felt bad for his poor roommate, about to get thrown out on his toned surfer's butt. But I was definitely not going to cover for that phony anymore.

So when my boss popped her head in to inquire about Grant's status, believing me to be her lifeline to him, this time I told the truth. I hadn't heard a thing from him. And when she said nothing but narrowed her eyes in annoyance, I had to admit, it was vaguely satisfying.

But of course, he still found a way to wreck my day. I had to work double-time again to keep up, handling all of my patients as well as many of his. As the bottom of the office food chain, I was expected to take up the slack. And I wondered if things would stay that way even after Grant was fired. I doubted I would continue enjoying my job for long.

I had to work through lunch to keep up. At close to 3 p.m., with a whole five minutes to spare before my next appointment, I ran into our office to catch my breath. Still no time to heat up my sad little frozen dinner. I plopped into my chair and savored the brief moment alone.

Until my grumbling stomach broke the silence. Ravished, I checked my desk drawers for a quick snack. No luck. And I knew my emergency purse-granola bar was long gone.

I sighed and sat back in my chair. But eventually my gaze fell upon Grant's desk next to me. Or more specifically, his bottom drawer. The one I knew housed all the contraband for his secret candy addiction.

He thought I didn't know about it. So he probably wouldn't suspect me if something went missing, right? *Actually, what do I care?* I was only in this situation because of him and his selfishness. And he was nowhere to be found.

I was going in.

After a quick glance over my shoulder, I dove into his chair and yanked open the drawer. I had more than once seen him futzing with something in the bottom. I shoved aside the pens and notepads littering the drawer and pulled out a shoebox.

The stacks of candy bars gleaming back from inside made me drool. I grabbed a Snickers and tore open the wrapper with vigor. My stomach began to slow its clenching the moment I took a bite.

For just a moment, I was perfectly fine with my lying, cheating coworker. One of his bad habits was now saving my life. Or at least my job, as I was otherwise likely to bite the head off the next imperfect patient.

I carefully shifted the remaining candy bars around to cover the hole I had created, then slid the box back into place in the drawer. The next step was casually scattering the miscellaneous office supplies across the bottom. I swished everything around to restore the obnoxious disorder to his drawer. No one would ever know I had been there.

But as I pushed the drawer closed, chewing my final gooey bite, I stopped cold.

A small folded card, like a thank-you note, blank on the front, had been amongst the detritus. But after the drawer-stirring, the card's inside now faced me, staring back at me with my hand on the drawer handle. The hand began to shake a little.

Bad manners to point fingers. Best to keep things to yourself.

The red scribbling on the inside of the card made my blood run cold instantly. There was no signature, nothing identifying. But I knew that message hadn't been meant for Grant.

The finger.

I stared at the words until they blurred, my mouth turning dry. *Do I call the police?*

I didn't know what Grant had to do with it. With any of it.

Maybe he just found it? But he was now missing.

A weird coincidence?

The intercom sounded from the phone on my desk. "Quinn, your next appointment is waiting."

I groaned and shook my head, jolting myself back to the present. I had to make an instant decision.

I stuffed the note in my pocket and slammed the drawer closed.

My mind never really left that pocket the rest of the day.

***

"I need to show you something."

We were like eerie twins, both proclaiming at the same

time. I slid into the booth at Joe's and faced my echoer. I saw the same fire of excitement in Sloan's eyes as I knew flamed in mine.

But I couldn't wait. The mysterious note was still burning and throbbing in my pocket. I slipped it out and flung it on the table.

"Me first."

Sloan eyed the note carefully from afar, as if the card-stock was diseased. After a reassuring nod from me, she reached to examine the message inside.

I felt less crazy about my suspicions when she looked back up with widened eyes. "You got another threat?"

I shook my head slowly. "I don't know that we ever officially decided the first *was* a threat. But I'm certainly leaning that way now."

Her face went dark as she returned to studying the handwriting.

"But it wasn't left for me," I continued. "I found it in *Grant's* desk."

Sloan tore her eyes from the paper to stare back curiously. She was clearly pondering the same questions that had been terrorizing me for hours. Finally she spoke, her face grim. "So what do you think this means?"

I laughed, despite myself. "For once I was hoping you had all the answers. Because I can't quite make sense of it. What does Grant have to do with this?"

Sloan sighed. "I'm not sure. Have you shown this to anyone else? I take it you didn't call the police."

I shook my head. "Hope that was the right call. Is this withholding evidence?" I thought better of it and waved my hand. "On second thought, I'm not sure I want to know."

She shrugged back. "Evidence of what? We need to find

that out first. It's not very likely there are prints on there besides Grant's. And now ours. So what would they do about it, really?"

"Sure, I'll buy that." I always appreciated her gray-area logic when it mattered. "But why would Grant have it in the first place?"

Sloan bit her lip as she thought for a long moment. "The way I see it, there are three main possibilities. First, the note has nothing to do with the, ahem, *present* that was left for you."

"You really think that's possible?" There was an annoying note of hopefulness to my voice. I was grasping for normalcy.

Her face was deadpan. "Not a chance."

I shrank back a little and began to doctor the mug of coffee that had appeared in front of me without my notice.

Sloan did the same as she continued to muse out loud. "Second, someone could have left the note specifically for Grant. Only . . . why would they want to do that? He had nothing to do with it."

"Unless the finger was originally meant for him?" I offered.

"Could be. But they got the wrong desk the first time? And then came back for the right one days later? Seems sort of unlikely."

"And the message would certainly be pretty lost in transit that way," I conceded.

"Right." Sloan took a sip before continuing. "So the only reasonable explanation I can come up with? Grant had something to do with the finger in the *first* place."

I had been hoping she would have some other insight. Something that didn't make my skin crawl.

"But the note isn't my only reason to suspect that," she

continued. "That's actually what I wanted to discuss." She dug into her purse and pulled out the cell phone we had retrieved from Grant's house.

"I've been poking around in the guy's phone." She unlocked the screen using the simple passcode his roommate had shared. "Unfortunately for us, his email is not currently connected. And his text messages have been cleared, no history. Weird, for sure."

I raised an eyebrow. "Paranoid, maybe?"

"Looks like he had reason to be," she continued. "There were some interesting pictures on here. And I don't mean the ones of him dressed in some hideous goth getup on the weekends."

I cringed.

She tapped the camera memory, bringing forth my living room. All over, from many different angles. Ending with the wall of family photos where he had been caught off guard.

"So he *was* snooping," I exclaimed. "Why would he photograph my apartment?"

"Oh, it gets better." She swiped over a screen and tapped a red icon. She tapped once more and rustling noise sounded from the phone speaker.

"Oh, Quiiiiinnn." My head snapped toward Sloan at the sound of my coworker's whiny voice. "I know you're heeeere."

"How do you know where I live?" The sound of my own voice was jarring. My jaw dropped and I stared back, gaping.

Sloan stopped the playback after a few seconds. "Sound familiar?"

"He taped our conversation? How creepy!" I heard the outrage in my voice and felt a quick stab of guilt. "I mean,

I guess we're not really ones to talk, huh? We've . . . sort of done the same before."

"Yes, but in the line of duty," she replied. "For a purpose. To help someone. So I think the real question is . . . who exactly is *Grant* trying to help?"

I heard a quiet vibration and Sloan glanced to her phone.

"Let's hold that thought," she said. "Looks like we have a distress signal from our voyeur's Aussie roommate. Maybe *he* has an answer for us."

SEVEN

We burst into Jackson's house without even a knock. He didn't seem bothered by it.

In fact, he looked downright pleased. He sauntered across the kitchen toward us and gave us a slow once-over. "Not so bad my roommate's gone, have to say. Seems a pretty good excuse to get you two in here on demand."

Was this some kind of ruse? Rage began to simmer. "Excuse me?"

Jackson's face immediately turned red at the sight of our indignant faces. "Sorry, mate." He ran his hand through his hair and shook his head, eyes to the floor. "I flirt when I'm uncomfortable. Terrible habit."

Eh, not that terrible. He was sort of handsome when he was embarrassed. "So what has you so upset? Have you heard from Grant?"

"No, but I think I've found something." He turned and waved us down the back hall. We followed him to the first door on the left. "I got a bit desperate, so I decided to check out Grant's room. See if he had any cash stashed in there to keep us afloat." He averted his eyes again. "I'm not proud of it."

But my thoughts darkened as I stared at the door,

considering the possibilities. He surely wasn't dead in there, if Jackson called us first. *So what, then?*

Jackson cleared his throat, but his voice came out froggy anyway. "Have a look."

He slowly turned the handle and swung the door open with a creak. I held my breath, unsure what we might see. *Please don't be my coworker's lifeless body.* I relaxed with a sigh as I took in the space.

The room was neat as a pin, everything perfectly in place. Precisely-made navy bedspread, orderly storage bins and shelves. No dirty laundry or miscellaneous anything. *Perhaps Grant and I have more in common than I realized.*

Then my eyes were drawn to the laptop, glowing on the corner desk. The screen was lit with a word processor, the document's writing visible but not legible from that distance. I glanced to Sloan and we all moved toward it in silence.

$200,000.
Unmarked bills.
No police. You know the drill.
We'll be in touch.

Nothing else on the screen. The words glowed ominously at us in the dim room. *Some kind of ransom note?*

Sloan reached toward the keyboard.

"No!" My arm shot out to stop her, grabbing her hand before she could touch it.

She pulled back and gazed back at me, amused but curious.

"I mean, isn't this evidence?" I heard the nervousness in my voice and tried to stay calm. "We need to . . . let the police dust for prints or something."

Sloan shrugged and pointed at the screen. "It says right there, no police. That makes our job a lot easier. No red tape."

"*Our* job?"

"Yeah. Looks like we have a bit of a kidnapping situation here." Sloan seemed completely unruffled by her own statement. "So . . . we have to help find him, right?"

"Yes, of course. But . . . " My voice trailed off as I really wasn't sure *what* to argue. Just was sure I should, somehow.

"*But* they wouldn't find prints on there, anyway," Sloan continued. "It's all pretty standard so far." She acted as though it was the most normal thing in the world as she counted off on her fingers. "No witnesses, gets too messy. Typed ransom note, not handwritten. No police. So leaving prints would be insanely amateurish and inconsistent, right?"

She is right. "Then how do we trace who did this?" I started to panic a bit. "What if he's in danger? He could be hurt, or scared, or . . . we have to *do* something."

Sloan put a hand on my shoulder. "Don't stress. We're on it. And nobody's going to hurt him if they're trying to get paid. There's just no need. And I don't really see Grant fighting back, do you?"

I took a deep breath, knowing she was probably right. *We have to stay rational.* I met Sloan's eyes and nodded. I was with her.

She nodded back and turned to the laptop. She tapped her finger on her lips, thinking. "The only thing that gets me is that the note wasn't left to be obvious right away. Why not the living room, the kitchen? I guess eventually someone would have to go in his room. But by that time, it might've been the cops checking out a missing persons report. It seems risky." She studied the screen a moment, then glanced up to Jackson, waiting quietly behind us. "Why did you check the laptop, anyway? Did you know the password?"

He shook his head. "It was just there, glowing away when I came in. Couldn't miss it."

Sloan mused some more, narrowed eyes staring at the screen. "We'll at least be able to see when it was created and edited, maybe."

Giving up on the fingerprints, I tapped the mouse-pad to minimize the document and satisfy my curiosity. A few standard icons littered the screen. Nothing else open, nothing obviously suspicious. The ransom note was unsaved and untitled.

Jackson edged closer, peering over our shoulders. "So if it's a ransom . . . who exactly is supposed to come up with two hundred grand? Surely whoever it is isn't expecting *me* to have that kinda cash."

Sloan and I glanced at each other. I cleared my throat. "I guess you weren't privy to your roommate's secret family either, then."

He raised his eyebrows at us.

"They have boatloads of money," Sloan said, matter-of-fact.

"Literally," I added. "They spend most of their time on a yacht."

"Oh." Jackson's brow furrowed as he pondered. "That would explain quite a lot, then."

I studied his face. "Such as?"

He shrugged. "Just his general attitude toward money. Always seemed to act like it was a never-ending resource, and I was a fool for not treating it that way. I thought he just made mad dough at his internship."

I grimaced. "That's definitely not the source."

Jackson nodded, considering. "That's why it was so weird when I found out he hadn't paid the bills. I thought he was literally rolling in it. He certainly always seemed like it." He cringed. "Crikey, I just referred to him in past tense. Can't say I really like the guy, but I don't wish him harm, you know? What do we do?"

"First, we try to figure out who has him," Sloan replied. "But we should probably contact his family, too. In case things go south and we have to get the payout instead."

Jackson paled. He looked about how I felt. I tried to shake it off and focus on the task at hand. Panicking wouldn't help anyone.

"He'd been keeping them quite the secret, lying to everyone." I mused out loud. "So then the question is, who *did* know about his family? Maybe that could tell us who's behind this."

"My thoughts exactly." Sloan surveyed the rest of the room, then turned to Jackson. "You have any empty boxes around here? We're gonna need *everything*."

***

"Nothing, nothing, and more nothing." Sloan shoved aside the last box in disgust. "What a waste of time."

I climbed from my spot on the floor, giving my knees a chance to stretch. The small pile of cardboard boxes littering my apartment held the meager contents of Grant's room. They had turned up nothing interesting. And thus, no clues to who held him captive.

I tried to think of anything we might've missed. "Should we have taken his clothes, too?"

"Maybe." Sloan shrugged. "But I don't know what that could possibly tell us. We checked all the drawers."

I gave the carton in front of me a little kick in frustration. "You'd think he'd have *something* personal in here. Maybe not a diary, per se. But mementos, hints to what he does in his spare time. Something."

Sloan hopped to her feet in one swift movement, reminding me of a ninja. "Nope. And no stash of pictures, either. Only those two framed ones." She reached to retrieve two black frames from the floor. "Him with what looked like his family at Christmas, surrounded by piles of glittering presents. And one of a fluffy little dog. No friends, boyfriends. Not even a holiday card."

I took a closer look at the photos she handed me. Five tanned, smiling faces peered back. "The family doesn't look all that bad. Wonder what happened with them?"

"You've met your coworker." Sloan smirked. "Probably *Grant* happened to them."

I grabbed an empty notebook from the pile and threw it at her. "Not helping."

She jumped out of the way, dodging the flying debris. The notebook slammed into the bookcase behind her, toppling a small basket of office supplies. Pens and notepads spilled onto the floor.

"Hmmm." Sloan pretended to study the pile. "I kind of like it like that, maybe you should just leave it." She grinned. "This mess wouldn't bother you, would it?"

I rolled my eyes and headed across the room.

Sloan stuck her hand out to stop me. "Just kidding. I got it."

She grabbed the basket and swept the contents back in in one swoop. Then made a show of putting the basket back, making tiny, mockingly precise adjustments to its position on the shelf. Clearly she found my tidiness hilarious.

Then she stopped moving the basket and just stared.

"Okay, I think you've made your point," I said.

Sloan didn't respond.

I got curious when I saw her head tilt, examining the shelf further but not moving from her position. She still said nothing. But her grin was now gone. "Sloan?" I leaned in, getting nervous. "What's up?"

She paused another moment before turning back, a bright new smile on her face. "Nothing at all." She straightened and moved to grab her bag from the kitchen counter. "But it's about time to meet Leo. He'll be waiting."

Her voice sounded perfectly calm and normal. But something was off. I was certain.

In a move so brief I wasn't sure it had happened, she pressed her finger to her lips as she hurried out the door.

Quiet.

EIGHT

After driving separately, at Sloan's insistence, I was more than ready for some answers by the time we pulled up to Joe's. *What had made her act so bizarrely?*

She continued to ignore my look of inquisition and headed straight to the back of the diner, where a familiar male head waited. His dark hair swished across his chiseled asian face when he turned his head toward the sound of Sloan's heels approaching.

"Evenin' ladies." Sloan's hacker friend Leo looked up with a sly grin. "Could I buy you two a cup of coffee? They'll put it on my tab."

"Very funny." Sloan smirked. "We both know you don't have a tab." She slid into the booth to face him. " And you should really stop charging things to mine."

"If you say so." Leo gave me a little wink as I took the seat next to Sloan, then returned his attention to her. "But you know you owe me a lot more than my shameful secret pie addiction will *ever* cost you."

Sloan gave a flick of her eyebrows in agreement. "Touché."

He looked satisfied with that response. "So, good news or bad news?"

With Sloan's added mystery-behavior back there, I was desperate to know *something* positive, however small. "Good news, definitely."

"So the good news is that I've found buttloads of information," Leo announced. "Plenty of dirt on this guy."

"Of course you've found stuff," Sloan objected. "You're you. That doesn't exactly count."

Boy, they work fast. One of the security guys had just dropped the laptop off to him hours earlier. "You've gone through his whole computer already? You're really good."

"I *am* that good." Leo winced. "But no."

Three coffees were dropped to the table in front of us. We gave a simultaneous thanks to our laconic but friendly, ever-present Southern waitress Dottie and reached for our cups.

Sloan slid the creamer over to me. "He's been doing a deep dive on Grant since I found that recording on his phone. Background, family. Second or third secret lives."

I stirred the fixings into my coffee, mind buzzing. There was no way I could focus on all the background info just yet, I was too distracted. I needed answers. "Sorry, Leo. But the bad news is going to have to wait." I turned to face Sloan beside me. "I need to know what happened back there."

"Mmm . . . a little drama?" Leo leaned in and plopped his chin on his fist, looking intently between us. "I'm listening."

I concealed my own eye roll with a little head shake. "No, but she has some explaining to do. Why did you zone out like that?"

Sloan stared at her coffee a moment. "I hate to tell you this." She carefully put down her cup and met my eyes. "But you were being watched."

Watched. I gulped and lowered my own cup to the table. "What do you mean?"

"There was a camera in your bookcase. Hidden under the lip of the shelf."

That can't be. "Are you sure?"

"Absolutely."

I shook my head, in major denial. "How can you be? You didn't get all that close."

"Trust me, I know hidden cameras. And this one was very familiar. And expensive."

I flashed back to our previous adventure. We had seen the comings and goings of a businessman's hotel room the night he died. Courtesy of a camera she had planted in the hallway, completely undetected. I had to believe her. "Why didn't you show me?"

"I needed to play it off." She shrugged. "We don't want whoever is watching to know that *we* know, right?"

Whoever is watching. "I think I'm going to be sick." She had been right in keeping it secret. I wouldn't have been able to react appropriately. That was my *home.* "So then who *is* watching?"

Leo cleared his throat dramatically. "I think I can answer that." He pulled a fancy laptop from the bag next to him. "The camera fits with what *I've* found so far."

"Right, the other bad news," I mumbled.

"So let me guess," Sloan began. "I'd like to think none of the reporters outside were *that* desperate for a story. So more likely, it would be the local mob itself. Someone in Sal's crew. We *did* help put away a nice chunk of their organization."

"Not on purpose," I objected. *Not that I regret stopping criminals. Right?*

"Be that as it may, we played a role. And they might

want to exploit our participation somehow." Sloan turned to Leo. "So what do you think, someone looking for dirt? They could try to discredit us or something."

"That's sort of what I'm thinking," Leo replied absently as he clicked on the keyboard.

"But you were doing research on Grant," I objected. "Why would *that* lead you to the mobsters being behind the camera?"

"Because it's one and the same." He spun the computer around to face us. "Hate to tell you, but I think you were right about your finger-delivery theory. There's evidence to suggest Grant here was your culprit."

I gulped, not wanting to accept his words. I had a traitor in my midst.

"Think about it," he continued. "He certainly had easy access, right? And was acting pretty funny. Asking you a lot of questions, suddenly being all friendly?"

I nodded absently, the truth of his words hitting hard and fast. "And then the pictures on his phone. Of my living room," I croaked, my throat suddenly dry. "That must've been when he planted it."

"I'd say definitely," Sloan replied.

"But why would he do this?" I put my coffee down to stare Leo down directly. It just wasn't adding up for me. "We weren't the best of friends, but how would the mobsters convince him to be so *devious*?"

"My guess," he replied, "is it didn't actually take much to convince him. Turns out Grant is definitely loaded . . . but now it's with debt. Beaucoup bucks on the credit cards."

He pulled a stack of printouts from his bag and laid it in front of us. "And it seems his family recently cut him off."

I glanced at the top sheet, an email from Grant to his parents. It was all caps and full of expletives, bursting with outrage that he would be deprived of funds. "That could explain him suddenly not paying the rent, then. Or his lunch tab. Our measly stipend from the internship would never cover the overhead on that house. Or his taste in designer duds."

"I see." Sloan nodded sagely. "So Grant gets himself in a financial bind, making him ripe for exploitation by the mobsters. They make him some kind of deal to spy on you, get on the inside. Most likely in exchange for some much-needed funds. Far as we know he only had a few more weeks here, with no permanent job lined up and no ties to the area. It was probably a no-brainer for him."

"Yeah, well," I muttered bitterly, "trusting that guy was clearly *my* no-brainer. I don't know what I was thinking."

"You were thinking you were a nice person, and you expect others to be the same." Sloan's sympathetic smile turned amused. "Don't worry, investigating will drive that impulse right out of you. Just give it time."

Great. I sighed, trying to refocus on the task at hand, not my bleary future outlook. "So it looks like he was helping the mobsters, trying to keep tabs on us. Maybe delivering the mystery finger on their behalf, as an unsuccessful warning. How does that fit in with his current situation? A kidnapping?"

"Maybe it's all the botching that got him there," Leo answered. "Think about it. If we're right, it looks like he messed up in delivering the finger without the note, rendering it useless. The police report would of course have had no mention, so the mobsters who hired him would figure it out pretty quick. Far as they know, you still have no knowledge of the connection, or the point." He shrugged. "And then you caught him snapping photos in your apartment. He might be *willing* to be devious, but he doesn't seem to be very good at it. So maybe he quit. Or more likely, they cut him loose."

"And I'd be willing to bet the mob guys don't just let things drop that easily," Sloan added. "Not if they can find a way to get something else out of you."

"Like a ransom," I said.

Leo shrugged. "If they figured out Grant's background, it would seem like an obvious choice for some quick cash. They're probably pretty desperate at the moment, with most of them in prison."

Pretty desperate. "You don't think they'd actually hurt him, right?" My voice quavered involuntarily as I pictured Grant in real danger for the first time.

"Don't worry," Sloan replied, unconcerned. "They just want money. And his family has plenty." She pulled me into a side-hug. "We can try to find another way first. But a payout is always our backup plan. Quick, easy and painless."

"Assuming they *will* pay out," Leo added.

I sighed, more confused than ever. "So where does that leave us now?"

"That depends on you, my dear," Sloan said. "It looks like Grant was working with our enemies, spying and plotting behind your back. Are you sure you even want to continue helping him?"

I let it all sink in a minute. They were right. It was a mess. But it seemed a mess mostly of Grant's own doing.

"No one would blame you for wanting nothing to do with any of it," Leo offered.

I should have felt no responsibility in the debacle. I was the one who was betrayed in all of it. But I couldn't help the nagging feeling in my gut.

"I agree, completely," I said. "And yet, I don't think I can just walk away. Not yet."

Sloan raised an eyebrow, seeming genuinely surprised.

"He may have been using me for his own gain," I continued. "But he would've never been in that position in the first place if it weren't for us. *We're* the reason those monsters went to him for his intel. And now for his money. I can't just leave him hanging."

Sloan and Leo shared a look. Their faces said it wasn't the answer they were hoping for—but it was the one they expected.

"Ok," Sloan said with a sigh. She turned to yell down the aisle. "Better get some pie for our friend here. Extra helping."

"Right up," Dottie called back.

Leo's face lit up with anticipation as he straightened in his seat.

"You want to pursue, we'll pursue," Sloan said with a shrug. "Really, what else do we have to do these days?"

NINE

"I still don't know what you're hoping to get out of telling them," Sloan argued into my ear as I drove to the office at the crack of dawn. I was honestly surprised she was up that early. She seemed a bit of a night owl. "There's no upside here. It's up to us. What are they gonna do?"

I was not buying her arguments this time. My mind was made up. I was telling my boss *everything*. "I really don't know. But maybe they can help get us some cooperation. A backup plan, at the very least." If Grant's family wouldn't believe us, maybe they would believe my employer. Once I convinced my boss to help, of course.

Our phone conversation with his parents the night before hadn't exactly gone as planned. Not only did they not offer to cover the ransom if necessary, but they refused to have *anything* to do with the 'supposed' kidnapping, as they called it. Didn't believe a word we said.

"We can try to convince the 'rents again once we know more," Sloan rebutted. "But if we do our jobs, it'll never even come to that. Let's just figure out who's behind it first. You can relieve your guilt when it's all over, if you must."

"I just feel in over my head, Sloan. I don't know what I'm doing."

61

"Who does?" she retorted. "You just make it up as you go. But *we* call the shots."

"I'm not so great at making decisions." I shrugged. "Much better at taking orders. I'm a *great* follower."

"I don't buy that. You're not giving yourself enough credit."

"I don't know." I put the car in park and stared down the front door to the building, resolving myself. "But if we can't call the police, I would just feel better if we could bring in some other 'grown-ups,' for lack of a better word. And since it's *my* coworker and *my* guilt, it's my call."

"*And* your funeral, I guess." Sloan replied with a sigh. "I'll check in later."

* * *

My heart was pounding when I arrived at my desk. I had a big conversation in front of me, and didn't know how long it could wait. My job was riding on how this discussion went. They certainly didn't have the whole story yet.

I opened my schedule on the computer and felt better instantly. My first patient had cancelled, leaving an opening. One just big enough to get this over with. I hoped.

I rushed down the hall to my boss Dr. Seymore's office and timidly knocked, requesting a discussion. She graciously invited me in and gazed down at me, curious, as I took a seat in front of her desk. "So what can I do for you? Has Grant made it in yet?

I took a deep breath, trying to do a final thought-gathering. I planned to lay out a detailed description of events, starting at the very beginning. An articulate chronological explanation, certain to get her up to speed and on our side.

That wasn't *quite* what came out.

"Grant's been kidnapped and it's all my fault," I gushed uncontrollably.

Dr. Seymore's eyes widened. Her mouth opened and shut. Then she crossed the room to close the door behind me, never taking her eyes off me.

She returned to her seat and took her own deep breath. "What are you talking about?"

I let it all out. It wasn't the coherent exposition I had hoped for, but it got the job done. I started with the appearance of Sloan, the dipping my toes into investigations. That before I knew it, I was facing down an angry businesswoman with a gun. Then just when everything had settled down, half the local mob was arrested and we were given most of the credit.

But now Grant was missing, and there was evidence to suggest he had been spying on me, possibly for the same mobsters. And that he had something to do with the chopped finger that was found. I finished up with finding the ransom note and the futile discussion with his parents.

Dr. Seymore looked grim as I wrapped up my rambled detailing. "That's . . . quite a story."

She sat back in her chair, quietly pondering for a long minute. Then she leaned forward and scribbled some notes on a legal pad. The wait was brutal.

She looked back up at me. "You told me the other day he had texted you that he was home sick. Was he already missing, or was that the truth?"

I averted my eyes. "I thought I was covering for him. Fellow intern and all."

"I see." She scribbled something on her pad. "And this . . . . evidence . . . that he had something to do with the finger. A note, you said? Did he show it to you?"

I shook my head. "I found it. In his desk."

"So you were searching in his private belongings, before anything even happened?"

"No. Well, not exactly." *Strange direction to take.* "Honestly, I was just looking for a candy bar. The note was just laying there, in his drawer."

"So he offered you a snack?"

"No, he was already gone. But I thought he was just playing hooky. I had to take over his patients for the day and didn't have time to eat anything."

"So you were helping yourself." She narrowed her eyes a little. "And do you have a habit of stealing from your coworkers?"

What is happening here? "Of course not. It was just, I was . . ." I started to stammer, embarrassed and confused. I felt my face redden.

Dr. Seymore looked back at her notepad, moving on. "So the ransom note, left on his computer. I assume you went to his house trying to find him? Trying to help?"

I sighed in relief. "I did. I started to get worried when he was gone the second day."

"But you didn't say anything to me, to anyone, choosing instead to 'cover for him,' as you put it." She pressed her lips together before continuing. "And I certainly didn't give you his address. You obtained it through other means, I guess?"

I nodded. "A friend."

"A . . . mutual friend?"

I lowered my head a little. "No."

She made another note on her pad. "And when you found this ransom note. Last night, you say. You then tried calling his parents? I understand Grant has nothing to do with his family. Hasn't for many years."

"Well . . . that's not entirely true. It seems he's recently been in disagreement with them, but they're definitely in touch. We thought they should know." I forced myself to stop nervously fidgeting with my sleeves. "And we wanted to have a backup plan on the ransom. Make sure we could get them to pay if we had to."

Dr. Seymore scoffed. "And what would possibly make you think they could pay? We've discussed Grant's meager background extensively in the past."

I gulped. I didn't want to be the one to explain all this. But there was no choice. "That story is not . . . entirely true either."

Dr. Seymore looked taken aback. Amazingly, she seemed more stunned at this than at any other facet of the story. "What part?"

"Well, all of it." I averted my eyes once again. "He actually comes from a wealthy family. Very wealthy. And definitely never lived on the street."

She gazed at me coldly. "So many secrets, I see. All a big joke on the boss. And Grant confided this to you?"

I tried to keep from squirming. "No." I could see where this was headed.

She leaned toward me a little, inquisitive. "Then how did you know about this wealthy family?"

I knew I needed to stick to short, sweet answers at this point. *Why am I suddenly on trial?* "A . . . friend told me." "This private investigator friend? The one that has drug you into this whole mess?" She pursed her lips again. "I take it you're still working with her, then."

"Not actively, no. I have taken a break from the investigating business."

"Doesn't really *seem* like it, now does it?" She dropped her pen on the notepad and pushed them both aside. "As I see it, so far you're snooping around in your coworker's desk. In his private bedroom. Stealing from him. Digging up his personal history. Hiding the fact that he's missing and lying about it. To me. What if something really is wrong?"

"That's why I'm here." I leaned forward, earnest." I'm certain there *is*."

"Then we need to call the police. What you probably should've done in the first place."

I shook my head and reached toward her, desperate to get things back on track. "I know. I want to. But the ransom note specifically says no police. We *can't*."

"I see." She grabbed her pen and made another note.

I held my breath as she sat back again and studied me, her face expressionless. *Surely she understands the gravity of the situation.*

"I'll have to get back to you on this," she finally said, smoothing her skirt as she stood to hover over me. "You should really get back to work."

TEN

It hadn't taken very long.

By lunchtime I was parked down the street behind my apartment building, waiting for Sloan. She had agreed to meet as soon as I sent a mayday signal. I wanted to sneak in through the backdoor in the basement to avoid the possibility of reporters that were sometimes still lingering out front. I couldn't take facing them. Not today.

Sloan appeared at my car window within minutes. She pressed a bottle of wine to the glass and gave me a sad smile. "Brought reinforcements."

I slid out of the car, grabbing my depressing little box of personal items on the way. I hadn't had much of a presence in my student-extern desk. Just a handful of organizational tools I had supplied on my own.

"You don't even like moscato." I straightened with a sigh, emotionally exhausted. "Go ahead, you can say it."

"Wouldn't dream of it. And you're right. That's why I brought another friend." She held up a brown paper bag, undoubtedly disguising whatever ingredients went into a martini. "But it's not about me. I'm not the one who got fired today."

"I'm not *fired*," I retorted. "Just on a leave of absence. A very, very brief one. Very." I started walking to avoid her annoyingly sympathetic expression. "I'll be back at work in no time. Just in time to get my hours in so I can graduate, in fact. It won't be a problem."

I just have to figure out how first.

"So why did you get sent home, exactly?" Sloan spoke carefully, as if afraid of upsetting me. "They're mad you're trying to . . . help your coworker?"

I sighed. "More like blaming me for his disappearance. Which I took full responsibility for—"

"And which *I* told you is crazy," Sloan interjected. "It's. Not. Your. Fault."

"Whatever." I waved her off. "But to them, none of this would've happened without me. And they're right. There would be no dismembered finger—"

"We can only assume," she interrupted again.

"Sure," I conceded. "No media circus harassing everyone at work. And now Grant's disappearance. I'm at the center of everything. And a *major* liability."

Sloan was aghast. "They said that?"

I nodded. "I've brought 'undue attention and danger to their doorstep,' according to my boss. So she just thought it would be best if I weren't there for a little while. Let everything cool off a bit."

"I see." Sloan raised an eyebrow to me. "And you believe her? That you'll just go back when this thing settles down?"

I took a deep breath, not wanting to face the question. "I have to. But to be safe, I think getting Grant back is really my only chance. If everything turns out fine, surely they'll let me finish my internship." I cringed. "Even if I don't get to keep the permanent job they offered me for after graduation. That's gonna be gone for sure."

Sloan narrowed her eyes. "You want that job, we'll make sure you have it. We can dazzle them with our brilliant resolution to everything. Don't you worry."

I nodded. I couldn't truly believe her, but her confidence did make me feel better. *We'll figure something out.*

"So I take it they don't want to help find Grant?" she continued. "Is she at least going to call his parents?"

"Wants nothing to do with it. Grant lied about his family from the very beginning. So she feels it's really none of their business to call parents they aren't even supposed to know existed."

"One way to look at it, I guess." Sloan pondered this as we started up the back stairs to my apartment. "And they agreed we shouldn't call the police? That actually surprises me."

"Another liability, as she sees it." I shrugged. "If they make that call despite the kidnapper's warning, and things go wrong . . . let's just say the prospect of being held responsible was suboptimal to my boss. Said that decision belonged to his family, and they are choosing to stay out of it. She will respect their wishes."

"Well, for once I happen to agree with corporate thinking. Or at least the result of it."

I shrugged and glanced to Sloan as we approached the landing. "Guess it's just us then."

"It's easier that way. No messy *wannabe* authorities in our way." Her eyes narrowed, quizzical, as she looked past me down the hall. "Isn't that your door?"

I whipped my head to see a rotund female figure dart down the hall, away from my apartment. A folded piece of paper was attached to the door with red tape.

"Can I help you?" I called after them.

The woman glanced back before continuing on, headed

for the front stairs. It was my landlord. I frantically tried to recall her name but couldn't place it.

"Sorry, in a hurry," she called over her shoulder.

We sprang toward the door and snatched down the paper. I gave it a once-over and handed it off as I rushed in the woman's wake. I could see her head bobbing a flight down when I reached the top of the stairs.

"Can't we talk about this?" I called down.

She continued on without a glance.

"Please," I tried again. "Let's work something out."

Reluctant, she paused her escape to glance up and meet my eyes. "Look. You're a nice kid, but I just don't need the headache. Getting complaints left and right. People traipsing in here uninvited, harassing people outside. I just can't renew you. I'm sorry."

The woman ducked her head and continued down the stairs, moving away as quickly as her bulky frame would let her. I watched her, fascinated, until she disappeared at the bottom. Then I turned back to a wide-eyed Sloan.

"Can't say I've ever had a landlord run from me before," I said with a half-smile, trying to lighten what I knew would be a terrible mood once this sank in. A foul, wretched mood to match my terrifically horrible day. *Good thing she brought wine.*

Sloan's face contorted strangely.

"It'll be okay." I shrugged and started back down the hall toward her. "I'll figure something out."

She bit her lip and took a breath, hesitating.

My face fell instantly. "What now?"

She reached a finger out and pushed my door open an inch. "Did you happen to leave your door unlatched?"

What? I leapt forward and shoved the door open, slamming it against the far wall. I sucked in a breath at the view. Beyond the threshold lay a wasteland of my meager belongings. The contents of my living room lay in a chaotic pile on the floor.

We walked through in silence. The bedroom and bathroom were in similar condition, but everything seemed intact and present. I hadn't had much of value to begin with.

My stomach roiled as I returned to the shambles of my living room. "At least nothing's taken, I think."

"Laptop?"

"In my car. That was lucky, at least." I tore my gaze away from the rubble. "Guess we call the police?"

Sloan took in the room once more, then shook her head, decisive. "Security can handle all that. I don't think we should hang around here." She grabbed our bags off the kitchen counter and tossed mine over. "We're going to my place."

***

"Don't tell me you changed your mind about moving." I glanced back at Sloan, still hovering in the doorway of her apartment.

Her face informed me that was most definitely not the case.

We inched further inside and surveyed the now-familiar scene. The contents of her large open room, previously stacked in neat boxes, now lay like rubble on her hardwood floor and rugs. Pots and pans adorned the tops of the piles. Empty cardboard was thrown to the perimeter.

"Not you too," I managed to eek out at a whisper.

Sloan stayed mute, just staring. Calculating.

"I just don't believe it," she finally blurted. "I'm so careful

. . . " She leaned down and picked up a picture frame. She gazed at it sadly, fragments of glass tinkling to the floor.

A noise at the back of the apartment made us both look up. Muffled thud. Then a toilet flush.

They're still here.

"Don't. Move." Sloan dropped the photo and sprinted behind us into the kitchen, dodging piles of overturned boxes. She crouched below the counter and disappeared.

I froze, unsure whether to obey or run. *Is she hiding?*

"What the . . . ?" Sloan exclaimed from behind the island. Her head popped up above the countertop, face drained of color as our eyes met. "Let's get out of here."

Before I could make my feet move, the bathroom door flew open and a figure began to move forward through the darkened back. We didn't have time to flee. I stopped breathing as I watched.

One last step brought his face into visibility.

"Just love what you've done with the place." Lucas beamed his megawatt grin at the two of us. "Knew you'd end up copying my style one day."

ELEVEN

Lucas and Sloan stared each other down. I gasped, finally breathing again. There was no danger here. No intruder. But my heart continued to race, regardless.

Lucas is back.

I would never have admitted it to Sloan, but my thoughts had wandered to her would've-been-brother-in-law a time or two since he disappeared. Months back he had helped us put the murder-for-hire businesswoman behind bars, and immediately hopped on his motorcycle and headed out of town without explanation. Leaving only memories of his impossibly handsome face to haunt my dreams.

"You," Sloan accused, gaping at the toned silhouette across the room. I couldn't tell if she was confused, angry, or relieved. Probably all three.

Unconcerned, Lucas shoved his hands in the pockets of his dark jeans and swaggered closer. He studied us closely for a moment, his amusement not well hidden. I watched both of them, waiting for someone to say something.

"And what style is that?" Sloan finally said. "Trash heap? You're right, that does ring a bell."

His grin officially broke loose. "Good to see you too."

Sloan's eyes narrowed. "It's no coincidence you finally show up again, right now." She stalked closer to him. "You can't tell me you just happened to resurface right as everything is going to hell."

Lucas closed the gap between them and gazed down at her, his dark chestnut hair grazing his eyes. "You're right. We both know that's not true."

Did he do this?

His voice turned soft as their eyes remained locked. "Of course I came as soon as everything started coming out. Did get a little delayed, though." He looked away, now quieter. "I'm sorry about that."

"So you just heard?" Sloan was trying hard to read him. "Or did you already know all this was coming?"

"It wasn't supposed to come out like this." Lucas shook his head, grimacing. "We were supposed to have some warning first. Enough to keep you out of it." He glanced at me. "Both of you."

"That's what Hudson said," Sloan spat, disgusted. "So apparently you, my business partner . . . seems like *everybody* knew what was going on but us. What happened to being a team?"

Lucas ignored her ire and stayed cool and collected. "Look, I'm here. I'll always back you up. But that doesn't mean I can always *tell* you everything, too. You know that."

Sounds familiar. Sloan seemed to have a similar outlook on our partnership.

Sloan sighed with frustration. "So . . . why do you know more than me? What do you have to do with it, anyway?"

"That's a . . . long story. Very long."

"You're in luck." She stomped across the room and plopped in the middle of the couch, propping both feet on an overturned ottoman in a dramatic sweep. She gazed up at Lucas, arms crossed and defiant. "Got nothing *but* time, these days."

Lucas hung his head before giving me a little wave, inviting me to the unavoidable chat. I took a seat next to Sloan. We both gazed at him expectantly as he settled on the opposite sofa.

"Look," he began. "I can't get into all the details—"

"But what are—" Sloan interrupted.

"—*But*," Lucas emphasized, taking over again. "You both now know the investigation you got caught up in had been going on for a long time. You came in at the end—"

"—helping get the ball rolling," Sloan interjected again, rolling her eyes. "We 'lit the match that started the fuse,' yada, yada. We've heard all that."

"Sure," he continued calmly. "But what you *don't* know is that I've been a part of that investigation from the very beginning. And as soon as I realized who and what we were dealing with—while you two were teasing out your confession like it was a little game—I started setting everything up. To turn it into the find of the century."

Sloan's eyes blazed. "So *you're* behind all this? You're saying you're responsible for turning our lives upside down?"

"Of course not." There was an edge creeping into his voice. "I'm saying you poked at a pretty big bear with your stunt. It had direct ties to the local mob. You would've had a pretty major problem on your hands no matter what."

Sloan and I exchanged a glance. She looked as sheepish as I felt.

Lucas sat back and crossed his arms, indignant. "But the second they had your people in handcuffs, I was helping make sure the fallout would be sent *up* the food chain, not back towards you. As quickly as possible. *And* making sure they would keep your names out of it." He sighed and shook his head. "But I guess something went wrong on that part."

I lowered my gaze, deeply uncomfortable with the new information. *He's been working behind the scenes . . . for us?* We had been careless. Acting like renegades, charging into things we knew nothing about. Like silly children getting in over our heads.

"Now don't get me wrong," Lucas continued, suddenly more chipper. "It was the best thing that could've happened. We really *had* been waiting for just the right thing to put an end to all this."

"But it's *not* the end," Sloan said. "For us, it's just the beginning. Our lives are torn apart. Our homes are torn apart. I can't go to my office." She motioned to me. "And she's even lost her job."

"It's just a *leave*," I argued.

Lucas really focused on me for the first time. "I'm sorry to hear about your internship. I know how long you've worked to get here."

You do?

What exactly did he know about me? I knew almost nothing about him. Except those dreamy, now agonizingly sympathetic emerald eyes. I stared back but said nothing.

His gaze turned inquisitive. "So you were fired, errr . . . put on a leave, because of the news? Just for having been involved? Not sure why it's any of their business."

"All the news didn't help," I replied slowly, trying to find the best way to explain. "And it *was* affecting the office, with all the media harassing people at work. But I think the final straw was my coworker."

Sloan jumped in to help. "There's a bit of a situation. Well, another one. It's sort of popped up."

Lucas's face contorted with surprise and annoyance immediately. He directed it at Sloan. "You're already caught up in something new? I won't be able to sweep up behind you forever, you know." He thrust his hand in my direction. "And now there's *two* of you."

I gulped.

Sloan was undeterred. "We didn't start this new one. If anything, *you* did. The mob was apparently *your* deal. We just stumbled into it, like you said."

He sucked in a deep breath and focused into the distance a moment, letting it out slowly. I had a feeling he was well-practiced at tamping down his frustration with his unruly sort-of sister-in-law. He turned to me, his voice unnaturally patient. "What is she talking about? And what does *your* coworker have to do with the mob, exactly?"

How to explain? "We . . . think my fellow intern could've been hired by some mobsters, to spy on us. Or me, anyway. We found a camera Grant planted in my living room. And I caught him taking pictures."

"Don't forget the dismembered finger," Sloan added. "I'd say that points to the mafia being involved."

"Finger?" Lucas's face was suddenly ready to explode. "What *finger?*"

"We'll get to that later." Sloan waved off his interest. "What is much more pressing is that Grant is now *missing*. And it appears the mob may be holding him for ransom."

Lucas sat bolt upright. He watched us closely, looking for signs of amusement. He didn't find any.

Sloan shrugged. "Not that I'm sure we should even get involved." She motioned at me. "He's never done anything for Quinn here, that's for sure. He's a lying, cheating scoundrel, far as I'm concerned."

"But *we're* the reason he's kidnapped," I said.

"So you say." Sloan sighed. "I'm not convinced."

"Well, my boss thinks we are," I retorted, "so we have to get him back. It's my best shot at being able to graduate. And I only have a couple weeks before it's too late."

"Now that's a reason I can get on board with," she conceded. "Fine. We'll find your frenemy, so you can get your job back and keep from wrecking your whole career. If you still *insist* you need another one."

"Good." My gut was beginning to question my own argument, though. *Should I have learned a lesson?* We'd caused enough trouble already. Our involvement could only dig ourselves in deeper. But I didn't see any other way.

Lucas cleared his voice dramatically, getting our attention. "Now that we have that settled, would one of you care to tell me what *exactly* is going on?"

We started at the beginning, taking turns. Lucas listened closely, trying hard to show no reaction to our story. But I did catch a few microscopic twitches of his jaw, particularly when we described finding my place also trashed a little while ago. He was concerned.

Lucas was quiet for a moment when we finished. "Quite a web you two have woven," he finally mused.

Sloan and I looked at each other and shrugged, resigned. We had no more fight left.

"We haven't done *anything*," Sloan said quietly. "Not since the original arrests months ago. We didn't know all this could happen."

"Exactly," Lucas snapped. "You'd be shocked what you don't know a lot of the time." His eyes softened as he turned to me. "I am sorry about your job, though. I'm sure we can get that sorted out later. But it'll make things a lot easier for now."

I stiffened. "What's easier? Me losing my career?"

"You not needing to show up at the office everyday," Lucas replied. "And your apartment. You actually got lucky with that lease. Now I don't have to pull strings to get you out of there. You're free."

To do what?

I truly didn't know the answer. I hadn't had time to process the fact that I was now jobless and soon-to-be homeless.

"You can keep yourself *safe*," Lucas continued, answering my silent question. "And stay out of all this while the authorities sort it out."

Sloan let out a chuckle. Lucas's head snapped toward her, eyebrows raised.

"Don't worry." Sloan raised her hands in the air in surrender. "I know I can't stay here now. It's compromised. Haven't found my new place yet, but I can certainly step up the search."

Lucas turned to me, now amused. "And just where does she think she's going?"

I shrugged. "Said she's going wherever the wind blows."

He forced a smile to Sloan. "Yeah, that's not gonna happen. You're both coming with me."

I tried to not sound alarmed. "Where?"

"Can't say just yet. We don't know who could be listening. Like she said, this place is compromised. So's yours, obviously. I'm gonna have to stash you two somewhere for a while."

I checked Sloan's reaction to help figure out my own. I couldn't read her.

Meanwhile my own panic was rising. "Are we going into witness protection or something?"

"Nah, nothing so formal for now," He shrugged. "You're

just going off the radar for a bit. But don't worry, it'll be an upgrade. I crash there sometimes. It's nice."

How would he know what's an upgrade for me?

"I'm not sure . . ." I trailed off, my mind whirling. Everything was moving so fast. A week ago I had a normal job and boring little apartment. I had no idea who to trust anymore.

Once again Lucas read my mind. "Just trust me." He finished his argument with a breathtaking smile. "And really, what else are you gonna do?"

He had a point.

I tried another glance next to me. "Sloan?"

She kept her eyes locked on Lucas, staring. Calculating. "Fine," she finally said, chin raised. "Like I said, I was planning on getting out of here soon anyway. I'm over this place. We'll try it your way." She turned to me, mood visibly lightened. "We can be roomies."

"Great." Lucas clapped his hands and sat forward. "We leave immediately. And don't bother packing. My guys'll handle everything."

"I'm guessing you mean *my* guys," Sloan retorted.

Lucas shrugged. "Like you said, we're a team."

"Fine." Sloan raised her eyebrows inquisitively. "But you took something of mine. Where is it?"

He gazed back blankly. She leaned forward, bringing her deadpan face close to his. "Where's my heat?"

Heat?

"Oh, right." He stood and reached to the waistband at his back, his hand emerging with a small pistol. "Almost forgot." He laid it on the coffee table between us.

Sloan grabbed up the weapon, checked the chamber and dropped out the magazine in one swift movement. Satisfied, she shoved it closed again and laid it gently back on the table. As if it were the most normal thing in the world to have sitting across from us.

We would have to discuss the loaded gun situation later.

"Why'd you take it?" Sloan asked. Her eyes narrowed. "And how'd you get into my safe, anyway?"

Lucas smirked. "I couldn't very well surprise you when you have that within reach, now could I? That doesn't sound very smart."

He turned and moved quickly across the room, turning back at the front door. "And I've always known how to get into your safe. Duh." He grinned and swung open the door. "Sit tight, and say nothing. Get some sleep. I'll keep a guy outside just in case. Someone'll be by to collect you first thing in the morning. No argument. No tears."

Just who does he think he is?

Sloan called out to him as he entered the hallway. "So how do we know it wasn't *you* who trashed this place, anyway? Seems like a nice way to scare me into submission."

Lucas turned back once more and surveyed the upturned room. Then he gazed at both of us and shrugged, a smug half-smile creeping onto his face. "Guess you never will."

Yep, would-be marriage or not, these two are definitely related.

TWELVE

These people move fast.

Trying to follow orders, we had done our best to not discuss the situation any further that night. Our worried eyes did most of the talking. We would have plenty of time to deliberate once we got where we were going. Wherever *that* was.

I woke from my dreamless, tumultuous sleep with my limbs contorted uncomfortably on the sofa. Sloan didn't look much more peaceful on the opposite couch. The gun lay untouched on the table between us. I averted my eyes at the reminder. *We're okay. For now.*

A loud rapping rang through the apartment, for what I realized wasn't the first time. The familiar pound had awoken me. It quickly began to get more insistent.

After confirming through the peephole, I opened the front door, still groggy. A dark mass of power and energy blew past me into the room. He marched straight to the den and stood over Sloan.

"You can sleep when you're dead," Hudson roared. He looked up at me as she stirred. "Time to get rolling."

Within minutes we were ushered into a large black Yukon XL out front, one of several identical vehicles idling in a row.

The crew of black-clad young men finished stuffing the other SUVs with the contents of Sloan's loft. We watched through the darkly-tinted windows as they hustled.

Apparently finished in what seemed like record time, the men slammed the rear doors closed and hopped into the vehicles. A moment later Hudson flung himself in our driver's seat and slammed it into gear. We took off in a burst of power, hot on the heels of the SUV ahead.

A block later I saw the first vehicle veer off, away from the rest. Then another. In less than a minute we were alone.

I finally found my voice for the first time that day. "Where'd everybody go?"

"They're gonna take the scenic route," Hudson said.

He glanced at me in the rearview mirror, noting my confusion. "Can't very well make a stealthy escape with a whole train of vehicles. We'll all take a different path and arrive at different times. Much easier for one vehicle to lose a tail."

I glanced at Sloan, for whom this was clearly not noteworthy, then back up front. "You think we'll have a tail?"

Hudson shrugged. "No reason to take chances."

Fair enough. "So then I guess we'll have to go do the same thing at my place?"

"All that's already on its way. Just sit back."

On its way. They had been in my place. With my things. Everything I owned.

Having already had my apartment raided, I was beginning to get used to the invasion of privacy.

But I didn't have to like it.

Sloan's voice interrupted my pensive sulk. "Before we get there, you're gonna need to put this on." She handed me one of the two brown shopping bags she had carried with her. "Your new uniform."

I peered inside, hesitant. *What now?* Thick navy fabric filled the top. I reached in and pulled out a hooded sweatshirt.

"That's just to get you started," Sloan said. "Don't forget the accessories."

In the bottom of the bag lay a pair of black-framed glasses and a single tiny silver loop earring.

I put on the glasses, curious. Fake lenses.

"No time to get your prescription," she added. "You can just wear your contacts."

"So by uniform, you mean disguise." I inspected the bottom of the bag, looking for the other earring. "You have a secret planning meeting with Hudson or something?"

"Nope. Just basic protocol. We need to lay low for a bit." She leaned toward me and lowered her voice a bit. "And then as other people, we can do whatever we want."

"We'll need to talk about that," Hudson called back, watching us sternly in the mirror.

"Sure. We'll see." Sloan reached into her own bag and pulled out a stringy mess of black and yellow. Wigs. She threw the dark one my way. "Can't forget the most important piece."

I inspected the mass. An above-shoulder raven bob with bangs. I smoothed the choppy layers flipping erratically at the bottom. "Hmm. So who am I supposed to be, anyway?"

"Personal assistant." Sloan slid the blonde wig onto her head and fluffed the long strands. "To a spoiled self-proclaimed overlooked actress. Ready to break out as a star any minute. In her own mind, anyway."

"Sounds like a blast." My sarcasm was biting this morning. I tucked my hair up under the wig, trying it on for size. "So why do *I* have to be the assistant?"

She raised an eyebrow at me and pointed at her wig. "You

wanna play the drama queen? I just thought the quiet, mistreated employee would suit you better. Being your first long-term role and all. But you're welcome to it if you'd like."

I studied Sloan's immediate melding into the look like a chameleon. *No way I could pull that off.* "No, you're right." I pushed an errant strand out of her face. "This suits you."

"You can have fun with it, though." She gave me a sly grin. "Maybe you're secretly writing a tell-all book about her as well. Give yourself ulterior motives. And secrets."

I laughed, trying to relax into the situation. "You really put a lot of thought into this, huh?"

Sloan pulled a brilliant blue rhinestone-studded scarf from the bag and flung it around her neck. "If we have to leave our real lives behind for a bit," she said, her eyes twinkling, "the least we can do is make the fake ones interesting."

***

"Please *do* be more careful." Sloan hovered beside the men as they hauled boxes out of the vehicles, cringing at every little jostle. "Anything broken will be sure to come out of your paycheck."

The men largely ignored her harassment as they hustled. I did catch one errant sneer, though. He continued on quickly. No one asked any questions or dared respond.

I stood awkwardly to the side, fiddling with the fake nose ring Sloan had forced on me. While definitely not my style, it *was* sort of fun to feel like someone else. And I was pretty sure even I wouldn't recognize myself.

Sloan directed her glare on me. "Maybe you should be helping too, rather than standing around twiddling your thumbs?"

So it begins. "Right. Of course." I cast around for something to grab, my face reddening. She was going to enjoy this a little too much, maybe.

I chose unwisely and struggled up the sidewalk with a box much heavier than it looked. I was anxious to get inside, curious what lay ahead in the downtown two-story Victorian we were now to call home. But a crack in the sidewalk halted my efforts. I tumbled to the ground on top of the half-spilled carton of books.

I hopped up quickly, hoping no one was paying attention. Perhaps my character was just a klutz? Yes, that would work.

A shadow darkened the pile as I bent to retrieve the contents. "Can I give you a hand?"

I looked up to find a dark-haired young man, not much taller than myself. His cute boyish face was partially hidden under dark-framed glasses that were a close match with my own. "That looked sort of painful," he said, his smile sympathetic.

"Not really." I gazed back uneasily, not ready for strangers. "Umm. Who are you?"

Now his smile was amused. I followed his eyes down to his blue uniform and the sack on his hip. The mail carrier. Obviously. "Oh. Right."

He ignored my embarrassment and squatted next to me, swiftly refilling the box. Flaps reclosed, he straightened and held out his hand. "Just moving in? I'm Levi."

A quick panic rushed over me. We hadn't discussed cover names. *Surely I can't be myself.* My finger reached to touch my nose ring, absently searching for inspiration. I blurted out the first thing that came to mind. "Daisy?" I grabbed his hand. "I'm Daisy."

Daisy?? I did not feel much like a Daisy.

"Interesting name. Welcome to the neighborhood, Daisy." The shake lingered a moment while he smiled intently at me.

A loud throat clearing nearby startled me. Lucas stood a few feet away, watching. Glowering. I quickly withdrew my hand.

"My noble director," Sloan exclaimed from behind, rushing toward Lucas. "So excited you've made it."

Lucas remained silent, reading our faces. Letting it play out.

Sloan grabbed his arm and turned him away, speaking a mile a minute. "As soon as they're finally done we can get right to work. I have *loads* of ideas. This place is an absolute goldmine." She pulled him toward the house, beginning a non-stop chattering. She turned back at the door. "Whenever you're ready," she called back to me irritably before disappearing inside.

"Director?" Levi said. "What is all this?"

I shrugged and nudged at the box with my foot, trying to buy myself time to think. "She wants to make a movie?" I glanced up at the house, looking for a hint. "A horror film. That's why we're here."

He raised an eyebrow. "You're an actress?"

No need to look quite so skeptical. "Personal assistant to Her Highness."

"Ah." He smirked. "Looks like a blast."

I couldn't help but smile back.

"And sounds like we both better get back to work," he said, finally breaking our eye contact.

"I think you're right."

"But I guess I'll be seeing you around," he continued. "Downtown, we hand-deliver. The box is at your door. And I'm usually here around this time." He turned away, flashing me one last grin as he headed down the sidewalk. "So . . . I guess you'll know where to find me."

THIRTEEN

Sloan said nothing as I entered. But I knew from her expression there would be questions later. I didn't necessarily have answers.

I dropped my box on the floor in the grand two-story foyer and shrugged at her. Lucas caught our silent exchange as he entered from the hall to the left. We both looked away.

He stepped closer and pinched a golden strand of Sloan's wig, inspecting it with a grimace. "Already scheming little roleplay games, I see." He shook his head. "That really won't be necessary, seeing how you're both going to be staying put. At all times."

Sloan scoffed. "We never discussed all that. We have our own interests to pursue. We have *lives*."

"Not anymore, you don't." Lucas's face was stern. "Your job is to stay here and be safe."

I looked to Sloan, not prepared to argue with him or the rest of the muscled men running around. She was busy staring Lucas down. Choosing her words.

Finally she broke the silence, her expression serious. "Fine, I'll make you a deal. You can send a team with us. They can follow us wherever we go, 24/7. But we go where we want, no questions asked."

Lucas opened his mouth to rebut. Sloan swiftly held up a finger to stop him. "In *exchange*," she continued, "we'll stay out of our normal lives. Play these characters, be somebody else while we're here. We already can't work. It'll just be a hobby."

Lucas glared back, but did not immediately respond. A tiny muscle twitched in his jaw.

Sloan reached out and gently touched his bicep, her voice soft. "We have to have *something* to hold on to. Let us have our fun. Nobody will pay any attention to these silly nobodies that moved in here."

Lucas appeared to be softening, but still raised a skeptical eyebrow. "I find that hard to believe."

She sighed. "Pretty please?" She put on what was clearly a well-practiced innocent face. Her bottom lip puckered ever-so-slightly as she gazed up at him hopefully like a puppy begging for a treat.

Two can play that game. When he glanced to me, I affected the same naivety, making sure to bat my big eyes just a little as I gazed up at him.

Lucas finally grimaced and looked away. "Fine." He dug into his pocket, pulling out several sets of keys. He shoved two of them in Sloan's hand. "But you're not here to make friends." He glanced at me. "Or flirt with the neighbors."

I averted my eyes.

"We're here to keep you *out* of trouble," he continued. "Friendly people lead to questions. We don't need questions right now. We need privacy."

"Fine," Sloan replied, indignant. "But speaking of privacy—no cameras. Not in the house. If we could hack into them, so could someone else. That's not negotiable."

I admired the way Sloan had no difficulty standing up to him. There was no way I had the nerve to speak to him like that. At this point I was lucky to speak to him at all. When my mouth would move properly.

Lucas stared her down again, eyes narrowed. "I'll cancel the install," he finally mumbled through gritted teeth.

"Great," Sloan said cheerfully. She turned to me. "Shall we check the place out before we run some errands? Might need to pick up a few things."

"If you insist on going out, the guys'll drive you," Lucas growled. "But no funny business or I'm locking you both in here. I mean it."

We watched as he turned and stormed back down the hall. I hoped Sloan wasn't also admiring the view as he disappeared. The man sure knew how to make an exit.

"Forget all that," Sloan said, waving a disinterested hand in his wake. "He's just grumpy he has to deal with all this. He'd rather be skulking around in the shadows somewhere, talking to no one."

Her comments did nothing to quell my fascination with the mysterious alpha-male with a clear soft spot for my maddening friend.

I nodded and took another look around, anxious to see the rest of what looked to be quite the spacious hideout. "Well, he's right, anyway. This place definitely looks like an upgrade for me." I reached down to grab up the too-heavy box again. "Oh, we're here making a horror film, by the way."

Sloan gazed up at the winding staircase behind us and touched a finger to her lips, thinking. She smiled. "That could work. Extra campy, I think."

***

"I . . . don't think they're gonna like that." The dark-skinned man in the driver's seat gazed disapprovingly at us in the rearview mirror. He looked torn as to how hard to argue.

Know what you mean. I wasn't sure I approved, either. Having just gotten into the idea of hiding behind a disguise for a while, I was hesitant about already ditching those covers.

"It's just for this afternoon, I promise," Sloan responded to both of our concerned faces. "Then we go right back to our roles. But we can't do this next part under cover. It'll never fly."

Before we could argue further, Sloan flung open her door and hopped out. I hesitated only a moment before doing the same. The tall, menacing fence of the regional jail loomed ahead across the parking lot.

"Will you at least finally tell me what we're doing here?" I hadn't even been able to unpack and settle in before she had whisked me into another vehicle, setting off on our next 'operation' with zero details. *This better be about finding Grant.*

"It's the finger," she said. "I got word about the print. The previous owner of the severed digit is not deceased, as we had assumed. He's in jail, awaiting trial. And we're going to pay him a little visit."

She began moving toward the building and I hustled to catch up. "He's *here*? Who?"

"An old friend we spent some time following a while back. He's quite the entrepreneur, if you recall. You particularly enjoyed his alfredo. *Not* so much his hospitality."

My throat constricted as her meaning dawned on me. "Salvatore?" I croaked.

"The very same." She glanced at me. "I'm curious to hear the story of how he happened to gift his own finger to you. Apparently he's not talking to the official investigators yet."

"I do want to know—but aren't we going to start working on Grant's disappearance? That's all I'm worried about right now."

"It's all the same thing, remember? We're pretty sure Grant planted the finger. So whoever sent him to do that could be behind his kidnapping." She turned to face the building ahead, resolute. "We need answers."

***

"Sorry, no can do." The prison security officer shrugged in the doorway of the interview room we had been waiting in. He did not look at all sorry. "Nothing I can do without an authorization."

"But they were supposed to get us the authorization," Sloan argued. "I was told it would be all set."

He glanced down at the clipboard in his hand again and shrugged. "All I know's it's not here. It's bureaucracy, what are you gonna do? You the guy's lawyers?"

"Not exactly," Sloan grumbled.

"Then you'll have to try again some other time. Can't bring him out today." He motioned for us to leave the room.

We both followed silently, Sloan sulking beside me. We could see several empty interview rooms through the plexiglass we passed. An irregular jangle rang out from the hallway ahead, echoing off the dingy cinder block walls. The sound chilled me.

The jangle continued closer and turned the corner, bringing with it an orange-clad prisoner, chained and led by a guard. I stopped in my tracks as recognition took hold immediately. *Salvatore*. I stared, breathless, as my companions came to a stop as well.

Sal's eyes moved from the floor as he sensed our presence, and he halted. His beady eyes glinted as he studied our faces, his own recognition setting in.

"Keep moving," his handler barked.

Sloan reached her hand out. "Please, just a second," Sloan said. She turned to our guide. "This is who we came to see."

Salvatore's eyebrows raised as he watched, silent but interested.

"It don't change a thing," our guard replied, indifferent. "No auth, no visit. Says right here."

"Just let us have one minute, right here," Sloan implored, directed to both of the guards. "Who's gonna know? Please."

The guards exchanged uneasy looks, silently considering the request. But apparently Sloan's pleas were undeniable, for the second time that day.

I really needed to learn her tricks.

"One minute," the drill-sergeant guard snapped. "No touching."

Sloan wasted no time. She turned to Salvatore, hand on her hip, her eyes now matching his icy glare. "What's with the games, Sal?"

His expression turned amused as he studied her face and beyond. "Games? I've taken up a little chess lately. Maybe some shuffleboard. But if you have something more *fun* in mind . . ."

Our eyes caught on Salvatore's hands as he gestured, hands outspread. The left was missing an index finger.

"What happened to your finger?" Sloan said. "I don't believe it was missing the last time we saw you."

He raised his hand to inspect, curious, as if just noticing the absence. "Oh, this. This is nothing. An accident."

"An accident, huh? And where's that finger now? You see a doctor?"

He shrugged. "I have friends. They take care of me. Really, it wasn't a big deal. I have nine more. You shouldn't worry about this poor old man."

"Yeah?" I said. "Then who should we worry about?"

"Why do you ask *me*?" His eyes narrowed. "Curious girls like you probably have plenty of reason to watch your backs. Clearly *I* can't do anything from here."

"But apparently your lost finger can." I inched closer, my eyes narrowed. "It somehow paid us a visit."

I watched Salvatore's face closely. There was a momentary spark of curiosity, then recognition, in his eyes. Understanding. And possibly amusement.

He quickly tried to hide it under a mask of disinterest. "Yes, the police asked me about that, just as you do. But I didn't know who found my poor finger. Haven't seen it since we parted."

"Well, we have." I glared at him. "So what do you think that could mean?"

He shrugged. "Probably nothing." His hands spread as far as the chains would allow. "But if I were the one pointing fingers, sending people to prison . . . well, I'd have trouble not seeing the irony of it."

"Funny, that's just what the note said." Sloan said. "Definitely something about pointing fingers."

"Interesting. The police, they didn't say anything about a note. But great minds do think alike, I believe they say."

"So do devious minds, apparently." Sloan was becoming irritated. "But that clever little threat ended up getting her coworker kidnapped. He's now being held for ransom after delivering it."

"This can't be, no. Surely they would know you're a

terrible ransom. You could never pay. If I recall, you're poorer than my gardener, who I sadly just had to let go."

"Well, his wealthy family might have something to do with it," I spat.

Salvatore looked away, considering. He mumbled something softly in Italian. When he looked back up, his face was serious, almost concerned. "I don't know anything about this. I can't help you."

"So if you had nothing to do with it," Sloan said, her tone now conciliatory, "surely you'd want to help. Might even earn you some goodwill towards your own troubles, I'd think."

He considered. "Tell you what. I'll ask around, I get any visitors. What's her name?"

"His name's Grant," I said. "Grant Parker."

"Grant Parker, your coworker." He raised his eyebrows. "Not your boyfriend?"

I shook my head.

"Ok, then, you have my word. I'll pass his name around. See what I find. You're right, maybe I can . . . improve relations a little." He flashed a hopeful smile. "A little good press couldn't hurt."

"Alright, time's up," Salvatore's guard called out. "Gotta go."

A voice boomed from down the hall behind us. "What the heck is going on here?" Footsteps rapidly approached, echoing off the cold walls. "Who are you and why are you talking to my client?"

We turned toward the sound. A middle-aged man in an expensive suit gaped at us, livid. Then what looked like recognition set in.

"You two," he snarled.

"You're right." Sloan flashed a smile at the guards. "Time's up."

FOURTEEN

"I believe him." Sloan dropped her mug to the table with a sigh. "Darn it, I think he's telling the truth. He doesn't know anything about this."

I pushed aside my discarded creamers and picked up my own cup, desperate for my regular fix of Joe's coffee. "But Sal certainly knows who had his finger. There was no accident."

"True." She pointed a finger my way in agreement. "I don't believe that for a second. Something happened. Maybe a fight. Or better yet, a warning."

"So the question is, who would he cover for? Why would he want to help the person that did that to him?"

She shrugged. "Probably just some criminal-code thing."

I considered. "No rats, you mean."

"Right."

I sighed, exasperated. "So it's a dead-end then." The reality of our uselessness began to sink in. "And I think it's time to call the authorities. We have no idea what we're doing. And Grant is depending on us."

"Whoa, slow down there," Sloan said. "You owe that snarky, lying intern nothing. We're doing this to get your job back."

"But that's the point, we aren't doing *anything*. We're just spinning our wheels." I stared into my mug, beginning to sulk. "And now we have no leads, either."

"Again, hold on. I never said all *that*."

I glanced up, trying to read her face. Coy, as usual. "What does that mean?"

"I said I believed he doesn't know anything about Grant." Sloan picked up her coffee. "I said nothing about it being a dead end."

I sat silently, waiting. Staring. I knew her games by now.

Finally she gave up. She let slip a little smile and her mouth opened to speak. But then promptly shut again as her eyes caught on something.

"What the . . . heck?" She stared behind me, fascinated.

I turned to follow her gaze. A flurry of pink, rainbow, bleach blond and feathers was shuffling up the aisle, head down, kitchen doors swinging in their wake. Enormous black hi-top Chuck Taylor tennis shoes made their way toward us, incongruous with the rest of the frilly spectacle.

I tried to process the figure that came to a stop at the head of our table. A long-sleeved pink leotard and tutu clung to what was clearly a man's frame. Below, rainbow leg warmers covered dark hairy legs. Above, multicolored boa feathers floated around the semi-muscular shoulders straining against the tutu material.

The stringy blonde wig atop the disconcerting sight shifted, finally allowing us a view of the figure's face. The thick dark eyebrows and straight white teeth were unmistakable. A clearly embarrassed Sayid lifted his eyes to us and gazed back, silent.

Sloan's eyebrows raised as she continued to gawk. "You look like Big Bird from my tween nightmares."

He sighed and rolled his eyes. "Go ahead. Get it out of your system."

"No offense, Sayid. But you make a very ugly woman. Without any makeup, anyway. You could've at least asked for some help."

"It's not a lifestyle choice, I promise," he said through gritted teeth.

"So you're not trying to get in on the covert work, too?" Sloan continued, amused. "Because I hate to tell you, but there are better ways to go undercover. You're sort of missing the point."

"So hilarious," he grumbled. "None of this is my choice. Believe me."

"Then why are you doing it?" I asked, desperately curious.

Sayid averted his eyes, his face now reddening. "I'm pledging. And someone asked me to."

"Pledging, huh?" Sloan said. "So by that, you mean hazing. Isn't that not allowed anymore, or something?"

"No," he said, shaking his head. "Not hazing. Just . . . playing around. Goofing off."

"Right," I said. "You look like you're having a blast."

He looked away again, shuffling his foot against the tile. "It's only for a few days."

"Well, I hope they're worth it," Sloan said, her face skeptical. "Personally, I don't believe in friends who enjoy tormenting me."

"Depends on your definition of torment." I flashed her my own skeptical look. "I do believe you've been known to have a little fun at others' expense."

"Not the same at all," she said, aghast. "That's *actual* fun. Not mean-spirited *torture*."

Sayid shook his head. "I'm fine. And it's all I want. Then

I'll be part of the crew." His chin lifted a little. "I just have to get through this first."

"Uh oh," Sloan said, straightening as she stared behind me once again. "Incoming."

Who now? I turned to see Lucas charging through the front door, brow furrowed. His expression evolved as he moved closer, anger morphing into confusion. He slowed as he approached, getting a read on the strange figure before us.

His hesitation was abandoned when Sayid turned his way. A wide grin split his face. "What the heck happened here?"

Sayid's head dropped again.

Lucas took a step closer to inspect. "Sayid?" He reached up to pull back a strand of long synthetic hair, revealing a red, grimacing face. "Anything new with you I should know?"

Sayid's lips pressed tight together as he took a deep breath. He kept his eyes solidly on the floor. "Nope."

"Ok, man." He let the hair drop. "Cool either way. You do you."

Sayid rolled his eyes, clearly biting his tongue.

"Be nice, Lucas," Sloan chastised.

"I'm being supportive," Lucas argued, smirking. "How was I not nice?"

"Anyway," Sayid mumbled. "Dottie said this would be my new uniform if I didn't come out here to say hello. So now that we've all seen the show, I can get back to work."

We watched him lumber back down the aisle and squeeze his tutu through the swinging doors. Dottie's uneven cackle echoed from the back as he disappeared into the kitchen.

Lucas turned to us, eyebrows raised in question. "Should I ask?"

I shrugged. "Stupid fraternity stuff."

"Frats." Lucas cringed. "Never got that."

"Good thing," Sloan said. "Because they'd never get you, either. But please be sure you don't make fun of him. You know he worships you."

Lucas glanced toward the kitchen, his eyebrows giving a little twitch of consideration. "Well, that's his own poor decision." He turned back, eyes now twinkling. "One of many, it seems."

He shoved himself into the seat next to Sloan. "But at least *someone* is using a disguise," he continued, his amusement rapidly disappeared, "unlike some people I know." He glared at both of us. "People who promised to not only stay under cover, but to stay out of their normal lives. Surely no one would think to find you two *here*, huh?"

For once, Sloan looked sheepish. "It's just a quick visit, since we were already out of cover," she offered weakly. "Disguises go back on for good as soon as we head home. Promise."

He scoffed. "I've heard that before. Earlier today, I believe." He glanced toward the door. "How did you even get away with that, anyway?"

Sloan perked up a little, proud of her persuasive abilities. "I convinced our driver he can use it to check for tails. If someone's looking for us here, they'll figure out who. He's on stakeout."

Lucas rolled his eyes. "And I hear you already had your own little 'operation,' as you like to call it." He grabbed the coffee from Sloan's hand. "Visiting Salvatore in prison doesn't sound much like staying out of your normal life, either."

"No operation," Sloan said, flippant. "Just a chat. And

Sal is definitely not part of my *normal* life." She yanked the coffee back from Lucas's hands mid-sip. "But finding her co-worker *is* my life right now. The only thing we're concerned with."

Lucas stared her down.

She was unfazed. "You said no questions, remember? We do what we want."

He gave only a frustrated groan in response.

"So, just curious," she continued, now playing nonchalant. "Obviously Sal's in jail, as are most of his guys. But what about *his* boss?"

Lucas glanced up, studying her face a moment. "What do you mean?" He glanced to me, looking for answers. "What boss?"

I shrugged. I had no idea where she was going.

"Far as I know," he finally said, his words careful, measured, "Sal's in charge." He sat back and propped an arm across the back of the seat, ropes of thick-but-not-too-thick muscles popping out of his black t-shirt. "Has been for a couple years now. Why?"

"Right, of course. He's the boss." Sloan fidgeted with her napkin. "But somebody's gotta take over now, I figure. Since he's out of commission and all."

"We're not sure if anyone has stepped up yet," Lucas said. "So far it looks pretty chaotic. You've taken them down pretty good." Concern edged into his face. "Why do you ask?"

Sloan bit her lip a moment, thinking.

His eyes softened. "Are you worried about who might be after you?"

Sloan hesitated. "Yes." She let out a heavy sigh. "I guess that's it."

"Good," Lucas replied, coldly. His face turned hard again

as he straightened, his casual posture abandoned. "You *should* be worried. Maybe now you'll get it." He turned to gaze at me across the table. "That goes for both of you."

I withered under his gaze. I didn't believe Sloan's little scared act for a second, but he could certainly intimidate me. *And he has a point, doesn't he?*

"You're right," Sloan replied solemnly, giving him a direct look. "We'll take it seriously."

She picked up the large bag on the seat next to her and shoved her shoulder into Lucas. "Now let me out."

He slid out of the booth and offered his hand to her. She ignored it and hoisted the bag onto her arm as she emerged.

"But first I just have one final loose end to tie up," she said. "I have to get changed for my date."

She twirled and strolled into the back hallway toward the restrooms, Lucas staring in her wake. He finally turned and directed his glare toward me. *Boy, he's good at that death look.*

"Date?" he spat. His green eyes bore into me. "What is she talking about?"

I gulped. The accountant from the other day had just walked in and was strolling up the aisle toward us. I didn't want to be in the middle of it. *Whatever* it was.

"Quinn, right?" The man approached with a friendly smile and reached his hand out, his formal manner matching his tailored navy sport coat and khaki slacks. "Sloan's friend?"

I returned a quick shake. "Yes, good to see you. She'll be right out." I glanced at Lucas, unsure how to proceed. "I'm just gonna . . . go see if she needs anything."

I scurried toward the back before he could stop me. But I froze just around the bend when I heard voices resume. The two men were interacting. And I *had* to know.

With only a momentary twinge of guilt, I slid silently to the corner to listen.

"Sloan's date, huh?" Lucas said, his voice lightly tinged with hostility. I pictured him looking the guy up and down. "You're not exactly her normal type."

"Guess I'm just lucky, then," Christopher replied cheerfully, trying to diffuse the situation. "We go way back. And you are?"

"A big problem." Heavy-soled shoes stepped forward. "For you. If you so much as look at her the wrong way."

Christopher's voice became uneasy. "Ok, man. You, like, her brother or something?"

"Or something." Light hostility was replaced with icy venom. "*Man.* Just keep your hands off, show her the pleasant, boring evening I'm sure you excel at, and then say goodnight."

There was a long pause. Finally Christopher's voice reemerged, now very quiet. "You got it."

"Then I think we'll get along just fine." Lucas's tone became overly smooth and easy-going. "But if you know Sloan, you understand you never *really* know who's in the shadows. So watch your back."

After another long pause, I heard the boots again, headed for the door. I was dying to see Christopher's face, but knew I would surely be caught peeking. I had done enough snooping for today.

I turned for the restroom, hoping my face wasn't red with guilt. Sloan emerged before I could reach it, looking amazing in a summery spaghetti-strapped dress.

"You look great," I threw out quickly, hoping to head off any show of surprise from her that would give me away to Christopher. I spun on my heels to return, as if I had been with her the whole time.

She flashed me a smile as we turned the corner to find a pale-faced Christopher. Sloan didn't seem to notice. Despite his appearance, he pretended nothing had happened. Cheerful and polite, just as before.

After quick goodbyes, they took off, leaving me to mull what I'd seen while I nursed my coffee. I was stumped. And I daresay, disappointed?

No, that couldn't be it.

Maybe Sloan is mistaken. Perhaps the protectiveness Lucas always displayed was not simply family protectiveness, as she believed. Maybe that annoyingly sexy display I'd just witnessed was a sign . . . he was in love with her.

He could've fallen for his brother's fiancé in his absence. Loss brings people closer. It happens.

And if true, could Sloan feel the same, deep down?

Maybe I would need a slice of pie, too, just for good measure.

FIFTEEN

After a quick survey of my new room in the safe house, all set up and partially unpacked for me in my absence, I was ready to wash the day off and pass out. New homes, new identities, new objectives. And no real privacy. It was all a little much at once.

At least my new personal space was nice and cozy. And utterly devoid of security personnel. There was even an old fireplace to add hominess.

But what thrilled me at the moment was the en-suite bathroom, complete with vintage clawfoot tub. I quickly undressed and headed in to try a long soak. It was a luxury not afforded to me as a student with cramped, shared spaces for many years. Almost eight, to be exact.

Within minutes steam filled the room and I felt myself begin to relax. It would be a welcome change.

Tub almost full, I surveyed the room for toiletries. Nada. The security guys had neglected to empty bathroom essentials. I stepped from the fog to eye the towering stack of unopened cartons in the corner of the bedroom. I was less than enthusiastic at the prospect of going through them. It was not the time to dig.

I flipped off the faucet and stared at the water in the tub, swishing and splashing, inviting me to ignore my missing bath products. *Just this once.* I dipped a toe into the warm water. It felt nice.

Who needs soap?

Just as I stepped into the tub, I noted the sudden lack of silence. I could've sworn everything had been quiet a moment ago. There was now a hum in the empty house.

It was water, coming from next door. *The shower.* Sloan had arrived home early.

I grabbed a towel from the rack and wrapped myself in it as I crossed the bedroom, on a mission. Sloan's door next to mine stood open. Her own luxurious bathroom lay just beyond the large bedroom, also with matching fireplace. She had won the coin toss for the master suite. The shower was nicer.

There was a thump from across the room, then the hum disappeared. The house was hushed again. Only quiet drips remained. *Perfect timing.* I rushed to the closed bathroom door and knocked hurriedly, now shivering in my towel.

After a few seconds the door yanked open, warming me instantly with a wall of steam. But gazing back through the haze was not Sloan. It was a glistening god.

Lucas stood in the doorway, hands busy tucking the corner of a plush white towel slung low across his hips. Beads of moisture clung across his torso, muscles gleaming. He reached to run a hand through his messy wet chestnut hair, shaking out moisture. I stood mute, watching.

After a long moment I gathered myself together and took stock of my unwitting reaction. I clamped my gaping jaw firmly shut and took a deep breath. But I couldn't quite remember what I was supposed to say. *Why am I here again?*

Lucas gazed back at me directly, the darkened wet hair making his emerald eyes glow more intensely. "Just hopped out, so you're a little late." His smirk was mischievous. "But I could probably be persuaded."

Reason returned rapidly as heat rushed to my face. *Who does he think he is?* My mouth made incoherent noise as I stumbled over my words for a response.

Lucas wet his grinning lips as he stared back, clearly amused by my fluster. He said nothing. Just let me flounder in front of him.

Finally his chuckle broke the awkwardness. "Relax, kid. I'm just playing." He moved to paw again at his hair in the fogged mirror before looking back at me, one eyebrow raised. "Unless maybe . . . I'm not the one you were hoping to catch?"

That's it. He was toying with me, trying to shake me on purpose. "Maybe that *would* be preferable," I snapped back, my voice returned. "But I'm just here for the shampoo."

He paused, seeming to notice my own towel-attired state for the first time. My stomach dropped as his eyes did a quick once-over. I did not own oversized towels. He suppressed a quick grin before averting his eyes and turning toward the shower. "Anything else?"

"Soap would be nice," I called to him. "What are you doing in here, anyway?"

He returned with bottles of shampoo, conditioner and bodywash. "You forget this was *my* hideout first. It's usually my room, on the occasion I need one. But I'm happy to be a gentleman." He glanced at the labels as he handed them over. "Hopefully this'll do?"

"It's great," I mumbled, turning to flee, bottles pressed to my chest as protection. "Thanks."

Lucas leaned casually against the doorframe, watching my hasty escape. His voice was teasing as he called behind me. "Be just down the hall if you need me."

***

The nerve of that man.

My annoyance and, I must say, embarrassment at the scene the evening before had occupied me through the night and was invading my fresh-start morning. Although I had to admit, tossing and turning over something other than the mob-related mess I had created was a welcome change.

Without a clue as to what a day in this new and hopefully temporary life would hold, I emerged from my room and headed downstairs. I was immediately assaulted by a heavenly aroma filling the first floor. Breakfast.

But my momentary dreams of coffee and fresh-cooked bacon were quickly halted. My appetite dropped away when I entered the kitchen. Lucas stood at the sizzling stove, spatula in hand.

Get it together. So what if we had been standing towel-to-towel last night? He probably didn't even remember. I had to be cool. "Morning," I called out.

Lucas glanced back, seemingly unaffected. "Morning." He nodded his head to the other counter. "Coffee's over there."

"Great." A welcome distraction. I headed for the pleasantly well-stocked coffee bar and busied myself with a fresh cup, dragging out the preparation process as much as possible. It was the most carefully-crafted cup of joe in history. The last thing I wanted this morning was some small talk with this near-stranger I'd just seen near-naked.

I lingered in place and sipped. And sipped. I had just about counted the number of tiles completing the back-splash, by color, when finally Sloan appeared in the door-way, looking fresh and cheery in her usual jeans and boots. She took in the two of us for a moment and grinned.

"You two sure are seeing a lot of each other lately," she chirped.

I sputtered coffee back into my mug, choking. I tried to give a little throat-clearing cough to play if off. But one glance at Lucas's amused face told me I hadn't fooled everyone. I looked quickly away.

Sloan cast a questioning glance at my reddening face but didn't say a thing. Lucas turned his back to us, focused again on the stove. I just knew he was silently laughing at me. Me and my awkward discomfort.

I grabbed a mug and held it out to Sloan, attempting to refocus her attention. She snatched it with a smile and poured herself a black cup, taking an appreciative sip as she moved to the banquette table in the corner.

I settled in across from her and took in the rest of the cheerful white kitchen for the first time. "Not too shabby for a hideout, I must say." I glanced back at Lucas, noting his striped, ruffled apron several sizes too small. It was fairly adorable. "Didn't know it would come with a per-sonal chef."

"Nah, don't let him fool you," Sloan tossed back jokingly. "He's just trying to show off. Doubt you'll ever see him in there again."

A soft scoff sounded from the other side of the kitchen. But Lucas didn't dare turn back. He pretended to not be listening at all. I caught a barely perceptible shake of his head. *Maybe Sloan knows how to embarrass him?* It was a satisfying thought.

I decided to feed the urge. "Sooo?" I gushed loudly. "You *have* to tell me. How was your date?"

Sloan read the situation immediately. She glanced to Lucas's back with a wicked grin. "I don't know. I think he might be it. The *one*."

"Oh." I hadn't expected that. I had just wanted to rub the date in Lucas's beautiful meddling face. "Really?"

For his part, Lucas continued to fake immersion in his cooking tasks. But I could sense the tension as he listened. His movements became very slow and deliberate. Forced concentration.

Sloan shrugged. "Who knows? Like I said, I think it's time to move on. He might be just what I need now."

Lucas threw down his spatula in disgust and marched over, dropping his disinterested pretense. "You've got to be kidding me. *That* guy?"

I watched silently, fascinated. *What is his motivation here?*

Sloan stared back, defiant. "And what is wrong with Christopher?"

"Christopher?" He sighed, annoyed. "Please. He would bore you to death. Mr. straight-laced accountant. That can't be the guy."

Sloan gaped at him. "I never *told* you he was an accountant."

Lucas looked away, holding his tongue.

Her eyes glowed with anger. "You researched my date?"

"Like you could honestly expect me not to," he snapped back. He took a deep breath and continued calmly. "But I just did a surface check. No deep dive, I swear. Not that there's likely to be much *to* that guy."

"Sure, okay," she retorted sarcastically. "So you're telling me you *didn't* follow us?"

He averted his eyes once again, lips pressed tight. "I never said that." He took another deep breath. "But not for long, okay? The guy just made me nervous. He's not what you need."

"And what *do* I need, someone like you?" Sloan hissed. "I tried that, remember? Your brother was perfect. But now he's gone." She crossed her arms and looked away. Her voice got softer. "And I can't do that again. Ever."

He opened his mouth to retort, but held back, wary. He seemed unsure how to proceed. The great uber-cool Lucas, uncertain.

"Not that it's any of your business, really," Sloan snapped. She leveled an icy look at him, daring him to argue. He didn't move a muscle. They had a long stare-down.

Finally she raised her eyebrows, a fake smile plastered on her face. "Those eggs aren't going to burn themselves, sweetie."

Properly dismissed, Lucas returned to his corner without argument, sulking silently. I took a deep breath as the tension in the room began to settle again. It was my first witness to any sort of real disagreement between them. And I wasn't sure what to make of it.

Earlier suspicions nagged at me once again. *He's jealous.* And I wondered if that was exactly what Sloan wanted, deep down. She *was* egging him on.

Sloan's face wasn't going to give anything away, though. She took a long sip of her coffee and sat back, cheerfulness returned as though nothing had happened. "So what about you? Maybe you want to give the friendly mailman a chance? He certainly seemed into you."

I glanced across the kitchen, embarrassed. "Oh, I don't know. I'm not sure he's my type."

"But you're not you, remember? You're . . . what was the

name? Daisy?" She raised her eyebrows playfully. "Maybe he's *just* Daisy's type. Why not try something different?" Her eyes bore into Lucas's back, daring him to turn around and interfere again. "I'm finding it quite refreshing."

I shrugged. This conversation wasn't really about me. "Guess I'll think about it."

A moment later Lucas appeared at the table bearing two loaded plates. My mouth watered as he carefully placed them in front of us and turned away. He threw his apron on the counter and stomped toward the door, disappearing without a word.

"After all that, he's not going to eat?" I asked. I felt bad for my earlier desire to make him uncomfortable. He really seemed affected.

Sloan glanced in his wake. "Probably already did. He devours his food like a caveman, they both did. Really don't know who taught them that." She shook her head and picked up her fork to dig in. "Boys."

SIXTEEN

He certainly hadn't burned our eggs after all. Breakfast was delicious, although tinged with wandering thoughts of the chef. I shoved back my plate, annoyed I had pushed through the pile of food to discomfort. Couldn't help it.

I sighed and sat back in my cushioned seat, hoping a few minutes of coffee would allow things to settle. It was time to poke around in some of my lingering questions. "So last night you asked Lucas about who's in charge of the organization now. Where did that come from? Is that your new lead?"

Sloan shook her head and copied my plate-rejection maneuver. "Unfortunately that seems to be a dead end. But I had hopes." She picked up her coffee and leaned in a little. "You remember when we were talking to Salvatore and he mumbled something before denying any knowledge? Well, it was Italian. All I caught was *Capo*. I figured he could've been referring to Il Capo, an old term for the big boss of a crime ring."

"And so maybe Sal suspected his boss was behind the finger message? However unsuccessful it might have been."

"Right. I really do think Sal had nothing to do with it."

She sighed, frustrated. "But apparently I was wrong about the boss thing. Because Lucas says there was no one above him around here lately. And if anyone would know, he would."

"And why is that again?" I tossed it out casually, hoping to finally get a little insight.

Sloan shrugged. "He's just very . . . plugged in. Remember, apparently he's been working with the feds on this for years. If someone else was calling the shots, he'd tell us."

I nodded, trying to hide my disappointment. *Working with the feds*. It didn't sound like he was one of them. So what *did* he do, exactly?

And why did I care?

"But that's okay," Sloan began again, interrupting my musings. "We have a better lead anyway."

"Holding out on me, I see." I straightened, perking up again despite my food coma. "You've got something?"

We both paused as a rustle sounded from down the hall. It was followed by footsteps, quickly headed toward us. I turned toward the doorway, halfway expecting Lucas to reappear. Instead a bloody, distorted nightmare of a face rounded the corner and stopped, standing motionless in the doorway. I gasped and fought back a scream as I processed the sight.

It was a mask. A rubber Halloween mask. It sat crookedly atop a slight male frame wearing a gray hooded sweatshirt and dark jeans, a weathered navy satchel hanging from the shoulder. They continued standing in the doorway, peering back through the uneven eye holes. We watched, waiting.

Finally Sloan spoke up, hesitant. "Leo?"

The figure sighed and hung his head. "Not even a scream," he said. "After all that, I at least hoped for a good scare." The man reached up to yank the mask from his head, shaking out his dark, sweaty mop.

I stared back, utterly confused. "What in the world are you doing?"

Leo strutted across the room toward us. "I heard there were disguises involved in coming here."

"You never have been good at disguises," Sloan replied. "Guess I shouldn't be surpr—"

"I *also* heard," Leo interrupted, "that your cover was something about making a horror film. So I thought it was a good opportunity. Fits right in, right?"

Sloan grinned at me, eyebrows raised. "The horror thing was your idea. Now you've only encouraged him."

Leo slapped the mask on the table. "Well, I neglected to think about your security out there when I came up with my brilliant cover. " He flopped down next to Sloan at the table. "They didn't seem to appreciate it so much. Almost got me killed."

I was more successful at hiding my amusement than Sloan. Leo glared back at us.

"Whatever." He waved a dismissive hand at us. "My mistake, covering up this mug. It deserves to be seen." He stretched his neck a little higher. "Don't know what you'd do without it."

Sloan cleared her throat, tamping down her laugh. "You're right, sorry." She forced a serious expression onto her face. "We're very glad you didn't die by Halloween mask. Really."

"So was the journey worth the risk?" I gestured at Sloan with my coffee. "She says we have a new lead. What've you got for us?"

Leo's eyes lit up. "I took a look at the video you guys sent me." He reached to flip open his bag.

"Video?" I glanced to Sloan, confused.

She smiled back. "Looks like we finally heard from the kidnappers. They sent something to Jackson last night. He forwarded it to me."

"Last night?" I gaped at her. "A video is huge. Why didn't you say anything the moment I saw you?"

She shook her head. "This is not for Lucas's ears. He doesn't need to know anything about what we're doing, or he'll be jumping right in the middle of things. Getting in our way." Her eyes narrowed as she glanced at the door. "In fact, I'm not certain it's safe to discuss here if he's still around."

"Long gone," Leo said. "He was leaving when I came in. Was even nice enough to become part of the welcoming crew." He rubbed the side of his head absently.

What did they do to him? I pictured the security team tackling him outside as he tried to approach in that ridiculous mask. Poor Leo.

I shifted my attention to his laptop, impatient for it to boot up. "So? What do they want?"

"We know what they want," Sloan replied. "They want two hundred grand. It was on the original note. Now we know *how* they want to get it."

Leo hit play and the screen lit up with the image of Grant's eyes, close to the camera. The lower half of his face was covered with a gag of some sort. Nothing else was visible. He stared straight ahead, blinking. Unmoving.

I gulped, trying to steel myself for the rest. At least he didn't look scared. More . . . resigned. Weary. I felt sick.

The video played on and on, nothing but him sitting there. Just blinking. I realized nothing was coming from the speakers.

"Is there sound?" I asked, trying to keep my voice from showing my panic. "Is this it?"

"No sound," Leo answered. "But there is a message."

Finally the screen changed. But only in the form of a piece of printer paper shoved in front of Grant's face. The camera light glowed against the words scrawled on the page.

Money's due.

$200,000 unmarked. Under bench, 21st Street dog park. Two days.

The message hovered on the screen for ten seconds before going black, the video abruptly ended. We continued to stare at the screen a moment, absorbing.

"So." Sloan finally tore her eyes away and looked to Leo. "What did you find? Could you trace where the camera is?"

My stomach lurched with hope. *I forget we have this kind of support.* We didn't have to be locked into the kidnappers' instructions. We had our own ways around.

"Sorry," Leo replied, shaking his head. "Not yet, anyway. Their signal is bouncing through all kinds of proxies, all over the world. Can't pinpoint the location."

I sighed, returning to reality. No quick fix here. Of course it wouldn't be that easy.

Sloan looked just as disappointed. "Well, at least we know the plan now. No more mystery. And he appears unharmed. So we have a couple days to find another lead . . . or persuade his family to pay up."

"I think that's probably our best bet," I said. "Just talking to his family again. Not that I know *how* to convince them it's not a hoax. But with another dead end, I don't want to waste time trying to find any more leads. Let's not take any chances."

"Oh ye of little faith," Leo exclaimed. "Giving up *so* easily." He whipped the laptop back around and clicked rapidly on the keyboard a moment. His face lifted in a wide grin as he twirled the screen back to face us. "I said I couldn't pinpoint the *location.*"

Our eyes widened. The screen was filled with video of a dimly-lit living room, featuring Grant slouched on an overstuffed brown sofa. His feet were propped on the coffee table as he stared straight ahead, a white fuzzy pillow tucked under his elbow and soda can in his clearly unbound hand. Flickering light from offscreen suggested he was watching television.

"I never said I couldn't get into the camera *anyway.*" Leo clicked another key to zoom in on the hostage. "We can certainly see a lot more when Grant's face is not the only thing in view."

I studied what I could, excitement growing. "Is this recorded? Because it's all dark there."

"Live feed," Leo replied. "Desktop webcam. Best guess is he's in a basement. Or they just covered all the windows. Doesn't take a genius to figure out you need a little privacy when you're holding someone hostage."

Sloan glanced up at me, eyes narrowed. "But your good buddy doesn't exactly appear to be spending his time bound and gagged."

He certainly doesn't. I felt a tiny sigh of relief. "Good to see he's not tortured or miserable. Just bored, maybe." I leveled a look back at her. "But you know he's just my coworker. Whose kidnapping happens to be all my fault, remember?"

Sloan rolled her eyes. "You have to stop taking responsibility for *his* choices. His decision to spy on you." She turned to Leo. "Anyway, won't they know you're watching?"

He waved away the suggestion. "I disabled the light. And even if they knew how to look, they wouldn't be able to tell we're there. But they're not that sophisticated, regardless. The protection they implemented is meager at best. Child's play, really."

"But what about all the proxies? They're hiding the location pretty good."

"Amateur stuff. I could teach even you two yahoos to do that in a day."

Sloan's face twisted in mock-outrage.

"No offense." Leo shrugged and gazed down at the screen. "But seriously, while this doesn't tell us who's behind things, it does tell us who is not. And that's any sort of real professionals. People who know what they're doing."

"That's surprising," Sloan replied. "I would imagine the mob guys have some experience in this sort of thing."

My stomach sank. "But it could still be who we think, right?" I had to cling to the story we knew. If we weren't certain who was behind this, then we knew a sum total of *nothing*. It was too much to consider. "The whole organization is in shambles. All their pros could be behind bars."

"Definitely still possible," Leo responded. "A desperate attempt to get much-needed funds, by whoever's left." His bottom lip puckered out as he considered, head tilted. "Not the worst plan, really. Get some quick, easy money from scared parents, and then walk away with no one hurt." He let out a quick chuckle. "Too bad they greatly overestimated the family's concern."

"And underestimated *our* involvement," Sloan added. "There's no way we're going to make it that simple for them."

It was comforting, her confidence. But had we really been any help at all, so far?

I returned her smile, not wanting to dim her enthusiasm. "So what now?"

Sloan tapped her finger to her lips, thinking as she stared at Grant on the screen. He stayed slouched on the couch, motionless other than the occasional sip from his soda. Finally she looked up, resolute.

"Since we're at a bit of a temporary stalemate, I'd like to talk to Jackson again," she said. "See if there's anything else useful we can get out of him. Let's find out where he is and pay a visit."

Leo cleared his throat, getting our attention. He looked between us, considering. Holding something back.

"What?" Sloan finally asked.

"He's at a golf course across town," he replied, a smile creeping onto his face. "So I'm guessing he's on a job. One of his landscaping gigs."

I glanced at Sloan. "And you know this . . . because?"

Leo looked bored with the question. "Because he doesn't look much like a golfer. But I could be wrong."

Sloan was not amused. "What did you do, Leo?"

"What?" He raised his hands in a gesture of innocence. "You can't send me messages and not expect me to try to track the person who sent them. C'mon now."

"So you used the forwarding to start tracking his location?"

"His *phone's* location," he said with a shrug. "But yeah. Why not."

Sloan sighed. "Fine. Share that with us. In the meantime, keep digging around. See if these unprofessional kidnappers messed up anywhere we can trace." She turned to me. "We're going to find him."

I nodded, hope beginning to reemerge.

"Okay, let's head out." Sloan nudged Leo to hop up and turned to me. "Don't forget to wear your disguise to leave the house." She gave me a little wink. "Not you, Leo."

SEVENTEEN

"**P**erfect. He's headed home now, says he'll meet us there in a few." Sloan glanced up from her texts. "Does that agree with what we know?"

I looked down at the little dot slowly cruising across my phone's map and nodded. "Jackson's on the move. We should be right behind him. Maybe ahead, actually."

"Only if we pick up the pace," she yelled toward the front, her tone joking. "We might make it there before tomorrow."

The driver of the SUV stayed silent, his face hard as he eyed us in the rearview mirror. Her attempts to rattle him and get him talking had thus far been unsuccessful. He was utterly unreadable. And apparently liked to drive very, very cautiously.

Something moved in the corner of my vision. I turned and discovered a vase propped in the back floorboard. It had somehow escaped our notice upon entry. Long flower shoots waved back and forth with the movement of the vehicle.

"Know anything about that?" I said.

Sloan followed my gaze. "Hmmm," she mused loudly. "Guess Benton has a crush on us after all."

The driver's eyes appeared in the mirror again, steady

on Sloan. "They were delivered to your office this morning. Just picked them up." His voice was very deep and matter-of-fact.

"He speaks," Sloan exclaimed, meeting his gaze. "And does he know anything else?"

Benton returned his eyes to the road, his participation ended as quickly as it began. Sloan grinned at me, amused, and stretched across the back of the seat to reach the small card tucked into the display. Her face was inscrutable as she examined the message and tucked it into her bag without a word.

Finally she looked up and responded to my impatiently questioning eyebrows. "Christopher." She shrugged weakly, with a smile to match.

Not exactly a typical reaction to 'the one.' Although it *was* Sloan we were talking about. Who ever knew?

"So," I ventured, unsure how much to pry. "Were you serious with Lucas this morning? Or just trying to mess with him. I couldn't quite tell."

"What, about the date? Are you asking if I'm *in love*?" Her smile was genuine as she mocked the words. "Definitely not. But Lucas doesn't need to know that. And I really am open to moving on, so I'll try giving it a chance." Her voice lowered to a mutter. "No matter how boring he may be."

"I *knew* it," I exclaimed, laughing. "Lucas is one hundred percent right, and you just don't want to admit it."

"I concede nothing to that man." She tried unsuccessfully to hide her grin.

Maybe she really does want him jealous, then, deep down. I smiled back and tried to swallow down the sinking feeling in my gut. It was none of my business, really.

The driver interrupted my pity party by clearing his

throat. He gazed at us in the mirror and seemed to hesi-tate. His expression was now sheepish.

"Sorry, ma'am," he said. "But we won't have enough gas for the rest of the day. Want me to just get some while you make your stop? It won't take long."

"Firstly, we aren't ma'ams," Sloan replied. She leaned over to peek at the map on my phone, swishing the screen toward our destination. "But I don't like my getaway vehi-cle getting away on me. There's a gas station just before his neighborhood, we can stop there. It's not a problem."

***

A few minutes later we pulled up to a pump at 7-11 and Sloan flung her door open without warning. She glanced back at me as she slid her sunglasses from her fake golden hair. "Let's stretch our legs while we wait, shall we?" Her smile was devious as she slipped the shades on and stepped out.

I had serious doubts about her need to stretch any-thing at this point in our brief journey. More likely she just wanted to people-watch while in disguise. Her own form of personal amusement.

But I could always use a coffee.

We strolled into the store, in cognito. *Okay, maybe anonymity is sort of fun.* I headed straight for the coffee station, glancing down aisles as I passed. Only a few stragglers in the quiet store.

I busied myself with inspecting flavored creamers while Sloan casually circled the room. I kept an eye on the beer cooler guys nudging each other as she was discovered. It seemed she drew the eye no matter what the attire.

I, on the other hand, felt even more invisible in my dark

wig and faux piercing. It hid my face nicely as I watched, head down. Sloan pretended not to notice the gawkers, but I knew better. She was aware of every move they were making.

Finally one of them decided to take a shot. I knew it before he spoke. He flicked his weaselly eyebrows at his friend and turned toward Sloan.

"Hey there," he called out.

She glanced up and gave a disinterested nod, ostensibly returning her attention elsewhere.

"What do you think we should get?" The skinny one persisted. "What kind do you like, darlin'?"

Sloan continued to ignore, but finally relented as the men stared her down. "I don't," she replied, her voice indifferent.

"See, we can't seem to make up our minds," he twanged, ignoring her reaction. "Sure would help to get the opinion of a pretty lady like you. We could even share."

I rolled my eyes. Sloan somehow managed not to do the same, continuing her cool play. She moved a little closer and faced the harassers. "Sorry, can't help you," she said cheerfully.

The man called out again as she turned away. "How 'bout your friend, then?"

My eyes widened as he turned his gaze my way.

In a flash Sloan was face to face with the loudmouth. She towered over the slight man in her tall heels.

"My *friend* is not interested, either," she said. "So I suggest you just finish your sad little mid-morning beer dilemma and get on your way."

The man clearly didn't pick up on the fire behind that calm, direct gaze. "Just being friendly, now." He reached a hand to touch her arm. "No need to get all upset."

I blinked and almost missed it. Within seconds Sloan had the man whipped around backwards, his offending hand twisted awkwardly behind his back as he leaned forward at an unnatural angle. He yelped with surprise and pain, eyes wide as he looked up at her. All bravado disappeared.

A disturbing faux smile played on Sloan's face as she gazed first at his shell-shocked friend in warning, then down at the meddler. "Like I said. Time to move along."

They shared a long look. Then Sloan carefully released him and stood her ground. The man shook out his arm dramatically and turned away, gesturing to his friend. They both shot her an icy look as they stalked away, headed for the exit.

The man paused by the front counter and stared down the attendant. "Not even gonna do anything, man?"

"Ain't see nothin' here," the large, bored man replied. He glanced up from the scratch lottery ticket he was working on. "Well lookee that, a free ticket. My lucky day." His hard smile dared the man to say anything further.

His response elicited outraged sighs before the men continued on their way, cursing under their breaths. The few remaining patrons went back to their browsing as the drama died down in the store. I fit a lid on my coffee and waited for my heart rate to slow down again. *That. Was. Amazing.*

Sloan moved to the front to watch the men disappear in their truck. Then sidled up to me and spoke quietly. "All set?"

She appeared as if nothing had even happened. *Bet that barely even registers in her day.* "Yup."

"How's the progress on our guy?"

I flicked on my phone and studied the movement of the

red dot. But there didn't appear to be any. "He's stopped." I pinched out to zoom in.

"Already home?"

"No." I blinked as I stared. "He's . . . here?"

"Aye, mate," a voice broke the stillness of the store. "Where's the rest of the energy drinks?"

Our heads whipped toward the drink coolers. In place of the departed harassers stood Jackson, cold air wafting around him from the open door in his hand. It reminded me of Lucas and the steam from the night before. But undoubtedly without the same effect, despite his objective attractiveness. I tried to shake off the memory.

"What is *there*," the attendant drawled back slowly, "is what we got." He continued his methodical work on the tickets, intently focused.

Some spies we are. We had just let our person of interest get the drop on us. And he didn't even know it.

Sloan and I exchanged a glance and immediately set to work, separating. She followed slowly as Jackson moved away from the coolers. I circled around to the medicine aisle, casually browsing.

We had no reason to suspect Grant's roommate of anything, but I figured we might as well use our anonymity to get to know him better. Sloan had taught me that it never hurt to know too much. And despite my determination not to listen, her impromptu lessons had apparently begun to sink in.

Quick glances caught Jackson breezing through the junk food aisle, grabbing two bags of potato chips and a two-liter from the top shelf on his brisk way. *Chips, soda, energy drinks?* It didn't really compute with what we knew of this guy so far. Was the kitchen stock we saw just for show?

Suddenly he was headed my way. I focused on inspecting a box of allergy medicine, keeping my head down. Jackson brushed by and came to a stop at the candy rack. He stood, taking in the selection, his arm weighted down by the small basket overflowing with his gluttonous purchases.

He grabbed up a handful of candy bars and threw them into the basket. Then another. I caught a quick sigh as he rushed off, headed for the checkout counter. He had been intent in his mission, paying no mind to the female strangers keeping an eye on him.

I stayed put, my pulse quickening again. Things had just taken a turn. He could be up to something after all.

Snickers.

He had grabbed loads and loads of Snickers.

What were the chances he and his roommate shared the *same* candy addiction?

***

We watched from down the street, waiting for Jackson to head into his house. Our hasty exit right behind him allowed us to arrive within seconds of him pulling up out front. I wanted one final validation of my suspicions before we entered. Finally he started toward the house, hands empty.

"Yep," I said. "He left the bag of junk in the car. Now why would he do that?"

"Interesting," Sloan replied. "Don't tell me you're thinking . . ."

"Can't help it." I shrugged and watched Jackson disappear through the door. "You saw that guy's kitchen. And you've seen him."

"Mmmm. Good point. There's no way he lives on a diet of that stuff."

"Especially the staple of his little shopping trip. Snickers, and lots of it."

"Definitely not the best choice, I'll agree." She raised an eyebrow. "But I take it that means something to you?"

I faced Sloan, excitement rising again. "They happen to be Grant's biggest weakness. Trust me, I know."

Her face lit up to match mine. "Well, now we really need to pay a visit. Shall I call you, then? I've been looking for an excuse to finally try out our new setup."

I pulled out my phone and grinned, pleased to see Sloan making use of the hearing aids I had fit her with. While she didn't need them like I did, the devices would allow us to stay connected the whole time, discreetly and without fancy surveillance equipment. Only a streamed phone call was needed. *But what exactly would we use them for here?*

Connection successfully tested, we removed our wigs and accessories to revert to our normal selves. There was no need to read Jackson in on our disguises. The driver pulled up to the house and we hopped out. A glance through Jackson's car window as we made our way up the driveway confirmed the bag of junk food still present. A box of Pop Tarts spilled out into the passenger seat.

"Might never have suspected anything of this guy if we hadn't seen what we did," I said, continuing on to the porch. "Don't tell me that's what you had in mind going in there?"

"Never really know what might come up." Sloan shrugged. "Always have the antenna ready. It's all useful experience."

"Also entertaining. Wouldn't have wanted to miss your

little takedown in there." I lowered my voice at the front door. "So . . . can you teach me how to do that sometime?"

"Now it's my lucky day." Sloan grinned broadly as she reached to ring the doorbell. "Thought you'd never ask."

EIGHTEEN

"Ladies, ladies," Jackson said as he ushered us in. "Good to see you. Sorry we can't meet under better circumstances." He turned back to lean his head out the doorway, peeking left and right before straightening and slamming the door shut. Both locks were immediately flicked into place and double-checked with a yank. Finally he turned to face us. "So what can I do for you?"

Sloan and I exchanged a glance.

"You feeling okay, Jackson?" Sloan asked carefully. "Has anything happened?"

"Yeah, something's happened," he snapped, indignant. "My flatmate's gone missing and I'm supposed to come up with a couple hundred grand to get him back. And I don't even like the bugger."

"Right," I said. "Sorry."

Jackson sighed. "I don't mean to snap at you. Think I'm just hungry." He began moving quickly toward the kitchen. "Haven't had time to eat just yet. Mind if I whip up something while we talk?"

"Please, help yourself," I replied. *Not in the mood for your junk food stash, I see.* I was curious to see if my original assumptions about him were correct.

"Hope you ladies like smoothies," he said. "My new kale and carrot recipe is epic."

Yep, spot on.

Sloan's nose wrinkled in disgust. "Darn. We just had a late breakfast. But thanks."

I suppressed a giggle at her response, curiosity winning out. "I'd try just a bit."

"Excellent." Jackson emerged from the refrigerator with an armful of fresh greens. "Won't take but a minute."

We watched him jam vegetable after vegetable into the blender. Just as he fired up the machine, Sloan threw out the first question.

"So have you had any new thoughts," she yelled over the racket, "on who might be behind that video?"

"Any what?" Jackson hollered back.

This is going to go just great.

But Sloan knew how to make the best of things. She sidled up to Jackson, leaning in close before attempting her question again, right in his ear.

Jackson glanced down at her hand on his shoulder before responding. His lips were barely an inch from her ear as he leaned in to speak.

After a few back-and-forths, leaving me standing awkwardly on my own, Jackson turned his attention back to the blender for a moment. As he stuffed another handful of leaves into the machine, Sloan took the opportunity to tap at her phone, barely glancing at the screen before blackening it again and placing the phone on the counter.

Jackson paid no mind when I clicked to answer my phone a moment later, my hearing aids immediately connected to the call just as Sloan's were. I too darkened the screen and placed the phone back in my pocket. I would have no need to speak for the next task.

"Mind if I use your restroom while you finish that up?" I asked, itching to get out of the room for multiple reasons.

"Yeah, sure." He barely noticed my presence between his blender work and Sloan hovering nearby. "Down the hall."

"Can't wait to try the smoothie," I called back as I left the room. Once out of sight, I rushed to the first door available. It actually was the bathroom.

A quick search of the tidy space brought forth nothing new. Not even anything interesting in the medicine cabinet. Although it did confirm that Jackson was legitimately on insulin. The vials there were valid prescriptions in his name. I sighed with relief we didn't have a drug addict on our hands.

The next room was obviously Jackson's bedroom. It was not as neat as Grant's OCD playground, but it could've been worse. It looked more like a teenage boy's room, with mild clutter and all the surfing paraphernalia.

I scanned the contents quickly, afraid to touch anything. A laptop and tablet in the corner caught my eye. But nothing that screamed 'Into something bad.'

The blender noise stopped and Jackson's voice reappeared in my ear, interrupting my search. "Maybe I should go check on your friend," he said. "The toilet could be acting up again. It does a thing sometimes."

"Oh, I'd leave her be," Sloan said quickly. "She might be a minute." Her voice lowered to a whisper. "She has IBS."

My jaw dropped. *Really? Nothing else you could come up with?*

But I couldn't blame her. The lie was for my benefit. My extremely slow, non-clue-finding benefit.

"Oh." Jackson left that alone. "Alright, then."

"Besides, it gives us a minute to get to know each other better," Sloan continued. I pictured her leaning in casually. "Nothing wrong with that."

Distracting with flirtation. *Of course.* I could really learn from a master.

I shook off my embarrassed annoyance and picked up the pace, determined to find something new. My career depended on us figuring this out. And right now it was all on me.

There was just no time to tear apart Jackson's bedroom, with him steps away. *I'll surely be caught.* I snapped a few quick photos as an inventory and retreated.

There was one final door at the end of the hallway. I held my breath as I reached for it. It had to hold the key.

No such luck. Nothing but a linen closet. I sighed and glanced over the contents, disappointed. Shelves of towels and bedding, clearly divided by roommate. The items on the upper shelves were hastily thrown in place and disheveled, while the lower shelves appeared to be arranged with mathematical precision.

Pretty sure they don't store their secrets between their bath towels. I sighed and accepted my failure, still unsure about what I had been searching for in the first place. Secret notes laying around in plain sight? A confession letter? The whole search seemed downright silly, if you asked me.

I swung the closet door closed, resigned. But something made me hesitate. *What was it?* A glint of light. Something had flashed in the corner of my eye.

I quickly tuned in to the kitchen conversation to gauge my remaining time. Sloan giggled amiably, followed by a quick chuckle from Jackson. They'd be just fine without me for another minute.

Quietly, I reopened the door and took another look. The shelving stopped a few feet from the floor. And there, on the ground below, were two shiny metallic bowls.

Surrounded by small stuffed animals and toys. Piles of them.

Odd. I leaned in to inspect. They weren't just any toys. They were mostly bone-shaped, with ropes and dangles coming out of them. The type a dog would use.

Chew toys.

I picked up one of the bowls and found an inscription. 'Mr.'

The second bowl had matching script. 'Pennington.'

They have a dog named Mr. Pennington? There had been no mention. And no other signs. Definitely no dog in the house or yard. I had just checked everywhere.

Maybe something happened to it. The stash could've been their sad little memorial. Unwilling to part with the items just yet.

Or . . .

An idea formed as a memory flashed in the front of my mind. Possibilities swirled.

I returned everything to its previous state and rushed back to the bathroom to flush and finally emerge, being sure to make plenty of noise for my return. Jackson barely noticed my reentry.

***

A few sips of a disgusting, heavily-spiced vegetable smoothie and a couple quick queries about the kidnapper video were all that was needed to get things wrapped up and us headed for the door. Sloan followed my lead in trying to get rolling quickly. She saw the excited glint in my eyes.

"Sorry I couldn't help, guys," Jackson said, holding the door for us. "Let me know if you find anything. Truly, I just hope they're okay."

His words made me stop in my tracks. "They?" I turned to face Jackson. "What makes you think there's more than one?"

"Well, yeah. I, uh. . . " he stammered. "I just figured. I mean, there's probably a whole bunch of poor kidnappees, you know? I don't know why it would be just Grant. Honestly, I feel lucky it's not me too."

Mmm hmm.

Sloan flashed a sad smile at him. "We'll be in touch."

***

"I know that look," Sloan announced the moment the car door was closed. "You saw something."

"Maybe," I ventured, uncertain of my certainty. "But it's really just conjecture at this point."

"Well, I have some conjecturing of my own." Her face hardened. "That convenience store junk was not for Jackson. There's just no way. And I think that'll lead us right to the crime."

I perked up again, thrilled to have another clue. "What are you thinking?"

"Clearly we think those purchases could be for Grant, which means the whole thing may be a ruse. And that flirtatious Aussie may be in on it."

"Right."

"So all we have to do is follow the trail of Snickers. He's going to have to get them to Grant somehow, right? I say we just watch and wait for him to deliver the goods to the junk food feind. And then we catch them both red-handed."

I wasn't thrilled that we were now assuming they were both frauds. I had thought Grant was my friend. Or was at least beginning to be.

CARRIE ANN KNOX

But I couldn't argue with the facts as they stood. Something funny was definitely going on.

"So simple it's brilliant," I said.

Benton cleared his throat loudly up front. We both snapped to attention. He met our eyes in the rearview mirror again.

"If you mean the bag of stuff from that car's front seat," he gestured with his eyes toward Jackson's car in the driveway. "I think that's going to be a problem."

We shared a quick glance, disappointment stabbing quickly.

"What kind of problem?" I asked.

"The kind where the items don't exist anymore," he replied solemnly. "At least here, anyway. Someone came and retrieved a shopping bag from the car while you were inside."

Our eyes widened. We had never thought to keep an eye on his purchases, too.

"And you didn't think to do anything," Sloan spat, frustration rising. "Or warn us, let us know in any way?"

"What was I going to do, tackle 'em?" He gazed back steadily, not intimidated by her anger. "As far as I knew, you were here to chat with your friend. And I have been explicitly instructed to mind my own business and drive. No information means I can't report back on your goings-on, remember? It was *your* idea."

"Jeez. He's right." Sloan sighed. "Sorry Benton. Maybe it *would* actually help to read you in a little, huh?"

"I still work for *you*," he replied, his eyes softened. "I can feign ignorance to the others just as well as the next guy."

They shared a long look in the mirror for a moment, coming to some sort of unspoken agreement.

"Okay," I finally broke in, hoping there was still

salvageable information here. "So what did they look like, this mystery bag-retriever? Did they break in?"

He shook his head. "Appeared to be unlocked. And they kept their head down, under a baseball cap. Never got a good look, not that I was tryin'. Not a big guy, though. Pretty average. White. Dark, maybe black hair under the hat. That's 'bout it."

"How about a license plate?"

"Came in by foot, around the side of the house. Then back the same way."

"Well that's not suspicious at all," Sloan muttered. "Can't believe we missed that. And now Jackson won't be delivering anything. Our potential tracking device is gone."

"Well . . ." Excitement perked up in my gut again as I reconsidered my original line of thinking. "We may not need it."

She raised an eyebrow. "What've you got? Is it the multiple hostage thing? That weird comment?"

"Sort of."

Sloan nodded. "It was random. All I can figure is Jackson's just trying to play dumb." She shrugged. "Why would there be more than one? There's no evidence."

"Actually," I began, a grin creeping in. "There's reason to believe there *are* two hostages. And I think I figured out who the other one is."

Sloan's eyes lit up. "Do tell."

"First, does Leo still have Grant's phone?"

She considered. "I think I have it now."

"Perfect." I took a deep breath to calm my racing pulse. "We'll need that, and the live feed of Grant. Because if I'm right about who might be there with him—I have a hunch they can lead us right to both of them."

NINETEEN

"There," I said, pointing to the screen. She had pulled up the live feed from Grant's hostage lair. "That little fuzzy pillow on the other side of the couch. It's not a pillow at all." I looked up to watch her reaction. "I'm pretty sure that's Grant's dog."

Sloan's mouth formed an 'O' in surprise as she put the pieces together. "Right. The framed picture in his room. How could I forget?"

"*And* I found his stash of toys and bowls. Hidden in the linen closet."

"Ah," Sloan said. "Which is why his roommate is cryptically worried about 'them,' not 'him.' He knows the dog is gone, too."

"And yet hasn't said a word all this time."

"He even tried to cover up his slip when he mentioned it," she agreed, nodding. "So I think that pretty much guarantees Jackson's in on it, then." Her lips pressed tightly. "The big, cute phony."

"Or he's behind it," I added. "It's far-fetched, but we really haven't considered that Jackson is in on something, but *Grant* is not. That he really is the victim. We have to consider everything."

"Good point, we definitely don't have all the facts." She narrowed her eyes. "But you know my money's on Grant being behind all this. Never did like that guy."

Just then the pillow's eyes opened as he uncoiled himself to stand and spring from the sofa. He shook himself out and stretched after his nap, moving to sit in front of Grant. His owner kept his focus on his video game.

"There you go, proven right," Sloan said. "That's a good find. But I'm not yet following on how that gets us their location?"

"That's where the phone comes in." I gestured toward her bag. "I could be wrong, but I have a hunch."

"I'm intrigued." She retrieved Grant's phone and handed it over. "And a hunch is really all we have right now, so go for it."

I swiped through the phone until I found it. The app icon featured a puppy face, my initial tipoff. I had vaguely noticed it the first time I browsed, but didn't think anything of it at the time.

I pointed it out to Sloan before clicking.

"We already went through all his apps," she said, skeptical. "You know something I don't?"

The program opened and I breathed a sigh of relief. It appeared I was right. "It looks like a game. Because they turn it into one, by adding scores and collecting points. So I'm sure it was quickly dismissed." I clicked around, digging through the program. "But it's actually much more than that."

"Interesting." She narrowed her eyes at me. "And how do you know about this random program?"

"Just before I met you, I was thinking of getting a dog. I was a little bored and in need of some complication. But in the end I decided I couldn't afford it yet." I glanced back at Sloan. "And that was lucky, because you brought *all* the complication I could handle. And then some."

Sloan grinned slyly. "You know you love it."

Except for the ruining my life part. "Anyway, I had read about this app that uses GPS to track your dog without a monthly fee. Which they somehow gamified."

I clicked into the map tab and the GPS zoomed out, thinking, before zooming back in with the same little puppy icon as a pinpoint. I handed the phone over, excitement beginning to churn rapidly.

"Their location, madame," I said. "Both of them, I believe."

Her eyes were wide as she took in the screen. She pinched in and out, getting her bearings and checking out the neighborhood of the location. Finally she looked up, her face grim. "They're only a few blocks from Grant and Jackson's house."

"Those fakers didn't even have to go to much effort," I said, aghast. "He just strolled down the street and set up camp on someone's couch."

"Apparently all you need to plan a fake kidnapping and extortion is a webcam and a charming roommate willing to lie. And a rich family, of course."

"Don't forget the gullible coworker," I added, deflating at the thought. "We seem to be the key to everything here. But why?"

She shrugged. "Probably needed someone to convince that rich family. If we believe it, then maybe they will too. He didn't exactly have the most trusting relationship with them."

"Right. He needed a true believer." I shook my head in disbelief. I had been such a fool. "And after learning about our previous exploits, he figured we would jump right in and try to save the day. Make the connection to the newly-imprisoned mob and blame *ourselves*. That connection was probably all made up too."

"Maybe." Sloan nodded in agreement. "And I'd be willing to bet that story coming out is what gave him the idea in the first place."

"Great," I muttered. "More good things coming from my participation. When will the party end?"

"Oh, don't you worry. The real party is just getting started." Sloan's eyes became fiery. Devious. "Let's go find our guest of honor, shall we?"

***

"So are we just gonna go knock on the door?" I stared at the front of the small nondescript brick ranch sitting in a sea of plain-vanilla fifties ranches. The neighborhood near Grant and Jackson's home was in a lower tier, but mostly well cared-for. "How do we confront him?"

"We're not going to directly confront him if we can help it," Sloan replied. "Not yet, anyway. He would probably just run right out the back door if we tried that. And then we've gotten nowhere."

"Then maybe we should just walk away," I said glumly. The idea, just a seedling at first, began to sound appealing as it bloomed in my gut. "Actually, yeah. If he's behind all this, we don't owe him anything. What if we just ignored the whole thing?"

"Not a bad point," Sloan conceded. "We certainly can if you want. This is your case." She gave me a direct look. "But you did point out that we don't know for absolute certain that this is Grant's doing. I mean, we know, but we don't *know*."

The fleeting feeling of relief vanished quickly. I sighed,

frustrated. "You're right. I wouldn't be able to live with myself without knowing for absolute sure. Plus, we'll at least get some answers."

I sat up straighter and refocused on the house, still sitting dark and unmoving. "So we're finally here, but we aren't going in to confront-slash-rescue him? Surely you have some trick up your sleeve for this sort of thing."

"I'm sure I could come up with something to get in there. But it's much safer to make him come to us. We just need to find a way." She settled back in her seat, getting comfortable. "So first, we wait."

I wasn't ready to relax. "Wait for what, exactly?"

She propped her feet up. "We just have to get a feel for the situation. See who comes and goes, who might be inside. Make sure our assumptions are correct. We don't want any surprises."

"And after the waiting," I said, impatience setting in. "Then we pounce?"

Sloan laughed. "Indeed. And then we pounce."

***

Unfortunately for our attention spans, the comings and goings of the house were limited. Very limited. As in, zip. Zilch.

Not even a twitch of a curtain or flicker of light. For hours. Days, it felt like.

I yawned and slouched further in my seat. "At least we know it's not likely a big operation. Couldn't be very many people involved here."

Sloan looked just as bored. "Definitely." Her voice was sleepy. "That's good."

I sighed. "Maybe we could take a five minute break? I think a coffee run could do us good."

"We shouldn't." She straightened, shaking herself awake. "But I don't think we have a choice, really. We're useless. And it's not like we're going to miss anything at this non-stop action house anyway."

I perked up at the thought of a steaming cup of caffeine. "Better put our disguises back on." I reached for my paraphernalia and called toward the front. "Benton, let's hit the 7-11 again."

Sloan followed my lead, sliding on her wig. The driver put the car in gear and slowly nudged the gas.

"Wait," Sloan called out suddenly. "Don't. Move."

The car froze. I followed her gaze, now riveted on the house. And the little white ball of fur, barely noticeable as it blended in behind the white picket fence in the backyard. It trotted along the perimeter, sniffing.

Mr. Pennington.

I sighed with relief. My app theory had been correct. And that was definitely the dog from the video.

Which meant Grant was certainly inside as well. *We're so close.*

"Is that enough?" I looked to Sloan, pleading with my eyes. "Do we go in now?"

"It's enough for proof, definitely. Now we're certain he's here." She met my gaze. "But we aren't going in. I have a much better idea."

Sloan rummaged in her bag, retrieving a black flip phone. Then she flung open her door and looked back at me. "Be right back."

Before I could respond, she was gone. Her long fake-blonde strands bounced as she strolled down the street toward the house in question. She hooked a right at the yard and slipped casually through the back gate, peeking around the side of the house before continuing. It appeared she was moving onto the back deck.

My heart raced as she disappeared from view a moment. *Is she charging in the back door?* I didn't understand why she had suddenly gone all renegade on me. We were supposed to be a team.

But a moment later she reappeared, turning the corner with a fur ball tucked under her arm. She slipped quietly back out the gate and made her way to the vehicle, nonchalant. I noticed Benton put the car back in gear as he watched her return.

"Drive?" he said as soon as she stepped in.

"Drive," Sloan confirmed.

He hit the gas and we were down the street and out of view in seconds. I looked down at the fluffy little creature lying calmly in her lap, watching us carefully with little brown eyes.

"What's happening?" I said, my own eyes wide. "What are we doing with that?"

"Oh, this little guy's not a *that*. His name's Mr. Pennington." She grinned up at me. "And he's going to help bring Grant right to us."

***

"So how was this better than just knocking on the door, again?" I eyed the dog on Sloan's lap as we sped across town, making sure my face read the appropriate amount of skepticism.

"We would have no leverage," she replied. "What reason does he have to tell us anything, much less the truth? I, for one, want some answers."

"Oh, I see." The reality of the situation began to finally sink in. "So he has to talk before he gets his beloved dog back. He's the leverage. He's *our* hostage."

"In a way." She picked up Mr. Pennington and snuggled him to her face. "But he'll be a *spoiled* little hostage. And hopefully it won't take very long. We can set up a meet right away."

"A meet?" I was always paddling hard behind, trying to catch up.

"Somewhere nice and public. And on our own terms."

"And how do we set that up?"

Sloan looked down at the dog as she stroked his head "Let's just say I set up a new line of communication. One that cuts Jackson out this time." She raised her eyes to mine. "Grant's new cell phone. I left him a burner. We could call, but . . . that could get awkward. So I'm thinking we just text. Leave him messages on where and when."

"And you think he'll just drop this whole charade and show up?"

"Absolutely." Sloan grinned. "If he wants his dog back. His little game is over. And he'll come to realize that very soon."

TWENTY

"Well, well, well," Grant called out as he approached the meeting spot. We were stationed in the middle of the 21st Street dog park, nice and public. No place to hide. "If it isn't the long-haired Hardy boys, come to save the day."

"Stay right there, Grant," Sloan ordered. "Don't come a step closer."

Grant's grin had a new edge to it I'd never been privy to in my time with him. Something a little sinister. "Or what, exactly?"

I scooped up the fluffy little ball next to me. "Well, you don't get your dog back, for one."

"Mr. Pennington," he gushed, reaching his hand out as he moved toward the dog in my arms. The dog gave a little yip at the sight of his owner.

Sloan took a step forward, her arm raised in warning. "I mean it."

"Okay, okay." Grant raised his hands in surrender and stepped back again. "So what now, tough guys? You figured me out, I guess."

"Really didn't take that long." Sloan glanced to me. "Gotta be the shortest extortion in history, wouldn't you say?"

"Or the dumbest," I added.

"Hey, I was working under a lot of pressure." Grant's voice was almost whiny. "There was no time to get it perfect. I think it wasn't so bad, given the circumstances."

"Which were what, exactly?" I said. "What would make you use your coworker like that, for such a silly little stunt?"

Grant gave a little chuckle. "Oh sweetie, it's not about you. Nothing ever is." He shrugged. "I was about to be thrown out. My parents cut me off and our sad little stipend certainly wasn't getting me by. And even that was about to end. Since you took my permanent job and all."

"So the whole thing was a con? To trick *us* into convincing your family you were in danger?" I was in utter disbelief. "Who even comes up with something like that?"

"Actually, those mob guys got the whole thing started. They cornered me one day and offered me good money to keep an eye on you. Dig up a little dirt on what you're up to."

"So you *were* spying on me," I said, disgusted. "Betraying me for some cash."

"It's not personal. I told you I was hard up. I'm not the kinda guy who gets evicted. It was a temporary solution. Very temporary, because as it turns out, I was not very good at it. You wouldn't give up anything useful. And when they saw how I got caught taking pictures, they knew you'd be suspicious." He shrugged. "Plus I left you that nasty finger, but sort of forgot to put out the note with it. So you'd get the message."

"Don't worry, we got the message. I found it later."

"Oh good." He smiled, proud of himself. "See, it did work. I was hoping you might poke around in my stuff. Helped lead you right to the desired conclusion after all.'

"Which was that you got involved somehow, and that ended in you being taken for ransom?"

"Precisely. Which is exactly what you thought, was it not?"

Sloan and I shared a look. As frustrating as it was, he had succeeded for the most part.

"Until we wised up, thanks to your sloppiness," I retorted. "So the mob dumped you after you were no help. Then what? How did that turn into your master plan to steal from your family? And use us to do it?"

"You gave me the idea, you and your little crime-fighting duo. I told you, I was desperate. Once I heard the news about your secret hobby, I knew you wouldn't be able to resist. And the possibility that there might be men after you, too . . . well, that just gave it plausibility, now didn't it?"

"So your idea was to use our curiosity to manipulate us," I said.

"Sure. But don't forget your interest in saving the day. I think you have a little superhero thing going on, wanting to right the injustices of the world. Or something."

I stared back, amazed at the stranger before me. I had been trying to help this person. Risking everything in the process.

"And don't forget guilt," Grant added, directed at me. "Admit it, you felt responsible for me going missing. I bet you thought it was *all* your fault." He stuck his bottom lip out mockingly.

My stomach boiled with rage. To be manipulated and used by someone so callously.

"I wanted to use that guilt to help me get out of a jam, is all," Grant continued. "Just tell me, would it have worked? Were they going to pay up? I've been dying to know."

I stepped a little closer, pleased to deliver some bad news. "Your family wanted nothing to do with you *or* your little game. And clearly we should've listened to them in the first place. They knew you were full of it."

Grant shrugged. "Ah, well. Guess I overestimated their concern. And your powers of persuasion. It was worth a shot, anyway." He reached his hand out. "Can I have my dog back now?"

I took a protective step back. We stared at him, silently pondering the depths of the guy's derangement. He seemed to have no remorse for anything he'd done. So much for bringing him to task for his actions.

But there was one way he could pay a penalty.

"Why would you risk your career on something like this?" I gazed at Grant directly. "Once the director knows what you did, you'll surely be fired. And then you won't graduate. It can't be worth it."

"Who's going to tell them, you?" He smirked at me knowingly. "Go ahead. Sounds pretty far-fetched to me. You might sound like a crazy person." He shrugged. "Not that it matters. I'm about to quit anyway."

"You're leaving audiology? Why would you come this far to quit at the end zone?"

Grant gave a quiet laugh, one eyebrow raised. "I'm not leaving the field, my dear. I already have all the hours I need to graduate. Paperwork's all done, I'll have to head home for graduation soon. I don't know why I was considering staying the last couple weeks on that measly pay anyway."

It had never occurred to me. He must've been ahead of me in the patient contact hours requirements before he got there. He really did have nothing to lose. At work, anyway.

I tried to hide my disappointment. "But what if we had ignored the warnings, and gone to the police anyway? You could've been in serious trouble." I was suddenly regretting my decision to avoid the authorities. *Is it too late?*

"Like you would've taken that risk. I knew there was no way." He raised his arms in a wide shrug. "But besides, all I did was leave a note on my own computer. I was just an amateur filmmaker playing around, and everyone else got the wrong idea. They would never charge a wealthy white boy for his artistic pursuits, now would they?" He grinned, satisfied. "People like me get YouTube channels, not criminal records."

I wanted to smack the smirk right off his smug face.

"Either way, it really wasn't a bad idea," he continued. "I like to think it would've worked. And with more time, you could've convinced my family to pay up. You just needed more convincing yourself."

"Doesn't really matter now, does it?" Sloan said.

"Actually, it could," Grant slowly replied, still looking at me. His gaze turned intense. "You could still go through with it, you know. Get them to send the money, to save their son. It's an awful lotta cash."

A harsh chuckle escaped my throat at the thought. "And why in the world would I want to do something like that?"

"You can't go back to work." He shrugged. "They may let you back for your last week or two, pretend everything's fine. But they'll never keep you on permanently after all this. Too much liability. You bring chaos, far as they're concerned." His eyebrows knitted with faux concern. "You know that, right sweetie?"

A sick dread settled in my stomach as I considered his words. He was probably right. The signs had already been there. They were looking for an out.

And I would soon be starting my career with nothing.

"But we could split the money instead," Grant continued, jolting me out of my mental spiral.

His face was serious as he took a tiny step closer. "It could be seed money, to start your *own* practice. You don't need them. You could go out on your own, with none of their rules. No more grunt work. I know that's what you really want."

Of course it is. For the briefest of moments I imagined the possibility of being my own boss. In my own place. No more judging looks from coworkers. Free to do as I pleased, office hours or not.

But the idea was beyond even my wildest dreams at this point. It was ludicrous. And I was no criminal.

They were both watching me closely as I shook myself from my reverie. I straightened my shoulders and gazed directly at Grant, ready to put a damper on the new hopefulness in his eyes. He really thought he could buy my integrity that easily.

"Sorry, *sweetie*," I said, my voice acidic. "But that's never going to happen. Besides, you're my ticket back into their good graces."

His face darkened. "How do you figure?"

I finally allowed myself a little smile. "Once you tell them all about your devious plans, I'll be off the hook. Things'll eventually settle down with the mob case, and my life'll go back to normal, especially with you gone. I'm not worried. About *my* future, anyway." I pulled a phone from my pocket and waved it a little. "So, ready to start your confession?"

Grant's brow furrowed in skepticism. "And why would I possibly do that?"

"That's why we're here, right?" Sloan asked. "You want

to trade for your dog back. Surely you knew there would be some concessions." She gave him a dubious look and shrugged. "Or Mr. Pennington can come hang out with us for a while longer. Your call." She glanced over and eyed the furball. "Then again, maybe he'll just go to a pound out of state. We'll see."

His lips pressed together as he watched us, considering. Finally he thrust out his hand. "Fine, give it to me."

I tapped to open a recording app and handed the phone over. Grant hit the start button with a sigh and began talking. He started at the beginning, telling his story in his own biased, snide way, but getting the overall point across.

I figured we would be able to cut out his final commentary accusing us of our own kidnapping and extortion plot with his dog. I didn't think anyone would need to know how the sausage was made. That was our trade secret.

"There." Recording complete, Grant handed over the phone. "Happy?"

I took it and paused to glance at Sloan. Her face told me she was as satisfied as I was. It was the best resolution we were going to get. She reached to tousle the dog's head, then nodded at me. I did the same and stepped forward to hand him over. I was going to miss the little guy.

"Mr. Pennington," Grant gushed as he pulled him gently into his arms. He snuggled the dog to his face a moment, then settled him into the crook of his arm to face us again. "Well, I guess our business here is done. But it's not too late. Let me know if you change your mind. Trust me, my family's got plenty of dough to spare. Might as well get a piece while we can."

He turned to walk away. After only two steps he whipped back around to lunge at me, yanking the phone from my hand. Before I could react, he was leaping over the small fence and sprinting across the park, Mr. Pennington tucked against his chest.

My eyes were wide as I glanced to Sloan and made a move to follow. She grabbed my arm to stop me. My eyes got wider with confusion.

"He's getting away," I said, panicked. *With the key to saving my career.*

She just stood there, watching. At peace.

"Aren't we going to do something?" I gaped in horror at his retreating figure. All that work, for nothing. *Back at square one. Or worse.*

"It doesn't matter," Sloan finally replied, turning to me. Her voice was calm. "Why do you think I had you record that on a burner?"

I stared back, trying to understand. Hope flickered. She must have something up her sleeve.

"We don't want his canned, coerced confession," she continued. "We have the whole story, from the beginning. I was recording on my phone since we got here. Every last whine and excuse." She pulled out her cell phone, pressed stop, and handed it toward me. "You'll just play that for your boss, and everything will clear up just fine for you in no time. Trust me."

I turned back to watch Grant finish his sprint across the park lawn. He was a pretty fast runner. I would've never caught him. He slowed when he reached the parking lot and saw we weren't on his heels. I turned away, tired of the sight of my apparent new nemesis.

A moment later a screech of tires made us both turn back. A white van had appeared in the lot, headed rapidly toward Grant. The side door slid open as it rolled and two men in dark clothes and ski masks jumped out and sprang after him. Grant immediately turned away on instinct.

He was fast, but not that fast. Within seconds they had wrestled the dog from him and were dragging him toward the van. Mr. Pennington gave a scared little squeal as they shoved them in and slammed the door behind them. The van took off again immediately, the screech of the wheels echoing through the park as it disappeared.

Shocked, I looked around. The meeting was intended to be public, but the sleepy park was no longer very populated. And no one had seemed to notice the incident that had lasted only seconds. We were the only witnesses.

Sloan's breathing was ragged and erratic, just like mine. *What just happened?* We both stared at the now-empty spot in the parking lot, not comprehending.

Finally she looked up, her eyes wild. "Did that really just happen?"

I shook my head. "I don't know. And if it did, was it real? How do we know?"

"Exactly. It could be another one of his tricks. Right?" She began to sound desperate. "Right?"

We both jumped when male voice appeared from behind us. "Sloan?"

We spun to find her recent date, Christopher. He looked different in navy athletic shorts and a gray t-shirt. A basketball was tucked under his arm. "What are you doing two doing here?"

"Not right now, Christopher." Distracted, she waved him off.

He stepped closer. "But—"

"I can't," Sloan snapped. "We're in the middle of something. Please." The stress oozed from Sloan as she turned her back.

"Okay." He took a few steps away, still facing us. "But I just wanted to let you know . . . your buddy Sal appreciates all your help on this."

Our heads snapped toward the retreating figure.

He called out with a knowing grin as he turned to jog away. "All that money'll sure come in handy for legal expenses."

TWENTY-ONE

"That lying weasel," Sloan exclaimed, seething with disgust. "I can't believe I ever considered that rodent. For even a second."

"A nanosecond. What a slimeball."

I slid the carafe toward her and began fixing up my coffee, ecstatic to be back in the familiarity of our booth at Joe's. Too many things had been changing and happening too fast. I needed the comfort of our second home. Despite our promise to Lucas to stay away.

Once again, we hadn't bothered with disguises. But I was no longer fighting it. *Let us be spotted*. If they wanted to find us, they would. They certainly already had been.

I glanced up to see Leo approaching, his typical smirk on his face and laptop bag on his shoulder. He slid in next to Sloan.

"So, got outplayed by the players, huh?" he said. "Guess you had it coming."

Sloan nearly spat out her coffee. She gaped at Leo. "How's that?"

Leo shrugged and reached for a mug. "*You* started everything with a trick, the way I see it. Ended up sending Sal and all those guys to jail. And then you go drop him a hint there was money to be had in your coworker's little scheme. What did you expect to happen?"

"First of all," I corrected, "we didn't drop any hints. Not on purpose, anyway. And we didn't even know it was Grant's scheme. We thought it was *their* scheme."

"You're just naming mistakes." Leo lifted his coffee with a smirk. "You got played from all sides, when you look at it."

My gaze dropped. I had been trying hard *not* to look at it that way. It was pretty embarrassing, how badly we'd proceeded in this whole thing. One ruse after another, with us following along like pathetic little puppets. Being used.

Sloan looked just as sheepish. I had a feeling she had never been in this situation before. Ashamed of her actions in an investigation. Embarrassed to have been so manipulated.

Maybe I'm the bad influence. I was apparently just too gullible and willing to pursue without any hard evidence. My instincts were clearly off.

And now I had gotten my coworker into trouble, for real this time. He was being held against his will somewhere, probably scared to death. And us mentioning him to Salvatore seemed to be the reason it was happening. *We* were to blame.

Grant had pulled the deception on us in the first place. But I couldn't focus on that right now. We had to get him out of this first. The actual, *real* kidnapping.

Leo dropped his mug to the table with a clunk, shattering my little bubble of self-loathing. Sloan seemed to shake back into reality as well. He pulled out his laptop and waited for both of us to give him our full attention.

"Well," he began dramatically. "You sure know how to

pick 'em, S. Going out with the star accountant to the mob? Doesn't really sound like you."

"I don't believe it." Sloan shook her head, processing. "I knew him a while back, a client several years ago. And trust me, he did not work for those guys back then. He was just a nice accountant that needed some help. Almost too nice. Annoyingly nice." Her eyebrows raised as she lifted her eyes to us. "It never even occurred to me he would've made a switch like that."

"So then," I ventured, uneasy about the possibility of offending anyone. "Do we think maybe he . . . targeted you? That running into him was not a coincidence?"

She shrugged off the idea. "I had never bought him just running into me in the first place. He knew my spot. But I assumed he just wanted to look me up. Finally try asking me out." Her face darkened. "Turns out, all he wanted was to spy on us. I guess now I understand all the questions about my work. The little sneak."

"You had no way of knowing." I shook my head sympathetically. "So did you talk much about what we were doing? What does he know?"

Sloan shook her head. "He got nothing. My lips were sealed. In fact, I suggested we not talk about work at all." She gazed down at her coffee. "Which also explains why I never got any hints about his new loyalties. I bet I would've sensed something was off, if I hadn't done that."

"You don't know that," Leo said. "He could be a really talented liar. Probably has to be, in that line of business."

"True." She gave him a small smile. "And at least I didn't let him drive me home. He kept pushing really hard to let him drop me off. I thought I knew why." Her face reddened a little. "But apparently it was to find out where we were staying. For his criminal bosses."

"I'd be willing to bet he had multiple motivations," Leo said. "But after this, you guys might need to consider instituting a background check on anyone you fraternize with. In this business, you just never know."

Sloan sighed. "I hate to agree, but you're probably right. And I really don't appreciate being used." She straightened, getting serious. "Anyway, we need to focus on the task at hand. Did you find out anything else on this faker? We need to figure out our next step in finding Grant."

"I've got the basics," he said with a shrug. "Address, social media, banking info. Divorce papers. Nothing that seems too helpful. Not surprisingly, he started really making the big bucks about two years ago, when he went off on his own and began doing freelance work for some pretty questionable dudes. I'm guessing he must have some skills in money laundering. I'll try to dig up some evidence."

"So what about now, for finding Grant?" I asked. "Where should we start?"

Leo considered. "You have Christopher's number, right? That's at least the most direct line of communication we've had so far."

"That's true." Sloan looked at Leo hopefully. "We at least know who we're dealing with now. But you can't *track* him just from that, right?"

"Maybe one day. Not today." He narrowed his eyes as he gazed back. "But I'm guessing if you put your mind to it, you could figure out your own way."

They shared a long, secret look. A little twinkle of understanding in Sloan's eyes told me she was following his insinuation. *She has a plan.* The possibility alone made me excited.

I was just about to give in and ask, when Dottie

approached. She looked unusually tired. I'd never noticed dark, drooping circles under her eyes before.

"You guys eatin' anything?" she said with a sigh.

"Maybe, if Sayid's cooking," Leo replied. "He wearing anything crazy today? I heard about his last getup. *Truly* sorry I missed that."

Dottie's face drooped further. "He called in. Not like him at all. Those frat boys are runnin' him ragged. Not a good influence." She leaned in and lowered her voice. "And I think it's more than just funny costumes and dumb pranks. I think they're torturing the poor kid." She shook her head in disbelief. "Why he'd put up with it is beyond me."

We all exchanged a glance across the table. "Torturing him, how?" I said.

"Maybe not torture. I guess I'm being dramatic." She shrugged. "But he did come back with a nasty black eye the other day. And I think they like to humiliate him, 'specially in front of girls. Even though that's the whole reason he joined in the first place, for help in talkin' to 'em. The poor shy thing." Her voice lowered further. "Not to mention making him do all their homework. I think they figured out he's a smarty, and they're makin' it worth their while."

Sloan's brows furrowed. "He's told you all this?"

"No way." Dottie waved her off. "Just some grumbles and mumbles is all he'll give me. But I can put it together, I'm no dummy. Don't know if his own grades'll hold up, though, all the work he's doing for everyone else these days. A smart kid like him should not have to deal with all that."

"Agreed," Sloan replied. "But hopefully it's just a phase? Then as soon as pledging's over, things can go back to normal."

"I'm sure you're right, sugar." She picked up the empty

161

coffee carafe to refill. "Now, you'll need something to fuel all that plottin' ya'll are doing back here. Pie all around?"

Another shared glance confirmed. "Perfect," we said in unison.

TWENTY-TWO

"Well, well, well," Sloan said, her voice acidic. "Look who's decided to show up as himself this time."

Sloan's eyes narrowed at her former date standing in her office doorway. Christopher looked much more like his accountant-to-the-mob title now, in his sharp dark-suited attire. He also looked a lot more sleazy.

She nodded at the security guys surrounding him. "I think we can take it from here."

They looked him over, hesitant, but finally walked slowly away. Back to watch over the company's suite, I figured. For several days their team had been required in order to usher anyone into the building without too much media hassle. It was our first time in the office since everything had gone down. We had an important meeting planned.

Christopher followed her in and tipped his head to me in greeting. I looked away, trying to tamp down my anger. So much deception, from all sides.

"Thanks for accepting my invitation," Sloan said flatly as she crossed the room.

"You know I'd never turn down your call," Christopher replied, taking in the room. "Boy, this place hasn't changed a bit, huh?"

"Wish I could say the same for you." Sloan stopped in front of a small black wall safe. She spun the oversized wheel to open it and placed her cell phone inside, adding mine beside it. Then she turned to face Christopher, hand extended. "Need your phone before we go any further."

He eyed the setup with suspicion. "I don't remember this part from before."

"Our conversations were never this sensitive before." Her face was hard. "And I was never this paranoid. Everything we've said and done so far has been used against us. *Including* you."

"Fair enough," he said good-naturedly. "But what is that going to do, exactly?"

"It's a Faraday cage." She tapped the edge of the safe proudly. "We need our privacy, I'm sure you'll agree. No signals can get in or out of this little marvel. No GPS, no eavesdropping." Her smile dropped and she thrust her hand out again, impatient. "I'm trusting you long enough for this conversation, but that doesn't mean I'm taking any chances. Humor me."

He handed over his phone without further argument. Sloan placed it behind ours in the safe and locked the door. She turned back and eyed Christopher.

"Anything else on you?" she asked.

"Just this." He pulled another small electronic device from his pocket. He placed it on the edge of the desk and flipped a switch. A barely-audible high-pitch squeal emitted from the side.

He looked up, checking between both of us. "I assume you don't mind if I take my own precautions, then?"

Sloan raised an eyebrow.

"I'm not a fan of recordings either," he continued with a slight grin. "Never have liked the sound of my own voice."

"That's surprising," Sloan replied. "Considering you never seemed to shut up about yourself when we went out." She pursed her lips. "Did manage to leave out a few things, though."

"Lot of good all that did me. You weren't exactly chatty in return."

Sloan gave a quick chuckle. "So tell me," she said, "when exactly did you go from unassuming accountant with a little problem—to star fixer for the mob? I assume that's what's happening here?"

"Oh, don't be so dramatic." He took a seat in one of the leather chairs and shrugged up at us. "Money got tight. Did you know I got married since I last worked with you?"

We knew his whole history by this point. But he didn't need to know that. "So you, what, went dark for love?" I asked skeptically.

Christopher scoffed. "Hardly. That skank's already long gone. But she helped herself to half of everything I'd worked for, and then some. I was finally going out on my own, making a name for myself. But she made sure that wasn't going to happen."

"So then what?" Sloan asked. "They 'made you an offer you couldn't refuse,' or something like that?"

He shrugged. "I learned pretty quickly that some business activities are just more lucrative than others. For everyone involved. So I did a little accounting work for the right people. Eventually it lead to more responsibility." He straightened a little in his seat. "And respect."

"Sounds delightful," Sloan muttered.

"It's working out pretty okay for me, I think." Christopher held his head high. "Too bad you weren't interested in playing ball. It wasn't all a ruse, you know. You could just drop all this renegade-investigator nonsense and I'd be happy to take care of you. Maybe not before, but these days I'm in a position to give you everything you could possibly want."

I watched Sloan's face for a reaction. She was not likely to take well to such an implication. Her expression did not disappoint.

"Oh, swoon," she hissed. "Sorry to have ruined your scheme to gather inside information and settle me down at the same time. But it's not actually all ruined now, is it? What exactly is going on, Christopher?"

He sighed. "It's simple, really," he replied. "That friend of yours—"

"He's no friend," Sloan interrupted, "but go on."

"We had a simple agreement. Grant was supposed to gather some intel for us, find out if there's anything helpful for my people's case. Anything to ease their legal troubles. Ask a few questions at work, just keep an eye on things." He raised his hands in exasperation. "But he turned out to be completely useless for our purposes, and was causing far more problems than he was helping. We didn't need the added suspicion. So we cut him loose."

"And?" I prompted.

"And apparently the guy took it upon himself to turn around and use *us* as an excuse for some fake ransom plot. *And* he wasn't even very good at it."

Sloan rolled her eyes. "Tell me about it."

"Yeah. Well, my guys don't take too kindly to something like that. But they did see the opportunity in it. Once you two brought his little scheme to our attention."

My stomach sank as he confirmed my suspicions. Reminded me of my guilt. "So that *is* what you meant," I said. "About Sal thanking us. *We* are responsible for Grant being held for ransom, for real this time."

And must be the worst private investigators in the world.
"Don't be so hard on yourself," he replied with a crooked smile. "Sure, we never would've known how that little pipsqueak was trying to use our reputation, if you hadn't asked Sal about it. But we would've gotten here someway no matter what. You just helped it along." He raised his eyebrows as if delivering actual good news. "He's even forgiven you for accusing him, by the way. Seeing how now you're actually right, and all."

Sloan and I exchanged a wary glance. *Still causing more problems than fixing...*

"Once you informed us what was going down," he continued, "we knew all we had to do was watch and wait. Our cute little interloping sleuths would eventually figure it out and lead us right to him. *And* his family's money."

"So the plan is what, then?" Sloan asked, skeptical. "You'll continue where we failed? Try to get his family to pay up?"

Christopher's chuckle was harsh. "No, sweetheart. That's not our strong suit. I think you can handle that."

Sloan shook her head emphatically. "Not going to happen. It was a non-starter. They wanted nothing to do with any of it. Didn't believe a word."

"Well, you're just gonna have to try a little harder. After all, this time it's *really* real. Maybe that'll help you be a little more convincing, seeing how you know the truth and all."

I gulped. Now it really was dependent on us. *How in the world do we make this right?*

"Or what, exactly?" Sloan said, disgusted. "Are you really going to hurt him? And for what . . . a little extra dough?"

"Hey, we're only doing what we have to do." He was far too nonchalant. "Legal fees are about to kill the whole operation. And that hurts *my* bottom line as much as theirs." He narrowed his eyes at us. "But this problem is all due to the two of you, when you stop to think about it. So I actually think it's pretty generous of them to include you in trying to improve our situation. A chance to make amends, you might say."

"The only amends we're interested in," Sloan retorted, "is getting her coworker out of this situation. Since we apparently got him into this."

Christopher shrugged dramatically. "Seems to me it was all his idea in the first place, but whatever gets you going." He settled back into his seat. "But you've got two days to bring in the dough. Oh, and the price has doubled. We need four hundred now. Cash. Unmarked bills, yada yada."

Sloan's face reddened rapidly, matching my own growing frustration. We shared a momentary look of frustration and panic, then turned to stare at Christopher in silence, waiting. He stared back, indifferent. Apathetic.

Finally Sloan hopped from her seat and stood fuming over him, arms folded. "Then if there isn't anything else, Christopher, I think our time is up."

He returned a subtle smile and stood, buttoning his jacket. "My phone, then?"

She retrieved it from the safe and shoved it into his chest.

"So rough," he chuckled playfully. "Wish I'd gotten to know *that* side." He leaned in toward her and lowered his voice. "All this would've been a heck of a lot more interesting."

Sloan glared ruefully at him, silently waiting.

"Okay," he said, hands up. "I'm going." He turned toward the exit, stopping at the door. "But tell you what, I'll make it easy for you. Why don't you two just stay out of it, from here on out. Leave the rest to us."

Sloan and I exchanged a glance.

"Wait, so we don't have to convince his family anymore?" Sloan said. "Do your dirty work?"

"I'm suddenly rethinking that plan, now that I'm here." Christopher stared down Sloan, slowly reappraising her face. "I'm not sure I can trust you two to play straight on this, without some kind of underhanded scheme," he finally continued. "The last thing we need is another double-cross. And let's just say we have ways of getting something like this done a little more . . . efficiently. Certainly we can top your friend's sad attempts to scare his family. So I think we'll just take it from here."

"And we can just walk away?" I asked, incredulous.

He returned a sly smile. "Actually, I'm ordering you to. You've been more than enough help already." He swung open the door and gave us a direct look before disappearing. "So I don't expect to see you two around anytime soon. For your own sake."

TWENTY-THREE

As soon as we reached Sloan's room I flopped immediately on her deep, comfy chair in the corner. It had been quite a day, between the park confrontation about a fake kidnapping, a real kidnapping, and an unproductive intel meeting. And I wanted nothing more than to go to bed for the next week.

But our job was not done, no matter what Christopher had instructed us.

"So what in the world do we do now?" I said, trying to keep the despair out of my voice. "That's great we're not being forced to *help* with the ransom. But do we really just sit back and let them do it?"

"Honestly, we probably should, you ask me." Sloan sank onto the end of her bed. "He asked for it when he started it."

I shot Sloan a panicked look.

"But relax," she continued with a sigh. "You want to save him, we'll do whatever we can." Her voice did not exactly impart enthusiasm for the prospect.

I shrank back into the cushions. "Which is what, though? We didn't exactly hit a goldmine of information with Christopher there. How can we possibly take on these guys, without a single lead?"

Sloan chuckled softly to herself. My head shot up, senses suddenly on high alert. "What?"

"Nothing, just amused." She gazed back with a tired smile. "You thought the point of meeting with Christopher was to give him a little 'how dare you' speech?"

I tried to cover my surprise with a disinterested shrug. "And see if we can get any intel, I guess. Sure."

Sloan shook her head. "Don't worry, we got plenty of intel to get us started. It just hasn't arrived yet."

I straightened, now fully re-energized. "Meaning what?"

"The first step to getting ahead of something," she replied, "is acquiring an inside man. And Christopher was kind enough to volunteer when he willingly handed over his phone."

"When you put it in the safe?" My brow furrowed as I replayed the scene. "I thought you were blocking signals."

"The safe does block all signals, all right," she said. "But only until my guys take it out from the other side." Her mouth lifted into a wide grin. "And download everything on it."

My jaw dropped as I processed. "The whole thing's a trick?"

"Actually, no." She shrugged. "It does double-duty. The safe really does block everything, which is helpful for privacy. But sometimes it's also useful for gaining access. Our little meeting was plenty of time for my security team on the other side of the wall to not only access, but also mirror and track his phone. We'll be able to know everything he's doing from now on. Untraceably, of course."

I settled back into my seat, eyes wide. For the first time since I had watched Grant get shoved into the van, I felt hope. We might actually be able to help him, with this kind of access.

"So do you know what they've found?" I asked. "Any leads so far?"

She shook her head. "Still working on it. Leo's going through everything as we speak." She sat up and crossed her legs on the bed. "But I got word Christopher's calendar does have another meeting scheduled for tonight. Kinda late. And, reading between the lines on an email, he suspects it has something to with Grant's little dilemma."

"So that's next? We try to listen in on this meeting?"

"Absolutely," Sloan replied. "But it's not 'til later." Her mouth quirked up in the corners, mischievous. "So there's a little something else I think we should do first. Much more fun."

I eyed my friend, suspicious. "For some reason that makes me nervous. Does this fun happen to be illegal somehow?"

Sloan scoffed good-naturedly. "Who you think I am?" She paused dramatically to think about it. "I guess you never know, when things get carried away. But that's definitely not our intention."

I could do nothing but laugh and shake my head at the faux-innocent smile she flashed me. For some reason, I knew I was just going to go along with it. Whatever the not-purposely unlawful activity was.

"We'll definitely need disguises for tonight," Sloan continued.

"Right. Back to our alter-egos." I straightened and reached for my dark wig, hoodie and faux piercing. They'd come to be a bit of a security blanket for me. I could escape my out-of-control reality while hiding in them.

"Not *those* disguises," Sloan said, eyeing my bundle. "Those are just enough to fool the neighbors. They don't know us." She grabbed the hoodie from my hands and tossed it on a chair across the room. "But Christopher and his gang do. We'll need to step it up a bit for this next part. Keep 'em distracted."

I narrowed my eyes at her. "What do you mean, distracted?"

She walked to her closet and peered in. "Remember that escort disguise you tried out last time? The one for the photos with Walter?" She began digging through the hangers, shoving dresses forward as she searched in the back.

I didn't want to remember the shenanigans that had gotten me into this mess. "A short, tight dress is not going to be enough of a disguise." I shook my head. "Like you said, these guys know us. Unlike last time."

"True, but it's a start." She emerged from the closet with a garment bag and a gleam in her eye. "Next comes the stepping it up part."

***

I froze just before I turned the corner, as soon as I heard the voices. Sloan had apparently finished getting ready and just beaten me downstairs to the kitchen. And she wasn't alone.

"Where in the world could you possibly be going," Lucas said. "Like *that*."

"Just . . . out," Sloan replied. "*Dad*."

There was a long pause while I felt them glare at each other. I was glad I wasn't there for the showdown. A protective Lucas against a strong-willed, independent Sloan made for a little more tension than I longed for at the moment.

"You *demanded* disguises if we want to leave the house,

did you not?" Sloan asked innocently. I could feel her batting her long eyelashes just to annoy him. "We're just following orders."

Another pause. *She must've really gone all out.* I glanced down at my own ridiculous getup. I thought I had been uncomfortable last time, due to the overall slinkiness of the dress. But this time she had made sure I understood what a real full-on disguise looked like. Sloan-style.

"Fine, just," Lucas stammered. "Just take the security with you. Extra. And then some more. We already have some mailman hanging around outside, taking a *little* too long to deliver your junk mail. And now this. Our guys leave your side, or you two ditch them in any way, and I'm locking you both up in the house. No more games. I'm not kidding."

Once again, I had to wonder about their relationship. *Does his overwhelming protective instinct mean anything more?* I still felt there could be something between them, despite Sloan's protestations. He certainly cared about her. And clearly was having a reaction to her appearance.

"Whatever," Sloan replied, uninterested. She raised her voice. "Good to see you, too."

I realized too late that she had been calling out behind Lucas as he stormed out of the kitchen. I gulped and cast about for an exit, anything out of his path. There was just no time.

Lucas turned the corner and plowed straight into me. His eyes went wide as he watched me crash to the floor with a heavy thud. Then got wider as he took in my ensemble.

"Whoa. So . . . sorry," he said, visibly flustered.

I yanked on the hem of my dress and straightened my long, layered necklace, trying to pull myself together. The outfit was definitely not meant for lying splayed ungracefully on the hardwood floor. I scrambled to stand, finally accepting his offered hand for help as I tottered to my feet on my over-the-knee black boots.

Finally dusted off and vertical again, I grudgingly looked up to meet his eyes. He immediately flipped the switch on his megawatt smile. His entire face lit, glowing with charisma and allure.

"We really have to stop meeting like this," Lucas said, continuing to hold my hand an extra second.

I felt a blush creep into my cheeks unbidden. He sure could turn on the charm when he wanted. It was just not fair.

I felt Lucas look me over, his eyes roving from the boots up across the little-too-tight cocktail dress. Taking it all in, the megawatt smile fading. Then he studied my face a moment, seeming confused. Probably wasn't a fan of such an overdone look. Sloan had taken a heavy hand on the makeup, particularly with a deeply smoldering smokey eye. I had hardly recognized myself.

"I know," I said, averting my eyes and pulling at the ends of my dark wig self-consciously. "It's a lot."

"You, uh . . ." He stammered, shifting his gaze away. "You . . ."

Sloan sure had him flustered with these outfits. I gave him a little encouraging smile when his eyes met mine again.

The charm suddenly disappeared. He cleared his throat and gave me a direct look, his face now hard. "You two want to play silly games," he barked, "fine, I can't stop you. But you better keep the security. And don't do anything stupid."

I didn't trust my voice to respond, with the sudden knot that formed in my throat. I simply nodded and averted my eyes. I didn't want him to see how his disappointment affected me.

There was a long pause. I could hear him breathing but didn't dare look up again. After a moment Lucas grunted and headed down the hall, without another word. I could hear him grumbling under his breath as he disappeared out the front door.

TWENTY-FOUR

"By the way," Sloan said suddenly, shaking me back to the present. "How's your accent game?"

I was grateful for the interruption of my Lucas-related ponderings as we drove. "Never really thought about it." I tried out a snooty, severely nasal inflection. "Mmm . . . I guess I could always be a wealthy woman of great, great means. Not quite British, but not quite *not*, either. What say you?" I had to stifle a laugh as I watched for her response.

Without missing a beat, she raised her nose in the air and looked to me through mockingly half-closed eyes. "Mmm, true true. However, the correct term is *comfortable*, you see dear, never wealthy. And while this might do fine in the theatre, *dahling*," she enunciated dramatically, "It won't quite work for us right now. *Obviously*."

"Course, of course." I twirled my fingers in the air playfully before being distracted by the SUV pulling to a stop at the curb. We were at the edge of the local college campus. It was near downtown, a small haven of pristine grassy lawns and gleaming academic buildings slipped right in the middle of the city.

I looked back at her questioningly. "What are we doing here?"

Sloan shrugged and pushed open her door. "Did some checking. Turns out Sayid's fraternity is having a party tonight."

I sighed, sensing where this was going. "And let me guess—you always wanted to know what a real frat party was like?"

"How'd you know?" Sloan widened her eyes in mock-shock at me before hopping out of the vehicle. "But it's not a party *per se*. Apparently all the cool kids call it a *mixer*. Duh."

I rolled my eyes and followed her. "Right." We strolled across the street and up the covered front porch of a stately brick home, likely built over a hundred years ago. A low thumping from inside shook the ground at regular intervals.

A young man of no more than nineteen bounded into our path as we approached, blocking the door. "Welcome," he said with a quick grin. He paused and looked us both over carefully with satisfaction. "I'm quite certain I've never seen you two here before."

"First time," Sloan replied, her voice bubbly. "We're here to see Matt."

"Right." His face fell slightly. He tried to cover it with suspicion, narrowing his eyes. "Which Matt?"

Sloan glanced at me and giggled. "I don't know . . . the cute one?"

He rolled his eyes and moved aside, ushering us in with a sigh. "Whatever. Have at it."

Sloan gave him a little wink as she passed. We continued through the foyer toward the dimmed main room. The walls and floor now vibrated with the music overwhelming the space ahead. I had to fight the immediate urge to find the DJ and demand they turn down the volume at once.

"I'll . . . come find you later," the door guy called out behind us. "Make sure you found him okay and everything."

I leaned into Sloan as we reached the crowded room. "Who's Matt?"

"Got me." She shrugged back, grinning. "Place like this, there's always at least one."

We paused and took in the room a moment, watching the mix of flirtatious mingling and the beginnings of drunken dancing. It hadn't gotten too out of hand yet. The night was young.

"At least it's classier than the one frat party I attended in college," I yelled into Sloan's ear. "That was just a pitch-black basement with half an inch of beer on the floor. Pretty gross."

"Still kinda gross, you ask me. But they at least dress it up in the beginning. To sell all the pledges, I'm sure."

"Music level's the same though," I said, cringing as my head buzzed with the thumping bass. "Think I should tell them to turn it down?"

"No audiologist tonight," she scolded with a laugh. "You old lady."

I noticed some looks from passersby, both male and female, and wondered if we actually *were* already old enough to seem out of place. Then I looked down and remembered our disguises.

"At least everyone *is* pretty dressed up," I said, feeling self-conscious. "But we still stand out a bit, don't you think?"

Sloan looked over, quizzical. "And that's a bad thing?" She gazed back out at the room, taking in the scene as if looking for something. Her head bobbed slightly to the music. "No, this'll do just fine for our purposes."

I sighed, knowing I probably didn't want to know until too late.

"There," she finally exclaimed, pointing to the far corner. I followed her finger across the room to find Sayid. Or what I could only assume was Sayid.

The frilly pink bonnet tied under his chin was embarrassing, but not the most disturbing part of the ensemble. The giant makeshift diaper covering his entire midsection was the real eye draw. And it was succeeding.

Sayid wandered through the crowd, a sagging tray of sloshing beers in his hands. Partygoers laughed and elbowed each other before grabbing a cup without thanks. He was doing a good job of ignoring the sneering and snickers, but we knew him well enough to read the humiliation in his eyes.

"That's all I needed to see," Sloan said, overtly disgusted. "Time to make someone pay."

My eyes widened as I watched Sloan scan the room, intently searching again. I had followed her to the party, willingly, but was quickly beginning to rethink my participation. Sloan in a revenge scheme sounded truly terrifying.

"There," she stabbing her finger at a figure in the far corner of the room. The guy had a gaggle of cocktail-dress clad girls in front of him, all chattering loudly. He looked bored with the whole scene and began chugging his beer, foamy dribbles running down his chin. "That guy looks in charge, right?"

I watched as he drained the last of the beer, crumpled the cup in his hand, and threw it hard directly at Sayid. Sayid flinched in surprise as the plastic missile ricocheted off his face. He stabilized his beer tray and continued on, otherwise unreactive. My anger simmered hotter as the cup-thrower cheered and his retinue followed suit.

"I think so," I hissed.

Sloan pulled out a stick of gum and popped it in her

mouth. "Come on then." Suddenly she took off across the room, leaving me to chase behind on my wobbly heels. I somehow managed to catch up while maintaining my balance. Not necessarily my composure.

I was expecting her to march straight up to the jerk of interest, but she kept her eyes everywhere but on him. I copied her fearless strut as we paraded past, inches away, pretending to pay him no attention.

He took notice immediately, stepping forward to grasp at Sloan's arm. "What's up," he said, implementing his clearly phenomenal frat-boy conversation-starter skills.

Sloan's face was hostile when she turned back. "Back off, buddy," she sneered, brushing his hand away. "We're not here for you. We're looking for the guy in charge."

"Interesting," he said, eyebrows shooting up and then furrowing as he looked her over. "Only I don't recall approving you two coming in here yet." He puffed up his chest a little. "And as President, I get final say."

Sloan rolled her eyes. "So you're Devin, huh?" She had affected a subtle but unmistakable Jersey accent. "Well, I'd say we were already pretty well *approved*. Since your buddies is who sent us here in the first place. Like I said, we're here for you."

His eyes lit up a little as he hesitated. "Meaning what?"

She chomped her gum a moment, eyeing him right back with boredom. "Meaning, whatever you want. I didn't set no rules." She flashed him a sly smile, eyes twinkling. "Not my style, as you'll see."

"You only get even *more* interesting," he mused. "So who's your friend?"

My eyes widened. I tried to play it cool as he looked me over.

NO FEIGN NO GAIN

"I was told the more the merrier." Sloan shrugged. "But if you're not into it—"

"No," he interrupted, "It's not a problem." He tore his eyes off my dress to face Sloan again, looking energized. "Looks like my pledges have really stepped up their suckup game, huh? Let's take this somewhere a little quieter."

He slipped an arm around each of our waists, playing the big man as he led us toward a back hallway. His abandoned gaggle flashed us dirty looks in his wake. Lots of smirking male head nods were tossed at our guide.

I was just happy to be working on an empty stomach.

He pulled us into a small bedroom lit only by a lava lamp. *Figures.* He clicked the door shut behind us, plunging the room into an eerie silence. Suddenly the situation became much more real.

What does she have planned? I began to feel a little uneasy, walking into such a vulnerable position. I would never have done it willingly on my own.

Sloan stepped away from us, holding a cell phone aloft. "Where should I set this up?"

"Hey," the guy said, "is that my phone?" He tried unsuccessfully to swipe it from her.

"They said you'd appreciate a nice record of your evening," Sloan replied, once again bored. "You want to delete it, that's your call sweetie. But it would be a real shame. Shall I turn it off?"

He stared at the recording phone a moment, thinking. "Nah, let's see what we can come up with."

"Alright then." Sloan flashed a mischievous look as she handed it to me. "Maybe you can play cameraman for a bit? I know you like to watch."

"You got it." Still lost, I zoomed in and pointed the camera at the target.

182

She turned back toward our host, throwing a thumb toward the door. "You sure you don't want to bring in that fella with the diaper? He looks like he's into some weird stuff. Could be interesting."

"Are you kidding?" he scoffed. "Dude's as boring as they come. He's only doing that because I *make* him."

"Mmm," Sloan murmured as she moved slowly toward him. "So all those guys just do everything you say, huh? Do you make them all wear diapers and what not? That's pretty hilarious."

"Damn right, they all do as I say." He watched her carefully as she neared. "But only the outsiders have to pay like *that*."

I caught Sloan's glance. She had an evil twinkle in her eye. *I think I get it now.*

She reached Devin and fingered at the collar of his shirt playfully. "Outsiders?"

"You know, the affirmative action ones."

"So, what, you *have* to let guys like that in here?" Sloan scoffed, disgusted. "That's not fair."

"It's not so bad." He shrugged. "I kinda like to watch 'em squirm."

I cackled. "You're so *bad*," I said, fawning.

Devin grinned, his attention jumping back and forth between us. He seemed to notice the camera again and raised his voice a little. "What? It's not my fault a towelhead like that just doesn't belong, they're not one of us. But we need at least one." His voice became mocking. "Lest the world say we're some kind of *racists*."

He attempted to slide his arm around Sloan's waist and she slipped away gracefully.

"Please, like it's racist to want to keep to your own kind." She sat gently on the edge of the bed and began fiddling with the tiny strap on her heel. "It's just nature. He's lucky you even let him in here, I say."

"Exactly." Devin was enamored as she slipped the first shoe off. "Although, they do have their perks. My grades have never been better."

I giggled. "What, you steal his homework or something?"

He was busy watching Sloan flip her legs to tackle the other stiletto. "Nah, stealing's a strong word. But the president has the right to *inspect* anything they want." He glanced up to smirk at me. "Looks like I'll actually *pass* my engineering classes this time around."

"Niiice." Sloan glanced to me. "Say, I have an idea. Hand me that camera?"

I handed it over. Devin looked on, slight impatience creeping in.

"Sup?" he said.

"One sec," she said, punching at the screen several times. "Okay, all set." Sloan handed the phone back to a confused Devin before slipping her heels back on in a flash, straps tucked out of the way.

She straightened and stood tall in front of him, her grin tight. "I think we're all done here."

TWENTY-FIVE

Benton was waiting anxiously for us outside the vehicle as we made our hasty exit. A baffled Devin, left standing alone with his phone, had not followed us far. But some raised voices on our way out told me he definitely knew something funny had just gone down.

I watched the party scene recede as we sped away across downtown. Safely escaped, I turned to Sloan. "So, I have my guesses . . . but maybe you can fill in the gaps?"

She was positively glowing. "Oh, you know exactly what was going on. We were just helping their dear leader to be free with his feelings. Open up a little. Good for the soul, you know."

"It's probably also pretty good for his reputation." I raised an eyebrow at her. "Assuming other people find out about his little soul-bearing exercise?"

"What, you mean like all his family and friends?" Her face was playing innocent. "Acquaintances, university authorities . . . everyone he's ever known, really?"

I gaped, finally understanding the scope of her game. "What did you do?"

Sloan shrugged. "Just passed along his true feelings to everyone in his contact list. And his social media. Not that there was likely much doubt, but now Devin's unique point of view has been made clear for the world, just as I'm sure he would want. He *is* the president and all. A real 'man of the people.'"

I sat back a moment, letting the result of our little prank sink in. It was fairly sophomoric, but it felt so right. Sloan's face told me she had a similar satisfaction.

"And don't worry," she leaned in to say. "I don't think anyone'll be able to recognize us on the recording."

"Actually, I was out of the frame entirely," I said. "And I kept you in shadow. All you can see is his sleazy, bragging face."

She shrugged with satisfaction. "So no one has any idea who went in there and did that."

"Did what?" I said, flashing back a devious smile.

My instinctual pang of guilt had been quickly overtaken by a sense of justice. I didn't necessarily condone revenge, but some people deserved to be exposed a little. Hung by their own truth. And that guy had definitely been a prime candidate.

"Alright, time for our next stop," Sloan finally said, shaking me from my awe. "You never really answered earlier, so I'm guessing that's a no. Don't have any special accent skills up your sleeve, do you?"

Already onto the next deception. I shrugged. "Never really come up before." I thought back to my previous exploits in getting the businessman Walter alone. Back when we were trying to solve the original mystery that started this whole wild ride. "I did think I pulled off Southern pretty well before, though."

"Wasn't bad, I'll give you that." Sloan nodded. "It'll come in handy later. But I don't think it's quite right for our purposes tonight."

I narrowed my eyes. "And what purposes are those? Surely we aren't going for invisible, in these outfits."

"Can't." Sloan shook her head. "If someone already knows you, pseudo-invisible won't work. We instinctively seek out the familiar. Instead you have to try to distract. Make them notice everything but what's recognizable. Dazzle with the new and exotic."

"And thus, the over-the-top outfits?"

"Exactly. Normal could just call attention to our recognizability. The outfits were fine for hiding from Sayid in that obnoxiously loud party, among other purposes. And for keeping our anonymity in the aftermath." She grinned for a moment, thinking of it. "But we're going to need another layer for this meeting. Remember, Christopher knows my voice pretty well. And he just talked to you earlier today. We'll need voice precautions."

"What did you have in mind?"

"You remember that high-end escort you brilliantly sloshed out of the picture, when you needed to get Walter alone?"

I pictured the woman's face after I 'accidentally' soaked her dress with her martini, months ago during our inaugural case. The memory of her shock and anger filled me with pride at the success of my first real solo mission. "The eastern European one? With the high cheekbones?"

Sloan smiled. "Your cheekbones will do just fine. And your dark wig definitely lends itself. But think you can pull off her accent for a little bit?"

I chuckled quietly at the thought and shrugged, resigned to the adventure. "All I can do is try. If we're just observing, we'll probably be at a distance anyway, right? So it doesn't have to be too good?"

"Exactly. It'll just help disguise our voices while we're

in the background." She checked out the window as we came to a stop, then returned to face me with an excited smile. "No time for practice, unfortunately. They'll be here any minute."

***

I had to work to suppress my grin as we waited at the hi-top table, anxiously awaiting the arrival of our guests. I was just so impressed at our cunning. Thanks to our maneuvering, we could actually have a chance.

In addition to tracking Christopher's movements, which had told us he would arrive momentarily, we would soon be able to listen in on his conversation with no extra effort required. Sloan simply had to turn on the mic in his phone, which was sure to be in his pocket. I was amazed at the destruction of limitations possible when you had a tech genius like Leo on your side. And no qualms about the legal or moral ramifications.

My conscience was clear as we watched slimy Christopher stroll in and sidle up to a dark haired, heavy-set middle-aged man already planted at the bar. The accountant was still slicked up in his dark suit that was practically a clone of his companion's. A hairy wrist reached out to meet his in a brief shake.

"Here we go," Sloan said quietly, punching several times on the screen of her phone. The din of the room suddenly amplified in our ears as the signal kicked in. With each of us wearing one of my hearing aids, paired with her phone, we would both have an ear tuned in to the coming conversation at the bar. Completely undetectably.

Our eyes met with excitement, ready for the intel that would break open the case. The insiders would lead us straight to Grant's holding place. And we could stage a dramatic rescue, leaving the dirty mobsters stunned and without their needed funds. I could finally right my world again.

But it wasn't long before our faces fell, confused and disappointed. While we had a direct line into their conversation, it probably wasn't going to help our cause. Not if we couldn't understand a single word that was said.

"Don't suppose you know *Italian* in zat big brrrain of yours," Sloan said slowly, affecting a perfect Russian accent.

"Apologize," I said, timidly making my first attempt at a lesser version. "Was not one of zee electives, no."

We listened quietly a moment, trying to pick up on anything useful. But their conversation was low and rapid, and I knew not a lick of Italian.

I sighed. "I geeve up. But I have learned lesson, yes?" I tapped at my hearing aid-bearing ear. "I vill borrow even more advanced, next time. Vit right devices, we can understand no matter what ze language."

Sloan raised an eyebrow, an impressed smile creeping in. "Look forward to it."

My own words sank in and I blushed with realization. "I mean, if I still *have* job." I averted my eyes. "*And* if we ever do zis again. Which I don't promise."

Sloan didn't respond, only nodded sagely. I knew it was sarcastic.

We kept one eye on the unintelligible pair. Suddenly Christopher paused the conversation to check his phone. He mumbled a few more words in Italian and hopped from his stool, slapping some cash on the bar top despite having never ordered anything. The two men clapped each other on the shoulder and Christopher began to move quickly away, out the door with his fingers working rapidly on his phone.

I sighed and looked back at Sloan, expecting to see utter devastation. Our plan had failed miserably, and the whole scene was over with nothing to show for it. But instead she gazed back, bright-eyed and energetic. She held her phone screen low across the table toward me.

"He got an urgent text, calling him in," she said quietly, hopping from her own stool. "I need to find out what for."

I began a move to follow, but she threw out a hand to stop me. She leaned in to whisper. "We need to double our resources. I'll follow Christopher, and hopefully get some use out of our ability to listen in. You stay with this guy and see if you can get anything. Even just his name could be helpful."

"You want me to *talk* to him?" I stared at her, incredulous.

She shrugged. "Worth a try. Use your accent. And that outfit. See what you can get with it."

"I don't even know if he speaks English," I retorted.

"I think that was just for privacy. I've got a feeling he'll understand you just fine."

I narrowed my eyes at her. "When I say what?"

"Just do what you can." She grinned mischievously. "I trust you."

With that, Sloan breezed out the door, leaving me gawking in her wake. She was trusting me to . . . what, exactly?

***

After several minutes of twirling my drink and keeping an eye on the bar up front, trying to delay, I finally took a deep breath and slid from my tall stool. I smoothed down my dress and made my way to a seat at the bar, empty wine glass in hand. One empty spot sat between me and the hairy wrists that were just beginning on a heaping plate of fries and a steak sandwich.

I made sure to put him on my right side, where I still had a hearing aid. Sloan had run off with my left, leaving me at a disadvantage. I would need to hear every word. I wasn't going anywhere until I had *something*. Anything that could help.

I signaled to the bartender with my empty glass, then sat back, wondering how men did it. I was never one to blindly approach the opposite sex, attempting to start a conversation from nothing. Pull charm out of nowhere. It always seemed very contrived and forced when they tried.

And now, on the other side, it felt no less awkward. I was at a total loss. So I retrieved my fresh glass and sipped some more moscato, buying time. *What did she expect me to say?* I had to think.

***

Most of a steak sandwich later, I was still getting nowhere.

Certain that the accent would not fare well up close, I had hesitated, unable to speak. Not a single word had been exchanged. I had hoped that his few surreptitious glances my way would lead to him making a move, saying something to get us started. But alas, he was pretty focused on his dinner.

The man finished his sandwich and picked up his cloth napkin, giving me another silent once-over as he wiped the grease from his fingers, less inconspicuous this time. It was an opening. *Say something.*

My mind raced, trying to channel that high-end Eastern European escort in my memory for inspiration. She didn't just sit there, waiting to be talked to like the coward I was. She got in there.

And suddenly that gave me an idea. A fairly ridiculous one, but it was the only one I had. And it had worked for her, after all.

Slowly, carefully, I snaked my arm across the bar toward the man's half-empty platter. Just as I neared it, my hand shot out and snatched a long french fry from the plate in a quick swoop. I yanked the loot back toward me and took a quick bite of the end, glancing at the man flirtatiously.

Instead of the return surprised smile I expected, I was shocked to see the man's face flash with anger. Suddenly his arms lashed out protectively across his food. The full force of his hand slammed into his extra-large glass of red wine, which crashed onto his plate. Bordeaux began pouring across the surface of the bar and into the man's lap.

I gaped in surprise as the man hopped from his seat, his face now crimson with rage.

"You steal from me?" he bellowed, accent present but his English clear. He grabbed up his napkin and began to stab at the soaked material of his crotch. Meanwhile more wine poured from the edge, now down his pant leg and onto his dress shoes.

He felt the stream and jumped back, knocking over his stool. I grabbed a stack of cocktail napkins and reached forward as an offer of help, my face repentant. The man waved me away with disgust.

"Keep your germs to yourself, woman," he spat. He threw his napkin to the floor and stomped away, mumbling angrily in Italian as he headed for the men's room.

I sat back a moment, blinking. Nearby onlookers slowly

returned their focus to their own tables as the action died down. I surveyed the wet scene, wondering where to begin. And what had gone wrong. *Should I just run out of here?*

And then my eyes alighted on something amidst the rubble of the man's dinner. Realization hit me just as it lit up. And my mind began to churn with excitement.

No, that trick definitely hadn't gone as planned. But it had somehow brought a similar result. I was in. Channels of communication were now open.

He just didn't know it yet.

TWENTY-SIX

Five minutes later the SUV pulled in to retrieve me from the nearby coffee shop where I had taken refuge. I climbed in with fresh caffeine for each of us and found Sloan in the back, already buzzing with energy. She clearly had something to share as well.

I played it cool, wanting to keep the intel to myself for a change. I gave her a hopeful smile. "Follow Christopher straight to their hostage hiding place?"

She scoffed. "Almost didn't follow him at all." She raised her voice, directed toward the front. "Since our *driver* refused to go anywhere without you at first."

Dark annoyed eyes appeared in the rearview. "Just following orders," he called back. His voice lowered to a mumble. "Or trying to, anyway."

"I know, I know," Sloan muttered. "I don't make it easy." She returned her attention to me. "Luckily he came around, and agreed we wouldn't mention our little splitting up to you-know-who. Not that any of it seems worth it, anyway."

"So you didn't get anything?"

"Not exactly." She sighed. "Unless you count watching him waltz into the back of a run-down dry-cleaning business, where he said only a handful of words, none of which were useful. A couple yeahs and okays and a lot of long silences, with the other person inaudible. I couldn't even follow him in to see who he was talking to. And then we tailed him home for his bedtime. What a waste."

"Stinks," I said. "But maybe the location could be important? I assume we didn't know about that meeting spot."

"True," Sloan replied. "I'll have Leo check out the address." I thought a second. "Any chance that could be where they're keeping Grant? He could be anywhere."

"Good thought," she said. "The place seemed to be legit, and a little small to pull that off, but I guess you never know." She paused to pull her phone from her bag, her face lighting up again. "But I'm hoping we have another lead on that, too. Grant's family received another video. They've apparently cut us out of the loop, but Leo is monitoring."

She tapped on her phone and a new image of Grant appeared. This time rather than a close-up in a dim basement, he sat at a distance in a straight-backed chair, a bright light in his face causing him to squint away. The small room was draped floor to ceiling in tan sheets, with nothing else about the space distinguishable.

Then I noticed Grant's hand. His arms were lying on the sides of the chair, untethered. But his left hand had a thick bundle of white wrapped around it. A crude bandage. A tinge of red was visible on the lower left corner.

I stared at the image, finally comprehending. He wasn't just squinting away from the light. I was pretty sure he was wincing in pain. A sour sensation began to spread in my stomach, contents curdling with fear and disgust. This was all my fault.

I looked up at Sloan, terrified to know what was on the video. "What happens?"

She shook her head. "Nothing. Just a few seconds of him sitting there." She hit play and we watched in horrified silence. For ten seconds Grant sat unmoving in the otherwise empty space, only his tired eyes showing signs of life. The image bobbed slightly, making it clear it was being shot hand-held. Likely with a phone.

"So, his finger, you think?" I gulped. "They're barbarians. Who could do such a thing?"

"I intend to find out," Sloan said. "Whoever it is, looks like they definitely have an .MO. I'd be willing to bet Grant's family will be receiving a package very shortly, similar to the one left for you. Only the message will be a lot more clear this time."

"Christopher did say they had more efficient ways of convincing . . . " I pictured the gruesome scene to come as his family grasped the truth of the situation. The horror. What was previously a game for Grant had suddenly become much too real.

At least it now had a good chance of resolving, I realized. Certainly they would take the threat seriously this time. Who would take the chance?

"Hopefully then they'll pay up," I said optimistically. "And all this will finally be over."

"That's what I'm thinking," she said, trying to match my optimism. "In the meantime I've already sent this to Leo, and he's seeing what he can come up with. If we're lucky, he'll be able to work his same magic. Or maybe even get an address for us."

I gazed back, skeptical. "Except this doesn't look like a home webcam. And unlike last time, we're dealing with real professionals. I'm guessing they have some experience with this sort of thing. Extortion, at least. I don't know if we'll be able to get as lucky this time."

Sloan appeared to deflate. "You're right. I just wanted to believe. So far our leads haven't really panned out, huh?" She looked me in the eye. "I don't want to take any chances. I know we need to find him for you. Right now I'm just not sure how."

Just then I heard a strange ding from my bag. Sloan raised an eyebrow to me, clearly recognizing it was not my phone's normal notification sound. "Actually," I said, reaching to retrieve the source, "our tide may have just turned. If our assumption is correct that the Italian we just encountered has anything to do with this little kidnapping gamble, anyway."

The screen of the small black phone I pulled out was lit up with a fresh text message. I held it up proudly as Sloan stared, putting together my meaning. Slowly realization dawned.

"You stole his phone?" She gaped at me. "That's some serious criminal-detective work. Do you have secret pick-pocket skills I don't know about?" She narrowed her eyes playfully. "Or are you just *that* distracting?"

I laughed, thinking of how incredibly opposite the scene had been. "More like . . . I was that clumsy and inept. So much so that I made him run off in anger, forgetting his phone for the moment. By the time he came back, I was long gone. And I don't think he'll be able to find the poor-ly-accented woman who tried to flirt with his precious french fry."

Sloan continued to stare, grinning, her eyes bouncing between me and the stranger's phone in my hand. She seemed unable to decide where to focus. Finally she spoke. "I'm definitely gonna need that story sometime." She snatched the phone away, excited. "But let's see what we've got here first."

TWENTY-SEVEN

The fresh text message lingered on the screen. *Our friend cooperated. Tucked back in his basement for the night.* The sender was labeled only as 'D.'

"Okay, so let's just start with the assumption that Grant is the friend," Sloan said, continuing to stare at the screen. "Hopefully that means he's just doing what they say and is fine, then."

"Except for the whole missing a finger thing." I immediately tried to shake away the thought, not ready to approach that dark path again.

Sloan's eyes lowered in discomfort.

Another low ding thankfully distracted. Sloan read the message aloud. "Package delivery asap. Expect exchange within 36 hours. Be ready."

"Guess you were right," I muttered darkly. "I assume that's referring to his family receiving his missing body part. Then freaking out and giving in on the ransom, now that they can see the whole thing's real."

"Then maybe we have nothing to worry about," Sloan offered hopefully. "The guys seem confident it'll all go through. They get the money, Grant is released. Maybe we just let it all play out, then."

"Harm's already done, you're saying." I sighed, feeling a little guilty at the idea of resigning. But she had a point. "We don't have much time at this point, either. So maybe there really isn't a use in chasing after him. If it'll all end in the next day or so, regardless."

Sloan's eyebrow flicked up, surprised at my surrender. "The only real loser here is his family, having to give up the money. I'll sleep just fine. But you'll be able to live with that?"

I considered a long moment. Finally I shrugged, beginning to accept. "It was Grant's game to begin with. So it's really not our fault, if you think about it. And once he's returned, my career can get back on track." I took a deep breath, making myself say the words. "So . . . let's just let it go."

"Now you're getting it." Sloan broke out in a wide grin. "Benton, hurry us home," she yelled toward the front. "We're all done here."

"Glad to hear it," he called back, stepping a little harder on the gas.

"I'll get this phone to Leo to crack, just in case," Sloan said. "But I doubt it'll be much more useful anyway. The owner's sure to report it missing pretty soon, if not already."

I nodded absently and settled back into my seat to watch the city pass out the window, taking a deep breath for the first time in what seemed like forever. It wasn't all over just yet, but it looked to be rounding the corner on finality. Grant would soon be returned—and hopefully my life would be going back to normal.

Only I couldn't truly relax. Something niggled at the back of my brain, like an itch I couldn't quite reach. I wasn't sure what it was. But something bothered me about the situation. Despite all our declarations, it didn't feel settled. Not yet.

I picked up the phone and studied the texts again, searching for the source of my unease. My gaze focused in on the first message. "Real quick," I said, startling Sloan from her own reverie, "let's go back to the basement thing for a second. What do they mean, 'his' basement?"

"Dunno," she replied, looking at me curiously. "There's definitely not a lower level at his house. They're pretty uncommon around here. Not that they'd just let him go home, of course."

"Right. So their use of the word 'his' seems funny, doesn't it? Like it belongs to him, or maybe he's at least been there before?" I tried to come up with an explanation. "Maybe he was there before, when he was helping them spy?"

"Still wouldn't explain the 'his' part," Sloan replied, shaking her head. "You're right. Why would he be *back* in *his* basement?" Her eyes narrowed as she thought about it. Suddenly her face darkened. "Except there is one basement we *all* know he's been in lately."

"The hideout from his original scheme." *But why would they send him to his own turf?*

We mused in silence a moment, pondering the possibilities. I gasped as an idea occurred to me. The beginnings of hope creeped back in. We could settle the issue. "You had access to the webcam down there. Can you still get in?"

Sloan began tapping on her phone immediately, lips tight. "Let's find out."

A few more clicks and a video feed appeared. It was still live. And it showed, plain as day, Grant back on the couch, a small white dog's head resting on his lap. Kicked back watching television.

"Grant," I exclaimed. "*And* Mr. Pennington."

"So what do you think this means?" Sloan stared at the screen, confused. "That they were really a part of this all along? It just doesn't make sense they would let him go somewhere of his own choosing, does it?"

But it now made perfect sense to me. "They would let him go somewhere of his choosing . . . if he wasn't actually a threat."

Sloan stared back carefully, trying to follow my drift.

"What if by 'cooperated,' they don't mean he didn't fight them," I said. "What if Grant legitimately agreed to partic-ipate? He could be willingly helping at this point."

"You're right," Sloan replied, now excited. "They've even doubled the ransom. And why not? He already tried to get the dough that way the first time."

"*And* he offered to split with me to keep the ruse going," I added.

Sloan nodded vigorously. "So why wouldn't he just agree to help, and maybe they cut him in? It's a win-win for everybody."

"Except for his family," I said ruefully. "And people like us that got duped into caring." My mood sunk further thinking about it. "But could he be so desperate he would let them chop off his finger? That's quite a trade."

"Depends on your priorities, I guess."

I shuddered at the thought. Then slowly reconsidered the situation. "But really . . . what proof do we have that any of it's even real? All we know is he had a bandage and they have a history of that sort of thing. We just jumped to conclusions from there."

"Which could be exactly what they wanted us to do." Sloan shrugged. "I guess we'll know when the family receives the 'delivery.' First thing tomorrow, I'd imagine."

We both looked down as we sensed movement on the screen. Grant shifted in his seat, switching his right leg for his left on the coffee table. Then he lifted his left hand to lovingly ruffle the curls on the dog's head.

My mouth slowly gaped open as I watched. I turned to Sloan. "He sure does love his dog," I said. "But there is *no* bandage on that petting hand anymore."

Sloan's voice became acidic. "That's some impressive healing time, there. Really quite remarkable."

"I'll tell you what's remarkable," I muttered, disgust growing. "That I've put this much time, effort, and concern into trying to save that scheming little weasel."

Sloan grimaced at the con-artist on the screen. "Should we go over there and confront him? We certainly know where he is now. *Again.*"

I tried to calm my breathing and process. *Duped again.* For days I had been running around dedicated to trying to save this guy, someone I didn't even care for. Risking my own future, out of a misguided sense of duty and guilt. Trying to right a wrong.

But apparently *he* was the wrong all along.

And nothing good could come from what I was doing. From any of it.

"Nope." I looked up at Sloan, my entire outlook rapidly reversing course. I had seen the light. "We're not going to confront him, or do anything else at all. I am officially *done.*"

Sloan quirked an eyebrow at me. "You, giving up? I can hardly believe it."

The car slowed to a stop as we arrived back at our safe house. I sighed at the sight, happy to be home. Or as close to it as I had at the moment, anyway.

"You wanna walk away from his scheme," she continued, "I am all for it. He can have the goons all to himself."

"It's not just that." I shook my head. "Not only am I done with our little search for my lying frenemy . . . but I think I'm done with *all* of it. All of the lying, the deceptions. The false leads and the greedy ulterior motives. Every last maddening clue." I swung open my car door and looked back at Sloan. "I'm officially hanging up my PI hat for good. I'm out." I hopped out of the vehicle and headed for the front door before she could say another word.

TWENTY-EIGHT

Either Sloan was still sulking at my announcement, or she was giving me plenty of space to reconsider. Whichever it was, I hadn't heard a peep from her since our return the night before. I had expected relentless badgering from her about my decision. But the house was quiet. No one pestering at my door.

Instead I finally got to sleep in, a good, solid sleep for the first time in weeks. I awoke refreshed, feeling I had everything in front of me once again. It was only a matter of time before the whole Grant situation was resolved, without any further input from me. And then my life could just go back to normal. How that worked out was really none of my business.

I pictured it all as I took a long, hot shower, how everything would go down. Grant's parents fork out the money and he is released. The little weasel walks away with some of it, his family none the wiser. Everyone is relieved. Grant moves back to wherever he calls home to graduate and move forward with his life, probably still lying and scheming his way through it all. But again, none of my business.

Meanwhile, I get to waltz into work with a very special

tape in hand. I turn over the recording of Grant confessing to everything. Everyone is stunned by his outrageous stunt, and I am vindicated. The media craze has also subsided in our absence. Now there is nothing to keep me from finishing out my internship, just in time to get my final experience hours in and graduate in a mere two weeks. I was home-free.

I just had to get the tape from Sloan first.

I knew how she operated. As long as I smoothed things over, leaving open just the barest possibility of continuing with her someday, it shouldn't be a problem. But now that things were on the right track, I was never going back. My days of being someone's pawn in a devious, criminal scheme were over. I clearly wasn't cut out for all the lying and subterfuge. I was going to be an audiologist, plain and simple. And I couldn't wait.

A few minutes after my daydream-filled shower, I headed down the stairs and toward the front door. It looked like a beautiful day outside, and I wanted to take advantage. I had a free mind and conscience for the first time in what seemed like ages.

The spring in my step was caught short when a deep voice thundered behind me. "And where do you think you're going?"

I sighed and turned to find Benton stepping forward, curious.

"Just out for a walk." Now that I was shaking off the case, the details of our living situation were beginning to wear on me. I could barely keep the sarcasm out of my voice. "That's okay, right? I'm not a hostage here?"

"Not a hostage," he replied, now looking at me even more curiously. "But not all clear. You still have to use your disguise if you leave the house. You don't live here, remember? *Daisy* does." His mouth quirked up a bit at the corners as he said the name.

"Right," I muttered. "Daisy." I turned back, headed for my room. I could finish jumping through their hoops, fine. A disguise wasn't so bad. At least I was free.

"And I have to come with you," he called as I trudged up the stairs.

Perfect.

***

"So how does this work, exactly?" I watched Benton pull the door shut and hustle behind me toward the street. "We're taking a walk *together* now? I just wanted to clear my head."

"Clear away," he said, pausing to give me a head start as I began down the neighborhood sidewalk. "I'll just follow behind. Pretend I'm not even here."

"Right." I glanced back at him once more, still self-conscious. "And you're sure this is completely necessary?"

I startled when I turned back around and found myself face-to-face with a blue-uniformed young man. Levi. He must've just appeared from behind the neighbor's walkway hedge.

He smiled brightly. "What's completely necessary?"

I grunted. "The 24/7 surveillance I seem to have back there. Can't even take a walk without someone trailing me."

"Sorry for the intrusion," Benton called forward. "But I follow orders. You know how your boss is."

I glanced back again, my brow furrowed. "Boss?" *Is he referring to Sloan, or Lucas?* Neither sat quite right with me. I was my own person. Especially now.

"Yes, your boss." He gave me a direct look. "The *director?*"

"Right," I said, slightly embarrassed at the lapse. We had to keep up our covers. And the specifics were my idea in the first place. "I know, I know."

"Well, I happen to be walking too," Levi said. "Just with some stuff to do on the way, obviously. Feel like tailing someone else for a minute?"

Having a normal conversation with someone who wasn't part of the lying, scheming world of criminals and espionage? Sounded *amazing.*

I gestured at the sidewalk. "After you."

We turned and continued down the path, saying nothing for a few moments. He stopped to drop some mail in a box and gave me another little smile before continuing.

"So, how's the movie going?" he finally said.

"The movie?" I had to think. *We're making a horror film.* "Yeah. It's . . . disturbing. Lots of mind games and missing body parts. I think it might just work."

"Disturbing, huh? I'm intrigued." He glanced over, eyebrow quirked. "Any chance I could take a peek while you're filming? I've always wanted to see how something like that works."

More complications. But this was one request I actually hated to turn down. I wouldn't have minded an excuse to hang out some more. "Sorry, director keeps a tight set. No visitors allowed. Can't even tell people where or when we're filming."

"So is your boss paranoid or something?" he asked, glancing back at Benton. "Why all the security?"

I shrugged, making it up on the fly. "Just the money, I guess. When you're loaded, you never know who's out to get you. At least as she tells it. It took forever before she trusted me." I glanced back at our chaperone again. "You kinda get used to all the precautions, for the most part. But some days it's just a little annoying."

"I can imagine." He stopped at the next mailbox but didn't reach to open it. Instead he turned to look at me, his gaze turning funny for a moment as he stared.

I flinched as he suddenly reached his hand toward my face. When I realized he was headed for my fake nose ring, I quickly grabbed his hand and yanked it away. My other hand shot up to twiddle the silver loop and I realized it was hanging crookedly, about to fall off. I must've been a little too rushed in getting my disguise together this morning.

"Sorry," he said. "Looked like it was coming out."

"Yeah, you're right." I tried to straighten it without giving away the obvious fakeness. "Thanks."

It took me a moment to realize I was still holding onto him, his fingers cupped in my hand. And Levi wasn't making a move to get it back. He was just gazing at me pleasantly. I blushed and quickly released my grip.

"Listen, I was wondering," he said, hesitating. "I know you're probably busy with work and all . . . "

"Actually, I have all the time in the world," I interrupted. "Nothing but time now." I gave him a little smile and took a chance. "What did you have in mind?"

His eyes widened slightly. Then a shy grin appeared. "Well, I mean," he began, eyes casting about for what to say, "we could . . . you want to . . . I don't know, should we hang out tonight, or something?"

He really wasn't my type, but I had to admit he had a sort of understated cuteness about him. And I did find his awkwardness a little charming. I gave him a reassuring smile. "That could be fun."

A throat cleared loudly behind me. I glanced back to find Benton gazing at me expectantly.

"But I guess we'll have to have company," I grumbled.

Levi eyed the guard watching over us from the short distance. "Yeah, sure." He glanced at the sidewalk ahead. "Well, I guess I better get back to it. I'll be behind schedule. But maybe I'll come by around . . . seven?"

"Sounds great."

He took a step back, then another, still facing me. "Okay, then." One final backwards step caused him to half-stumble on a decorative rock edging a driveway. He laughed to hide his reddening face as he recovered his balance.

He met my eyes again. "Anyway, then maybe you can tell me all about your mystery, too," he said.

I gave him a quizzical look. "The movie? It's horror, remember?"

"No, no. Your mystery." He returned the funny look. "The investigation? Or do you just call it a case? I don't know the lingo."

I stiffened. My mind whirled as I tried to come up with a reasonable explanation for his words. It came up empty.

"You know, your secret crime-solving thing?" he continued, reading my confused expression. "Catching bad guys and playing dirty tricks? I'd love to hear all about it."

The alarm bells in my head were now at high alert. I had flashes of Sloan's face when she realized her date Christopher was on the wrong side and she had been used. Something was seriously not right.

I whipped my head toward Benton. He was watching us closely, his face hard. He had heard everything and was moving closer, slowly and carefully. I gulped for breath, suddenly having trouble breathing.

The next several minutes were a blur of movement and

NO FEIGN NO GAIN

sound. Benton yelling for support. The roar of men rushing up from the house, from down the street. Then more in cars, circling within minutes. I barely registered Levi's pale, shocked face as they surrounded him and forced him to the ground. Stern voices, shouting. Questioning. Accusing.

I was led back to the front porch to wait. I sat on the stairs and kept watch down the street, my pulse eventually returning to normal as my reaction evolved from confusion to anger. Finally seeing clearly. He was just another one of *them*.

I stared down Levi, eyeing every move of the little faker. His bumbling innocent act was fooling me no longer. He had failed.

And it concerned me no longer, because I was *done*.

***

Guess I can cross that possible love interest off my list. My very short, now non-existent list. I finally gave up on the spectacle outside, the ramifications of it depressing me more by the minute. I locked the front door behind me and cast about for my best friend, desperate to share the disturbing news. I had almost gotten played, just as she had been.

"Sloan," I called out excitedly, "you won't believe what just happened."

I rushed into the kitchen, expecting to find her near the coffee, but the room was empty. And there was no response from the rest of the first floor. I turned back and called up the stairs, louder this time. "Have you seen what's going on out there?"

Nothing, not even a stirring. *She's still mad at me.*

I started up the stairs, thinking of how to smooth things over. Certainly the incident outside would get her talking to me. But her door stood wide open, the room empty. *Had she even come home after my declaration last night?*

"Sloan?" Still no response from anywhere. The house was quiet.

Too quiet, I realized.

Just as I began to be concerned, I heard the sound of the shower turning on in her bathroom. *Of course.* I hadn't checked there. A moment later, pop music emanated from behind the door.

I sighed and shook my head at my own paranoia. *Just antsy from all the excitement.* I needed to try to calm down, as Sloan probably was. I headed toward the kitchen for a nice cup of tea.

But just as I reached the stairs, two large men in dark suits appeared on the landing below. They were not wearing the typical all-black of the security guys. And their faces were not friendly.

They're here.

Panicked, I turned back and sprinted toward my best hope. I made it into Sloan's room and had the door locked before the men caught up. The solid wooden door wouldn't hold them off forever. Hopefully she had her phone nearby.

I banged on the bathroom door, frantic. "Sloan. Open up!"

After a moment the door swung open, but it was not my friend this time. Or a glistening god. Instead another man in a black suit faced me, his cheeks distorted with dips and rivets. He flashed me a grin that made my blood run cold.

The man raised a small black gun and used it to gesture behind me. "Be a doll and let my friends in. Don't want them to get the wrong idea, you and me in here alone and all. I'm a married man."

Behind him the bathroom was empty. I had to take a deep breath before I could speak. "Where's Sloan?"

"Don't worry, we'll take good care of her. We packed her a nice bag and everything." He took a step toward me. "Now, you gonna open the door or what?"

TWENTY-NINE

Considering the gun and the lack of other exits, I did as I was told. The men entered silently and ushered me into the bathroom, their faces grim. They stepped in behind me and closed the door.

The older man in front seemed to be in charge. He smiled again, this time almost amiably, as though we were here to have a pleasant chat. "I appreciate you getting your men out of here. They've been hangin' around for days. Never giving us a chance to be alone, you and me."

I took a deep breath. If they wanted to hurt me, they would've already. They wanted something else. "Who are you?"

"That's really not so important right now."

"Okay," I said, trying to settle my shaking voice. "Then why are we in the bathroom?"

"You and your friend are known for being a little tricky, are you not? A little clever. For all I know, you girls have bugged up this entire place like a Moscow hotel room. Just like *before*." He looked around the room dramatically, motioning to the space. "But I figure nobody puts cameras and such in their own crapper. So it can be our own private little oasis. While we have a quick chat."

Steam was beginning to fill the room. The upbeat pop music still playing in the background gave the entire scene a disorienting, dream-like feeling. "A chat about what, exactly?"

"Don't worry, we'll get to that. But let's just make sure you don't have any *other* tricks up your sleeves first, huh?"

He motioned to the men, who moved forward to surround me. One patted me down while the other waved a small device across me. I didn't dare argue.

A familiar beep rang out when he got to my ears. Their detector could pick up the wireless signal from my hearing aids. The bulky man pulled my hair back and yanked the devices off my ears.

He held them toward me accusingly. "And what is this we have here?"

I didn't know if it was solely the accent or not, but goon number one didn't sound too bright. It gave me an idea.

I raised my voice and leaned toward him. "What?"

"These things, what is this?"

I shook my head as if frustrated and yelled louder. "I can't understand you. I need my hearing aids." I pointed to the items in his hand.

The man looked to the other goon, then his boss. He seemed stumped for his next move.

The man in charge waved in annoyance. "Give 'em back. Sal has some too, they're always setting off the equipment. Damned impossible to get anything done if he don't have 'em, though. Man's a freakin' 'huh' machine."

The goon hesitated. "I never seen 'em."

"That's because they're real small. Don't want nobody to know he's gettin' old." He began to look impatient. "Anyway, just do's as I say."

I held back a sigh of relief at my small victory as I slipped my devices back on my ears. If I had been able to have this conversation, hopefully so would Sloan. Wherever she was.

"Now we can get down to business," the lead man continued. "Those tricks you do—tell you the truth, I kinda like that. Takes spunk. I like spunk." He smiled as if in actual admiration, and then he narrowed his eyes, leaning in. "So I'm here to give you an opportunity. Let you use some of that spunk in a way that's mutually beneficial. We can help each other, you and me."

I glanced back at the men guarding the door. "Help each other how?"

"We're all in a bit of a jam here, you see. All our fellas are sittin' behind bars right now. And we're the only ones left out here, tryin' to sort everything out, keep it together. Puts us in a bit of a tough situation. And the way I see it, *you* girls are the reason for that."

I took a tiny step back as he moved toward me. He made a show of shrugging before continuing.

"Me, I think you didn't even mean to do it. That wasn't what you was after. So I think you should be given the chance to make it up to us, no? Undo all the damage you caused. You do that, and I say—all is forgiven." He shot a friendly smile that creeped me out. "Now what do you say to that?"

I took a deep breath, dreading whatever was coming next. "And how would we do that?"

"There's no *we* anymore, darlin'. It's just gonna be you out there. And meanwhile your girlfriend'll be spending some quality time with us. That's how we'll know you'll get it done."

"Ok. What do you want *me* to do?"

"Like I said, get yourself a do-over. I need my men. So

your job is to make sure they walk out of there, free as birds." He pursed his lips as if pondering. "Maybe not every one. That'd be tough, I'll give you that. But I don't have most of my guys back to work in a few days, we're going to have a problem."

"A few days? *I* get them out of jail?" I had no control over the sudden stammer in my voice. "How could I do that?"

He reached out to gently touch my face, letting his hand linger on my cheek a moment. The skin on his fingers was dry and rough. I forced myself not to flinch.

"We're not here to give you orders, now, sweetheart. I'm not your boss. You can handle this however you see fit." He moved his face in a little closer. "But if you want your little roommate to come home, you need to find a way to unravel this mess."

He dropped his arm and stepped back again. "So if I were in your shoes—which I'm not—I would think about maybe tampering with some evidence. Changing your story, so it don't add up the way they need it to no more. Couldn't be too hard to take it all back, I would think. And then my man Salvatore can walk free."

I shook my head, thoroughly confused. "So you need me to get the charges against your boss dropped? But we weren't responsible for *his* arrest."

His chuckle was loud and unnerving. "Trust me sweetie, he ain't the boss. He knows who the big cheese is."

The man let out another gruff laugh as he glanced back at the men behind him. They lowered their heads, deferential.

"That gift I sent you should've made *that* perfectly clear," he continued. "You remember, the little box on your desk? I like to think it was his favorite."

The finger. This man had been responsible for that gruesome find. I took another step back.

The man watched my face with satisfaction. "You never did say thank you. A card is customary, you know. Anyway, you don't need to worry about who's who. You just need to have another chat with the police, tell 'em you were mistaken. Girl like you goes in there and changes her tune—and before you know it, the whole thing's kaput. Suddenly they have no case." He twirled his finger in the air. "Just do your part, spin 'em up a few good lies, and we'll make sure Sal gets out. And so does your pretty friend. No harm done."

The man glanced back to his goons, giving a little nod. I shrank back as the dim one headed for me. But he stopped and held out his hand, holding a small flip phone. I checked their faces for confirmation before retrieving it.

"Like I said, I like you two," the man in charge continued. "And everyone else is put away for now, which you're gonna help me fix. So you get the rare opportunity to deal with me directly, kid. You just go change your story with the cops, and make it a good one." He pointed to the phone in my hand. "And keep that by your side. I'll be in touch, soon as we're square."

My stomach twisted as I tried to imagine getting away with lying. The police would see right through me. I was just getting used to little white lies in investigating. But the authorities? No way.

I can just tell the truth.

The man watched me closely for a moment, then stepped closer and leaned into my face. I had to keep myself from cringing at his stale cigar breath. "And don't go gettin' any ideas. We'll still be watching. Got eyes and ears everywhere, you know. Even on your fancy security guys. You go and try to talk to the wrong people, and your friend'll regret it, trust me." He smiled a little, amused. "The only cops you need to converse with are the ones you confess *all* your shameful lies to."

He stepped back and raised his eyebrows at me. "Capi-che?"

All I could do was nod in return. He gave me a disturb-ing satisfied smile, again chuckling, and jerked his head at the men. I felt a rush of cold air as they opened the door behind me, letting the steam escape from the room.

He pushed passed me and down the hall, his goons lum-bering out at his heels. The bang of the back door slam-ming closed echoed through the otherwise still house. And I finally began breathing again.

THIRTY

I hadn't wasted any time once the men left. Until now. And it was driving me insane.

Sick of pacing Sloan's empty PI office for the millionth time, I flopped into one of the leather chairs and let my leg bounce nervously instead. I could think of nothing to do but wait. And let my mind race with terrifying confusion.

Following Sloan's previous example, from back in our original-case days, I had attempted to send a message to the one other person who could help me sort out what to do next. A bat-signal, of sorts.

But knowing I was surely being watched, and possibly had been for a while, I had taken some precautions.

My first stop, a visit to Joe's Diner, had included a special request with my order. Sayid asked no questions when I slipped him a piece of chalk and a scrap of paper with a Dave Matthews song title. A shy nod told me he was in on the routine. I knew the alarming phrase would be written on the side of the diner's brick facade as soon as I took off.

All that was left to do was wait until dark. And hope the message would be seen soon, before I lost my mind.

After what seemed like an eternity, a faint tap sounded from one of the tall, dark office windows. I scanned the wall until I found Lucas's face, partially obscured by a dark beard and green trucker's hat, peering in the window.

I felt my whole body sigh in relief as I yanked open the window and he clambered in. *Lucas will know what to do.*

He straightened up and surveyed the room. "Where's Mac?"

"Sloan's not here. That's why I called you."

"Oh." A crooked grin swept across his face. "Interesting." His eyes took me in for the first time, strangely contemplative. "I thought it was kinda weird she would send me a message like that. But it was you . . . " He trailed off, lost in thought.

I blinked back, confused and anxious. "What are you talking about? I sent you that message so you would know it was *serious*. And urgent. *When the World Ends.*"

"Yeah." His smile didn't fade as he continued to gaze at me curiously. "That's right." The corners of his mouth were edged with humor. "And do you even know what that song is about?"

Frustrated we were off-track, I paused to fly through a few lyrics in my head. Quickly a blush crept into my face. *Oh. It's very dirty.*

Lucas laughed, clearly reading my reaction.

His response to such a signal was intriguing, but had no time to parse it. I shook my head to refocus. "That's not what I meant," I snapped sternly. "Next time I'll be more careful. But I need your help." I hoped my serious expression would bring him back. "Sloan's been kidnapped."

The grin slid off his face instantly. "What are you talking about?"

"Well, more like taken hostage. Mob men, I guess. Three of them showed up at the house and said they'd taken her."

"Kidnapped?" Fury reddened his face. "What happened

to the security? They were supposed to have you covered at all times. They swore." His voice lowered as he grumbled, more to himself. "Knew I shouldn't have trusted them to take care of it."

"They *were* there," I argued. "They were always around. They only left us alone for a few minutes to take care of Levi."

"Levi! Who the heck is Levi?" His angry gaze snapped to my face. "Is he another mobster you two were chasing, despite all my objections?"

I shook my head. "No, he was just the mailman."

"Oh, I heard about him. Skulking around."

"He had been . . . friendly." I hung my head a little, not wanting to get into it. "But it looks like he might've been working with those guys, too, so yeah. Maybe he was another mobster. And just using us. Or me, rather."

Lucas's arms flexed powerfully as his fists clenched. He took a deep breath and let it out before speaking again, calmly this time. "Okay. And?"

"*And,*" I said, trying to ignore his fury, "when we realized he might not be who we thought, the team swarmed in. I guess they have him, or are questioning him or something. In the meantime some mobsters snuck into the house and took Sloan. Everyone was looking the other way."

"How do you know that?" Lucas sounded frantic again. "And why am I just hearing about all this? Why hasn't the team contacted me?"

"They don't know yet." I waited a second, watching Lucas freeze and stare at me, blinking. "Only I know. And now you. *And* we have to keep it that way."

Lucas's strong jaw flexed and then bobbed as he swallowed. "Okay." He stepped to the nearest armchair and sat absently. His voice was more calm when he looked up at me, direct, and finally spoke again. "Start from the beginning."

I gave up on our stubborn secretiveness and filled him in on each step of the mess. Every detail I could remember from the last twenty-four hours, from figuring out Grant's duplicitous cooperation with the mafia to learning my new objective from that same ring of mobsters: lying, and lying big. In order to free the rest of the bad guys.

Lucas let out a long breath, when I finished my story. Relieved to have the whole thing out there, finally, I slid back in my seat and waited for him to process. It was a lot, I knew. But Lucas would have the answer.

After what seemed like hours, he finally met my eyes again. Only his were not the shining beacons of hope I was looking for. They were glazed. Dulled and unfocused with concern. "I'll be honest," he said, shaking his head. "I'm not sure how to get you out of this one. Not yet, anyway."

My stomach sank. *Surely he's just being modest.* He would have to think it over. Mull his plan.

Because if not him . . . who?

"I guess we could try to track her down," he mused. "Get to them before you're supposed to make your move. We won't have long, but maybe. I can make some calls."

"You can't," I retorted, panicked at the idea. "If they find out the authorities are involved at all, she could get hurt."

"Don't worry, I have back-channels. They won't have to know." His expression was pained. "I'm sorry, but I don't think the easy way is an option. Just getting them all set free, that can't happen. I can't help with that. Not after all that's gone into it. This case had finally made it all the way to the top." His eyes blazed with frustration. "We got 'em."

All the way to the top. His words bounced around in my head, trying to get my attention. Something wasn't right. I thought back to the man's words in that steamy bathroom. His evil laugh at the mention of his boss.

"About that," I said hesitantly. "I thought Salvatore was sort of in charge. And that's why the FBI finally brought everything down at once, because they got to the top guy. Like you said."

"That's right. The boss was the real target. Been after him for years." He paused and looked at me carefully. "Why?"

"Well, this guy, that took Sloan," I said, cringing as I tried to block the image, "he mentioned something about Salvatore *not* actually being the boss."

"He said that?" His brow furrowed as he narrowed his eyes at me, moving closer. "What were his *exact* words?"

I scrambled back in my memory, hesitant to fully replay the dark scene. "Trust me, Sal knows . . . who the big cheese is?"

Lucas's eyes lit up for a split second before his brow furrowed further, now an impossible clench. "So did he happen to say who that big cheese might be?"

The man's harsh chuckle at the suggestion that Sal was his boss played in my head again. "I . . . definitely got the impression *he* was really the one in charge."

Lucas froze and stared back silently, his face stoic. I could see the wheels grinding in his head. His gaze turned inward.

After a long moment, he pulled out his phone and flipped through numerous photos before handing it to me. "Tell me . . . is this the guy?"

I knew as soon as I looked down that it was him. I would never forget that pock-marked face. I nodded solemnly. "Who is that?"

"That's Vincent Tartalano." Lucas took another deep breath. "And he's been dead for over two years."

THIRTY-ONE

After that I sat alone for a bit, just watching. Head spinning. Trying to piece things together while Lucas barked cryptically into the phone, one abrupt call after another. It turned out that Vincent, better known as Vinny—the man I had chatted with in the locked bathroom earlier—was the true original head of the crime family. The main man.

Up until he was presumed dead in an explosion two years before.

Witnesses had seen him heading into the building just before the blast. The authorities considered it fortuitous timing for the local mob. They had been closing in on Vinny and his gang, with an arrest planned within days. It would bring down the entire operation, starting with the head for once. And then—BOOM.

After that, the case had come to a grinding halt and everyone had to regroup. Everything had rested on Vinny and his inner circle, all obliterated by the blast. They would have to inch their way up again, one lowly mobster at a time. Any moves on a lower-level guy before the timing was right could result in the whole thing going dark, key people disappearing and evidence moved or destroyed. So they resumed their patience and started again, this time prominent local businessman Salvatore squarely in their sights as their assumed new leader.

After the revelation of my encounter, however, the new working theory was that Vinny had still been pulling the strings all along. He had operated from a distance, all but his closest associates believing him dead after the assasination attempt. And once the indictments had started to fly, he had painfully seized Sal's appendage as a warning for him to keep quiet. Vinny had wanted to stay dead, to continue in the shadows, no matter what.

But he took the chance to come out of hiding once he saw an opening. An opportunity to undo all the damage and reemerge alive and on top, all turncoats and informants publicly outed. The feds' case against his people would be shattered, the results of all their years of hard work useless in a court of law as public trust in the intel and confessions that made up their case was destroyed. And I, apparently, had been the linchpin of that entire plan.

Finally Lucas stopped his pacing and put down his phone. He turned to stare at me a long minute, still saying nothing. I let him think, my own mind whirling.

"Okay," Lucas said finally, "we have a plan." He moved to sit in the other chair and faced me, solemn. "But I don't think you're going to like it."

***

It was insane. They had to be crazy, all of them. Whoever *they* were.

They wanted me to just give in. Do what the mobsters said. Follow orders, lie to the police about everything. And get Sloan back as reward. Easy, peasy.

"Is this really the best way," I said, trying to hide the skepticism threatening my voice, "just giving them what they want? Won't it ruin everything?"

Lucas nodded. "It does jeopardize the case, I'll admit. But it doesn't ruin it. With time, we should be able to roll everything back once we get what we want."

"Which is what? Certainly it's not just Sloan they're willing to do this for."

"No," he replied, his gaze steady. "They're not that charitable. Because of you, we know we were never really finished anyway. And now we can truly chop off the head of the monster. Vinny is the real goal here, he always was. Those guys are downright drooling for him."

"The feds?" I took a stab, trying to to finally pierce some of his mystery. "Like you?"

He gave a noncommittal shrug. "I'm not exactly . . . official. But yeah."

Still unclear. "Okay." I pondered his plan. "Two birds with one stone, then. As long as it helps, I guess." I looked back at him hopefully. "So it's just a setup, then? The police will know it's all a fake, that I'm just doing this to help?"

Lucas's lips tightened as he met my eyes. He hesitated. "I'll have some guys in the background who will know the whole story. Some feds'll be in on it. But the local police department can't be read in on this. There's no telling where the leaks are, and we suspect many. It's just too dangerous."

I looked away, my hopes for playing the hero rather than the fool vanishing. I would have to be the enemy here. No way around it.

"So," I mused, "I'm supposed to march into the police station and tell them I lied—"

"*Both* of you lied," Lucas interrupted. "You and Sloan."

"Right," I continued acidly. "Tell them *we* lied about everything that happened. The tapes of Carolyn Evans admitting she paid a drug dealer to get rid of her husband. I'm supposed to say that we, what, doctored them? That it was *all* faked?"

"Faked and manipulated." He looked away, rubbing his hands absently. "Trying to frame all of them. You tell them that, Mrs. Evans's plea deal gets rescinded, charges dropped. Her testimony is then rendered worthless because she will no doubt recant. So the guy she paid to do the deed then walks. And his testimony against all sorts of mob guys is also negated."

"And on and on, back up the chain," I said, feeling weary just thinking about it. "I get it. But what I don't get is how I'm supposed to go on after that. Will they be able to keep it quiet? Keep my name out of it?"

He glanced up before averting his eyes again. "I'm afraid not."

I took a deep breath, finally grasping the full reality. Not only would I have to fake my way through this, but I would be announcing myself for all the world as an unbelievable liar and scammer. I was going to be infamous. Ignominious. I was finished here.

Possibly finished everywhere.

"Just remember," Lucas said, interrupting my depressing spiral of dark thoughts, "it's not forever. The truth will come out eventually. I can make sure your real story gets told."

"But then *that's* my story around here. I'll never just be me. I'll be the girl who let the mobsters free, hoping they would catch them all again. Some people may never even get the whole story. *If* this even all works as you say."

I lowered my head, steeling myself a long moment

before facing him again. "But I guess that's better than all the alternatives." I raised my chin a little higher, displaying confidence I didn't feel. "I'll do what I have to do."

It wouldn't help to whine about it. I didn't have a choice. My friend's life was on the line, partially my fault. And in the end, greater justice would be done.

Just maybe not for *my* life.

"One more thing," Lucas said, drawing out his words. "You can't just go into the police station to do this."

He stared at me closely, waiting. I immediately tensed up, sensing his reluctance. Clearly there was more. And I wasn't sure I wanted to know.

"It's too risky," he continued, holding my gaze. "We can't have you being torn apart by questions the moment you try to tell your story. It would only slow things down, and the whole situation could easily fall apart. I'm sure you would agree."

I shook my head, trying to understand. "So what are you saying?"

"I'm saying," he said, reluctance returned, "unfortunately, they think that to make it work you'll need to do something a little more . . . public. Very public, in fact."

So much for keeping my head down.

***

Devastation. Pure, utter devastation.

It was the only way to describe what was happening. What I was doing in front of that crowd. The swelling, now-livid crowd threatening to turn into a riot on me.

I looked out at the growing horde. Their anger mixed with fearfulness, confusion, desperation, all directed at me. It played on every face staring slack-jawed at me behind the podium, including the sizable core of black and gold police uniforms, eyes narrowed with disgust as they watched my future unraveling. I had no disguise today, no way to hide in the shadows. Their ire was laser-focused on me. The *real* me.

I took a deep breath and refocused on the prepared words on the page, leaning toward the microphone again. I tried to make sure my face expressed the appropriate fake remorse as I wrapped up my monologue. "Again, I apologize to the good people of this city for my part in this dangerous ruse. Things got out of hand, and I truly regret how many others were affected by our abominable lies." My voice wavered as I sprinted toward the finish line. "I hope to help to clear this up as quickly as possible and assist in any way I can. Thank you."

I abruptly turned from the podium, more than ready to put distance between myself and all those hateful eyes. The crowd itself stood blinking at each other, stunned, as I rushed from the makeshift stage. The murmuring turned up a notch and some raised voices began to hurl insults behind me, rapidly becoming unintelligible as they blended into a stew of hate. The media at the fringes, however, were ecstatic. They immediately pounced.

Fortunately, so did my security team. A swarm of dark-clad men appeared from all sides, rapidly forming a ring that led me down the courthouse steps as quickly as my shaking legs would carry me. The reporters followed, shouting questions and shoving their mics, trying to cut through the protective muscle. Once again I ignored them all, keeping my head low. Only this time *I* was the villain of their stories. The questions fired at me were now accusing, full of barely-veiled outrage. Daring me to speak.

They chased us to the dark vehicle waiting at the curb.

I climbed in and hung my head in shame as we sped away, playing into the act. Despite my urge to scream that it was all a sham, I would have to feign humiliation for a while. Fake profound remorse. We had to make them all believe, for as long as it took to do what had to be done.

I sighed with relief as we sped through downtown and the crowds receded behind us, a trail of matching vehicles following with the rest of the men.

Benton was watching me closely in the rearview mirror. "You okay? Heard you did pretty good out there."

I sank back in my seat, exhausted. "Sure hope you guys are right about this, about the press conference. Because that was brutal."

"You just wait. Brutal hasn't even started yet. You'll need to prepare yourself for the stories they'll write about you." He eyed me again and flicked his eyebrows up knowingly. "Or better yet, don't. I think maybe no contact with the outside world for a while. Won't do you any good, trust me."

I knew he was right. I wouldn't be able to handle the things they would say. The meanness that would infuse all the stories. The glee with which they would denounce me and what I had done to the city. To the police. To justice itself. And they would be right about all of it. According to the version of reality I was giving them, anyway.

I closed my eyes and tried to let my mind drift some-where else, anywhere else. Mere hours had passed since I had been face-to-face with the true head of the local crime family and lived to tell about it. But as we drove away from the bomb I had just dropped on the entire local justice system, I realized my world was forever changed. Ineffably altered.

My burgeoning career in audiology had been everything

to me. But the likelihood of me overcoming all the recent events and returning to that career, reputation intact, was growing dimmer by the day. And I wasn't sure who I would be without it.

Maybe we would be able to right some wrongs, one day. If everything went just the way we hoped. But I knew, deep down, that things for me would never, ever be the same.

THIRTY-TWO

I had thought the waiting would be the worst part. Pondering what was going to happen, wondering if we had succeeded in our nefarious secret mission to undermine justice for the sake of supposedly even greater justice. But no. Actually seeing it work, seeing the results of our duplicity, *my* duplicity, come to soul-crushing fruition . . . that had to be the worst part.

They had been right, about all of it. It hadn't taken long. Once word of my confession got out, fairly instantly, a horde of lawyers had swooped in from every direction and made their case. Demanding, outraged. The mobsters must be set free, immediately. Every last one of them.

And one by one, most of them were.

Sure, a few of the guys didn't get quite so lucky. Rock-solid evidence still existed for a portion of the gang, leaving them watching enviously from prison. But they and their confessions weren't numerous enough to hold up the rest, who had been charged, at least partly, on the report of their buddies that had hung them out to dry. Once freedoms were assured, the tales those traitors had told were quickly rescinded. Suddenly, no one knew anything for sure anymore. Everyone had amnesia.

Meanwhile, prosecutors across the city were tearing their hair out, trying to stop the hemorrhaging of the local legal system. But there was just no stemming the flow of criminals. They had found a loose thread and were going to keep pulling until the whole thing was a useless pile of nothing.

The city roiled. Fear of violent criminals stalking the streets en masse infused every news story. Clip after clip of their releases played on every broadcast, turning up the heat on the spectacle more by the hour. People were angry, and my whereabouts were discussed with breathless regularity. I owed them all plenty of answers.

Tucked away in my new safe house, I watched it all from afar. There would be no public appearances for me for a while. Too risky, given the police department's demand for extensive questioning regarding my purported misdeeds. And the public's new preoccupation with witnessing my painful demise, of course. We had to hold them off.

I checked every news report with bated breath, both dreading and eagerly anticipating the news we needed. One by one the mobsters waltzed out, grinning like fools. And then, finally, *the* announcement.

Salvatore, they reported, was proclaiming vindication as a respectable businessman and citizen falsely accused. The city watched, aghast, as he marched through the ring of reporters crowding the courthouse doors, head held high. Free as a bird, as requested. All due to me.

Within minutes Lucas came bounding into the room, energized. "You did it," he announced. "He's out, and everything is in place. If it all holds up as expected, Sloan should be released any minute—and soon this whole thing'll be over. For real this time. And all because of you."

I had to admit, I did enjoy the glow of Lucas's admiration.

The megawatt smile was back, and it *was* all because of me. But I didn't want to celebrate just yet. I couldn't relax. There was more to be done. More to go wrong.

"It all depends on you guys getting to Vinny, though," I said, trying not to sound too pessimistic about bringing down the true mob boss. "That's the only way you come out ahead. You really think Sal will just go straight to him?"

"Not really." Lucas shrugged, enthusiasm fading only slightly. "I agree, he's probably smarter than that. But there's gonna be a fight for control now that Vinny's out of hiding. A transition of power, at the very least. His secret's out. And we can follow the chatter. We'll have taps on all the newly-released phones and know their whereabouts now. Someone'll tip us off, don't worry."

I sighed and sat back, more than ready to allow some of his enthusiasm to rub off. To finally feel the glow of some good news for a change.

It didn't come.

The door burst open again. "Great job on the press conference." Hudson strode across the room to stand at attention in front of me, hands on hips. "Seems to have worked. But we have some other intel, too. Your boy Grant has been released."

My eyes widened. "Because of this?"

He shook his head. "Looks like the 'rents paid up. Mom and pop moneybags just made a big bank transfer from afar and he showed up back at home, no worse for wear."

I took a deep breath. "At least that's over, then. Were we right, that he was in on it?"

"Every step of the way." Hudson grimaced. "Capped off by the ransom money being suspiciously split in half as soon as the wire transfer hit."

Lucas moved closer, his eyes narrowed. "We can try to

track the money, if you want. Could be pretty good proof of Grant's involvement in a fraudulent scheme, if we can tie it directly to him."

I looked away, exhaustion setting in. "I just want to stay out of it. I've had enough of digging into things that are none of my business for a while. Nothing good seems to come of it for me."

"Can't argue with that," Hudson said. His voice lowered. "And unfortunately, while we're on that subject . . . "

My head jerked up.

His face told me he didn't really want to have this next conversation. "There *has* been another little snag for you. Nothing that I think we can't clear up, of course. Once this is done and all."

My heart sank. I wasn't sure there was any more I could take. *Will it ever be done?*

"We've continued to monitor your phone for you," he continued, "and you received a message from your boss." He moved closer, his face softening. "Unfortunately, they're rescinding your permanent job offer, given all the news. And it seems you will need to get your final clinical hours elsewhere. They have . . . concerns. About you coming back."

Work. I had completely forgotten about it, with everything going on. "I'm not going to graduate," I croaked, my voice no longer working properly. My throat tightened with panic. *I'm never going to be an audiologist.* I closed my eyes and let the news settle in. My life was a mess. Everything was gone. And I didn't even have my best friend by my side to help.

I was now completely and utterly alone. Not counting all the tough, take-charge men running all around, of course. Placating me. Assuring me it would all be okay. But it wasn't *their* futures that had just gotten washed away in an instant.

"But like I said, let's just wait until everything dies down," Hudson continued calmly. "I'm sure we can find a solution. Surely *someone'll* allow you to get those last few hours of experience in. And then you'll get right back on track."

"Sure," I replied sourly. With a lifelong reputation for mischief, at best. And no permanent job lined up, either.

Yep, right back on track.

THIRTY-THREE

As the hours ticked by and we waited, readied patience morphing into anxious impatience, my fog of depression began to slowly lift. At least the worst would be over shortly. The next call should be from Sloan's captors, setting her free in gratitude. And I would soon have my friend back to help maneuver through the rest of the muck. It really would all be okay. Eventually.

The mobster's burner phone that had been warming my hand all day finally lit up with a text. But rather than the announcement we'd been waiting for—it contained only an address and a time. Two p.m., somewhere in the city. No other message.

The big meet.

All the guys huddled around as we scoped out the location online, and immediately I knew what we were dealing with. We were to meet in an old industrial area—the same vacant industrial area where we had first documented Salvatore's questionable business dealings months before. It had been a favorite spot for his after-hours activities. And it seemed like a message. In the end, nothing had really changed. They were already back on the old stomping grounds, taking charge once again.

Despite their misgivings, everyone agreed I had to be the one to show up. I was supposed to be the only person involved in this little charade, the only one who knew of my lies on their behalf. No one else could do it. A driver would accompany me but stay in the car. I would make the approach alone and return with our friend, safe and sound.

A fake-bearded Lucas insisted on driving me to the meet. I saw no reason to argue. Sloan was his family and it was just as important to him. His entire body was tense as we pulled into the crumbling parking lot. He watched the surroundings like a hawk through his dark aviator glasses, jaw working overtime while we waited for movement.

Within minutes a black town car pulled in and stopped at the other side of the lot. My heart froze for a second as I envisioned Sloan springing from the back. But instead a suited Christopher emerged, looking serious. The tinted windows were too dark to make out other potential occupants.

Lucas cursed under his breath and turned to me. A terse nod from him sent me out the door, ready to get this over with. I walked slowly across the lot, keeping pace with the smirking man headed toward me. We met in the middle and stared each other down.

He pretended to tip a non-existent hat at me, his face admiring. "Have to hand it to you, that was some exquisite work there. So far, so good."

"Exactly, you got what you wanted," I said confidently, summoning all my courage. "I did everything they asked. So now it's my turn. You know what I'm here for."

Christopher chuckled in surprise. "I didn't take you for the feisty one. Our girl must've been rubbing off on you, huh?"

I stared, saying nothing. Trying to remember to breathe. He eyed me, taking my measure. "You're right, you follow instructions well. So well, in fact, that I was sent to pass along another task for you."

I narrowed my eyes, alarm bells going off. "What do you mean, another task?"

"Nothing major, don't worry." Christopher raised his hands in surrender. "No need to get upset here. Just a little favor, since we're now friends and all. I'm certain Sloan would approve."

"Fine, I'll consider it," I replied, shrugging nonchalantly. "*Once* you hand her over."

Christopher laughed louder this time, a true cackle. "Nice try, that's good. Keep it up, sharp and determined. You can use that determination to convince him. I'm sure it'll take some work."

I blinked, trying to understand. "Convince who, what are you talking about? And where is Sloan?"

"She's been . . . delayed," he said, watching me carefully. "But I promise, she's just fine. We just have the matter of that one last teeny, tiny little favor. And then she'll be all yours."

My blood began to boil as I stared him down, finally grasping what was happening. *They're playing me.* She was not there, was never going to be there. And I was stuck.

I steeled myself and stepped closer. "That's *not* our deal."

"We *did* have a deal, that's true." He shook his head solemnly. "And I'm ashamed of myself, really. You see, I'm pretty good at making deals. That's why they hired me. But my boss, well, he's just not very good at keeping them. Always likes to push the envelope. Keep people on their toes." He took a deep breath and sighed heavily. "Unfortunately, once his mind's made up, there's just no changing it. And right now he has his heart *firmly* set on meeting with a dear old friend. We just need *you to get* that friend to come with you next time. And then we're all square. *Promise* this time." His face brightened. "So what do you say, think can you make that happen?"

"Depends," I replied, confused and wary. "Who are we talking about?"

"We came across something pretty interesting." His face broke into a smug grin. "In Sloan's apartment, the one she shared with her *fiancé*. Would you believe we've been desperately hoping to see him?"

Joel? I swallowed. "But he's . . . "

"Dead?" Christopher eyed me, suspicious. "I know." He spread his hands wide. "But the thing is, we don't really believe that no-longer-alive story anymore. It seems they're just not buying it. So we need you to dig him out of whatever dark hole he's been hiding in and produce him for us, and right away. It's long past time we had a little chat."

My chest began to tighten with panic as I realized I was truly stuck now. *How in the world can I produce someone . . . not alive?* "I . . . I don't . . . " I stammered.

Christopher ignored my reaction and checked his watch dramatically. "Now I really am sorry to demand and run, but I do have to get going." He looked up at me, one eyebrow cocked. "How about . . . this time tomorrow?"

There was no time to deal with the dead guy conundrum. This was it. The chance for any further intel about Sloan's whereabouts was now. And we needed clues. *Something.*

I straightened my shoulders, trying to buy time. "No."

He stared back in surprise. "No?" A softer chuckle escaped. "And what does that mean?"

"It means . . . " *What did it mean?* I thought quickly and levelled my gaze at him. "It means I need some kind of proof. What assurance do I even have that Sloan *is* fine, as you say?"

Christopher smirked. "Please, like I would let them hurt my dream girl." He reached into his inner breast pocket. "No need to mention that part to her, though, huh?" His hand emerged with a phone. "But I had a *feeling* you might want something like that."

He held the phone out, eyebrows raised. Carefully, I took it from him and recognition hit immediately. It belonged to Sloan.

He saw me take notice, a hint of a smile playing on his face. "She was kind enough to remove the password for us, so we could have a quick look around. Not quite as interesting as I had hoped." He reached over to tap the dark screen. "But I did take the liberty of snapping you a fresh photo of our mutual friend, just this morning. No harm done, as you'll see."

I turned it on and went immediately to the photo memory. And there, indeed, was a close-up of Sloan. She gazed ruefully at the camera, newspaper in hand. While she definitely looked annoyed, she did in fact appear fine and unharmed.

"Now that we have that settled," Christopher continued, "let's get back to it, shall we? You've got some work to do. You can keep her phone, she won't be needing it just yet. Just keep it handy and I'll text you the place. This time tomorrow you can walk away with your friend, no strings this time. All you have to do is show up with our long-lost buddy Dominic."

Dominic?

Who the heck is Dominic? I started to open my mouth to question, not knowing where to begin, but he raised his hand to cut me off.

"You have my word," he said, meeting my eyes with intent. "You just do what you need to do." He turned and strolled back to his idling vehicle. The car pulled slowly away, leaving me standing in the middle of the lot, alone. With no earthly idea where to go from there.

***

Lucas was cursing under his breath when I climbed back into the vehicle. I shut the door and avoided his gaze, dreading the next conversation. I clearly hadn't retrieved his sort-of sister-in-law, or accomplished anything of use thus far, really. I had failed. We all had.

But mostly me.

"So," I finally began. "Obviously, I have some bad news."

"Yeah, that little weasel has it coming," he sneered. "You just wait."

I paused, confused by his reaction. "He's . . . not giving up Sloan yet. They want something first."

"I know. Just another wrench to throw in there. Like it wasn't complicated enough already. Now we're supposed to produce their dead guy."

I froze. "'Wait, you were listening?"

"Of course I was listening." He waved off the question. "The question is, how do we play this from here?" Lucas crossed his arms and stared out the windows, his mind churning fast and far away.

I began to pat myself down self-consciously. *How could he have heard that?* Had he bugged me?

Maybe I didn't want to know. There were more important things right now. "Well, to begin with . . . who in the world is Dominic? I thought Sloan was engaged to *Joel*."

He turned to face me soberly. "Dominic *is* Joel. My brother was working with the feds, too."

Lucas paused for my gasp. Everyone was always hiding something, in their world.

Or was it *our* world, now? *My world?*

"They must've seen something, a picture of them together," he mused to himself. "And connected the dots." The corner of his mouth twitched as he stared out at the horizon. "Or at least think they did."

My mind flashed to Sloan, mourning a framed photo after the break-in. Beneath the glass fragments sliding to the floor, beaming faces proudly displayed a sparkling ring. "The engagement photo," I said. "There was this one—"

"I know the one," he interrupted, somber. "I took it."

"Well, it was moved during the break-in. Someone probably saw it. Before they smashed it."

Lucas nodded but said nothing. I stared him down as he pondered, just waiting for the whole story. No more mysterious mumblings. No more cryptic asides. I needed answers.

Lucas finally took a deep breath and continued, eyes locked on me. "So Joel also helped on this same case, this mafia group. A while back. Before the explosion that killed Vinny and the rest of those crooks."

My eyebrows shot up. *Even more history here.*

"He was actually the main source of intel at that time," he continued, "operating for several years under the alias Dominic Vichelli. He worked with them, was one of them . . . or so they thought. Until that explosion."

"Wait." My mind whirled with the new information. "The explosion? Is that how he died?"

"It is." He broke eye contact, turning to gaze out at the distance again. "And thanks to you, we now know Vinny actually made it out alive, when he was presumed dead. So I guess they suspect their guy Dominic might've actually done the same." He scratched at the back of his head absently, lost in thought. "Not quite sure what to do with that yet . . ."

I watched him a moment, quiet, trying to take it all in. Sloan's fiancé was in the mix with these guys from the beginning, from *before* the beginning? And she never said a thing? Not even a peep?

I could feel my blood pressure rising. Despite there obviously being more pressing matters, I was not going to be able to just let that go. "So . . . no one ever wanted to mention this connection to me, after all this time?"

Lucas's head snapped toward me, concentration broken.

I tried to keep my frustration in check as I continued. "Not even Sloan, who dragged me into all this in the first place?" My fists were tightening against my will just thinking about it. Always the one lied to. The one left in the dark. *She got me again.*

"Actually . . ." Lucas cringed. "That's really not her fault. She didn't exactly know either." His eyes returned to the front window. "I never told her."

My breath caught as I watched him carefully, waiting for more. Surely there had to be a good reason for such a colossal withholding. Something to explain all of the deceptions. If anyone had a right to know the truth, it was his own fiancée. *Especially* after he had been killed.

"It wasn't my call," he finally continued, his voice deep and firm. "And it wouldn't have changed anything. We were asked to wait. Once this whole thing blew over, and they were all finally behind bars . . . then we could tell her everything. But until then, it was unsafe. Her connection to him couldn't be known out in the world. She could become a target." He glanced over, indignant. "As we clearly now see."

I swallowed, absorbing the news. *All this time.* So even the secretive Sloan could become a victim of all the masquerades in their maddening clandestine world. She would be clobbered by the lies, too. The deceit could be devastating.

But there was no satisfaction in knowing that I was not alone for once. My friend did not know the truth of her own fiancé's death. Or life, it seemed.

As I replayed his words, trying to picture their side of it, my mind hung on a pronoun. "So who's *we?*" I ventured.

Lucas's eyebrow quirked up.

"You said *we* were asked to wait," I continued. "So, other people knew, besides the feds?"

He shrugged. "Just Hudson. He was aware of Joel's participation. And he agreed to do his best to keep everyone safe until it was time. Which was *going* to be any day now."

Her business partner, too. Sloan was going to feel betrayed once everything came out. I had a feeling she wouldn't take kindly to her own weapons being used against her.

But now was not the time to worry about it. First we had to get her home.

"Wow," I mumbled, feeling overwhelmed. "Let's just figure out what to do now."

I took a deep breath to push aside the new information and turn my focus on the current situation. We only had one more thing standing in our way. In order to retrieve Sloan, we would now have to produce Joel, a.k.a. the mob's quasi-friend Dominic. Which was not possible, for obvious reasons.

Or is it? A flash of inspiration hit.

I turned back to stare at Lucas, studying his face. Trying to remember the broken photo. The glass had been too shattered for me to be certain, but it seemed worth a try. *We have to try something.*

"What about you?" I finally blurted, unable to hold back.

Lucas raised his eyebrows at me. "What *about* me?"

"All I know is you two were pretty close in age. Any chance you could pass for Joel, under the right conditions?"

One side of his mouth lifted slowly into a half-smile as he pondered. "I'd like to think I was the better-looking one," he finally said, "but yeah, we might just be able to make that work. With a little help."

I sighed, releasing a breath I didn't realize I was holding. We had a new option. A solution.

"Not a bad idea," Lucas said, still smiling at me with satisfaction. "Thanks."

I beamed. "So what do we do now?"

"What we do now is take *you* home."

I perked up even further for a second. "Home?"

He flinched. "Your temporary home. You know what I mean." He whipped around to put the car in gear and glanced back in the mirror. "I'll need to make some calls. We don't have much time."

THIRTY-FOUR

J ust waiting. And more waiting.

I stayed curled up on the couch in my second make-shift home in a week, trying to not to gawk as Lucas paced around placing phone call after abrupt phone call. He had a way of mumbling into the phone, his voice deep and low, that made it impossible to make out what he was saying even when he was only feet away. But just watching him made me feel better. Things were happening. People were taking charge.

Finally Lucas slipped the phone in his pocket and turned to me. "We've gotten some intel. Think we have a line on where they might've taken her. Sal's restaurant." His gaze turned hard. "I think you know the place."

My eyes widened. "Fantastic." The place had seemed nice enough when Sloan and I had done surveillance in the past. No dark dungeon, at least. "Now we can just barge in and get her, right?"

"First of all," he said, eyes narrowed, "*we* wouldn't be barging in anywhere. But our people aren't prepared to go in blind, either. It's an unnecessary risk. They don't know what they're walking into."

I felt a panic rising. "But we can't just leave her there."

He waved off the idea. "We just have to be smart. We're going to be invited guests tomorrow, anyway. Now that we know where she is, it will help us plan it all out. The less unknown, the better."

"Right." I tried to hide my disappointment. It sounded like we would still be playing completely by the mobsters' rules. I had hoped we would finally get the upper hand, for once.

"We're moving ahead with your idea, by the way," Lucas continued. "We'll give them what they want. 'Dominic' will be going in there with you tomorrow."

I looked him over, curious about his acting skills. "So you'll be playing your brother, then?"

"Don't forget, it's my brother, *pretending* to be their old pal Dominic." His smile was crooked. "But I think I could pull it off just fine." He took a deep breath, his expression slowly flattening as he exhaled. "The only problem is Sloan's reaction. We don't know how she'll respond to her long-lost fiancé waltzing in. Will she believe it, or pretend to? Will she just freak out?" He shuddered. "Pretty disturbing, I'd think."

I gulped just thinking about it. *Poor Sloan.* It would be heartbreaking to be in such a terrifying situation already, and have a faux-loved one show up. I was certain I wouldn't know what to think. Or do.

A sudden voice in my ear startled me. "Battery," it blurted.

My hearing aids. They would die soon without new batteries. I would need to find my stash, hopefully included in my things that had been rushed to the new safe house.

"Excuse me," I said to Lucas, grateful for the momentary distraction. Finally, a problem I could solve.

I crossed the few feet of the small space into the first

bedroom, in search of my suitcase. Most of my belongings had been left behind. My entire shrunken world was now contained in the one sad little bag. I breathed a sigh of relief as I pulled out the box I needed. At least I would be able to hear. There was enough chaos without that added problem.

I pulled a new pack from the box and hesitated. I found myself squatting in front of the open suitcase, frozen, just holding the batteries. Staring at them.

Something had made me stop. Something was bothering me. *But what do batteries have to do with anything?* I studied the packaging, trying to find the source of my unsettled feeling.

And suddenly it hit me. It wasn't the batteries. It was what they represented. And that was a link.

A possibility.

I rushed back to the living room. "Where's Sloan's phone?" I blurted to Lucas, interrupting his millionth phone conversation.

"Hang on," he mumbled into the phone. He moved the handset away from his mouth and looked up, a little impatient. "Why?"

"I might have a way to get in touch with her. Get her a message."

"I'm gonna have to call you back," he told his caller. His eyes narrowed as he pulled Sloan's phone from his back pocket, hesitant. "I don't really see how."

"Just let me just see it," I snapped, grabbing it from his hand. I went straight to the accessibility settings and confirmed. There was a possibility.

I looked up at Lucas, excitement bubbling. "We can talk right to her. If she still has them in, of course."

"If she has what in?" His look was beyond skeptical.

"There's no way they let her keep some listening device, if that's what you're thinking. These guys are known for their meticulous checks. They've been burned too many times."

"I'm well aware, having been subjected to it myself. Which is why I have reason to believe she might've been able to keep something else. Something *just* as useful."

I held the phone screen to him, pointing to the listing of the hearing aids paired with the phone. "If we can get close enough, these could give us a line right into her ears."

He raised an eyebrow. "Since when does she wear hearing aids?"

"Since I showed her how to use them to communicate and listen in on things. It's actually a lot easier than the fancy setups you guys use, and a heck of a lot more versatile." I smiled, proud of myself. "*And* much more discreet. I convinced those goons to let me keep mine. So if she acted like she needed them, played hard of hearing, they might've found it easier to just let it go. Completely unaware of the true capabilities."

He looked keenly interested now. "So it's like a headset? We can talk to her?"

"She won't be able to talk back. But if they're in her ears, she'll be able to hear us." I watched the expressions play on his face, concern battling excitement. "You said we need her to respond appropriately when we show up. Now we can *warn* her."

Lucas nodded, pondering. "So you really think this'll work? That Sloan tricked them?"

I shrugged. "She's pretty smart. So it's worth a shot."

He pursed his lips, considering, before looking up with a nod. "Guess I can't argue with that."

***

By the time we pulled up next to the restaurant, Lucas's silent meditation had returned and become brooding as dark as the unlit parking lot. I peeked over from the corner of my eyes, unsure about breaking his trance. Or about what I could possibly say to lighten it. I fidgeted nervously with the ends of my dark wig, the rest of my disguise abandoned for the nocturnal mission.

He kept his gaze on the back of the white stucco building, eyeing the service door and the row of warmly-lit windows along the first floor. As usual, all the second floor windows were pitch black, not a flicker of activity. But we knew better.

By now, Sal's not-so-secret underground casino was probably back up and running full steam. It would be a nice way to shove their seeming triumph in everyone's faces. Back when Sloan and I had first visited the restaurant months ago, I had attempted to access that upstairs lair. We had been suspicious something more was going on, and were just beginning to scratch the surface of the truth.

I no longer wanted to get myself in. Only to get her out. And fast.

Despite the closed sign on the door, two dark-suited men exited the darkened front and crossed the parking lot, confirming our unspoken suspicions. I turned to see Lucas's face harden once again, his lips pressed tightly together as he watched them in silence. He finally looked back at me.

"I've seen enough," he said. "Now let's see what *you've* got." He yanked the door handle and stretched himself back to normal height as he exited the vehicle. I followed, trotting to keep up with his long stride as he crossed to the shadowy front corner of the building.

He handed over Sloan's phone, eyebrows raised in curiosity. I went straight to the special streaming settings, checking to see if the hearing aids showed connection. Nothing yet.

Lucas leaned in to peer over my shoulder, the proximity sending chills down my spine. "What now?" he whispered. "I was promised communication."

"I said we could *try*," I snapped back, trying to keep my voice low. "But there's no guarantee."

I took a step away, heading around the corner. Lucas reached a hand to stop me. "Where are you going?"

I pointed the phone screen at him. "We need to get closer. If they're on, the devices will show up here as connected. But only if we get near enough."

He considered only a second. "Stay behind me," he growled quietly, peeking around the corner to check before continuing.

I followed him down the side of the building, eyes focused on the connectivity page on my screen. Nothing was changing. I avoided Lucas's questioning eyes as he continuously kept watch of both me and the vicinity.

Staying as close to the building as possible, we maneuvered around the green cinder-block garbage area at the back and suddenly got a hit. The hearing aids lit up as connected. I had to suppress a shriek of excitement, settling instead for a sharp intake of breath. Lucas's head jerked toward the sound.

"She's here," I said, trying to remain calm. "She must be somewhere in there, probably upstairs above us. Or at least the aids are. We don't know for sure she's wearing them, but they're definitely turned on."

"So how do we talk to her?" Lucas's eyes were lit up, somehow twinkling despite the darkness.

"Just call her," I whispered. "All I have to do is answer with her phone. Your voice will be routed straight into her ears."

He shook his head, just a hint of a smile forming. "You're a genius." He pulled out his phone and dialed.

My head tingled from the compliment. *Now it just needs to work.*

Sloan's phone lit up in my hand, vibrating. I took a deep breath and hit the button to answer, connecting the call. The screen indicated it was being sent to the hearing aids.

Lucas met my eyes and I nodded, encouraging him to go on.

"Sloan," he said softly into the phone. "It's Lucas. Don't be alarmed. We're right outside." He paused, thinking. "I'm here with Quinn. We can't get you just yet, but we're coming in tomorrow. I promise." His voice cracked as he began to choke up. "I hope you can hear me. And I hope you're ok. I'm sorry you're stuck in there, all alone. After everything . . . "

He trailed off, seeming lost for words. *He really loves her.*

Fearing we would run out of time, I slipped the phone from his fingers and spoke, my voice low. "Sloan, you should know that there'll be a surprise tomorrow. Lucas will be coming in to get you, but he'll be pretending to be Joel. Only he will go by the name Dominic. It's confusing, I know."

I paused for a moment to listen, thinking I heard something. Nothing. I continued hurriedly. "But it's very important that you play along. Act like Joel never went anywhere. And then hopefully we can all walk out of . . . "

I was cut off as Lucas suddenly grabbed my arm, flinging me up against the wall. The phone clattered to the ground beside me. He swung himself into me, wedging us in the corner between the restaurant and the garbage wall. I gasped in surprise, searching his darkened face for explanation as it hovered over mine, moonlight highlighting his features from above.

"Shhh," he whispered. "Don't say anything. Just giggle."

What in the world? My back stiffened as his hands slid around my waist. He leaned in, pressing me firmly into the wall.

"Just do it. Right now." The stubble on his jaw tickled my cheek as he moved his face in close to mine, sending every nerve ending in my body into overdrive. "Giggle for me," he whispered again, his hot breath on my cheek setting my face on fire. I gulped, utterly confused.

And then I heard it. Footsteps headed toward us. Possibly more than one pair.

I sucked in a trembling breath and let out a shy giggle. Then a little louder.

The footsteps were close. And I understood. I began to wriggle around and push him coyly away a little. "You're so bad."

"That's my girl," Lucas purred in my ear. He slid a hand up my back and pressed his face into my neck, scratching my skin with his short beard, just as the spotlight settled on us.

I gave a little squeal and shrank back, hiding my face behind his shoulder. Lucas froze, not daring to turn around. After a long moment, letting them have a nice look, he groaned. "C'mon, man," he called out, his voice gruff. "Mind your own business."

The bright light dropped away as we heard quick

chuckles. "Get a room," one of the visitors yelled sternly in an Italian accent. "This is not the place." The two shared another laugh and strolled away.

We stayed like that, pressed close and listening to each other's breathing, long after there was nothing left to hear.

THIRTY-FIVE

I knew there wouldn't be much chance of sleep that night. But I didn't realize just how conflicted my insomnia would be. Tossing with worry about my friend and her impending rescue. And turning over my unexpected intimate moment with Lucas. And my embarrassing reaction to it. He was just trying to obscure our intentions, to keep us safe. *Could he tell how flustered I was?*

I certainly would never have known by his actions afterward. As soon as the coast was clear, he made another quick, mumbled phone call and announced he had last-minute things to take care of right away. Within seconds a mysterious dark sportscar peeled into the parking lot and pulled up alongside us. I assured him I would be fine getting myself back safely, and would do so immediately. He hopped into the car and disappeared with nothing more than a nod. And most definitely no eye contact.

I found my phone on the pavement, where it had shut down upon contact when I dropped it in surprise. Our connection to Sloan had abruptly ended. But hopefully she had gotten the message and understood her role.

And now all that was left was to march in and get her, everyone playing along in the Joel/Dominic ruse. Especially his faux-fiancé. My stomach tightened with anxiety as I dug through my suitcase, ready to start the day.

What exactly is the proper attire for a mass mob deception?

***

We all met up in the corner of the adjacent parking lot before the appointed time. Hordes of dark-attired men climbed from vehicles and swarmed, a small army setting up camp. A thick line of trees hid us from the restaurant's view but would give quick building access to the gathered federal agents when the time came.

I desperately needed to know when that would be.

"So you still aren't just barging in there?" I shook my head at the men, frustrated. "Why are we following their instructions, when there's probably more of you than them? Surely you could take them."

"Not without undue risk," the tall agent with the thick silver mustache replied, his voice patient. Given his constant vigilance, I had pegged him as being assigned my 'handler' for the moment. "We need our guy to get a feel for the situation first, find out what's in there. And make sure the main target is present and accounted for." He leaned his head down to me a little. "I'm real sorry you have to be dragged along in the meantime. We sure appreciate your cooperation, ma'am."

Yeah, yeah. There was no sense in arguing. But my mind was hung up on one phrase. *Our guy.*

Lucas.

My stomach tightened as I pictured waltzing into the building, fake mobster by my side. I had no idea what his real experience with this sort of thing was. Or with *any* sort of thing, really. He was still quite a mystery. "Where is Lucas, anyway?"

"No Lucas today, remember?" a voice behind me growled, low and serious.

I spun toward the sound. And there he was, only feet away. Sort of.

His face itself seemed normal. Strong, chiseled jaw and perfect masculine features. But nothing else rang true. Lucas's thick, lovely chestnut hair had been chopped off, razed to just a thin covering on his scalp. Gone, along with the facial stubble that had affected me so only the night before. I felt my face heat up just thinking of it.

The short sleeves on his too-tight black t-shirt showed off a jagged fake tattoo banded across his right bicep. And thick dark-rimmed glasses shadowed his eyes, assisting him in expertly avoiding my gaze.

Crap. *He's uncomfortable.*

Dark thoughts from my sleepless night rushed back. Clearly I had embarrassed myself when he got too close. Of course he was going to avoid the girl who couldn't handle a little pretend makeout session under duress.

I tried to ignore my shame and took him in quietly, realizing that the plan might just work after all. He looked entirely different. And was probably the spitting image of his brother in that getup.

So if he needed to take on the part immediately, I should not get in the way. "Right," I said, shaking it off. "Hi Joel. Or, umm. Dominic?"

"Let's just get in there," he said. He locked eyes with my handler, Robert, one eyebrow raised. "We have the go-ahead?"

The man bowed his head. "Invite's been received. And

luckily they're staying put, as expected. We're clear, whenever you're ready."

"Then let's do it." Eyes focused intently on the path ahead, the fake Joel flashed me a little wave to join him and took off for the trees.

Now? I scrambled to catch up, my mind lurching into panic mode. I still had no idea what the plan was, what we were supposed to be saying or doing besides simply showing up. No one had filled me in on a thing.

We reached the back of the restaurant in less than a minute. As we neared the kitchen entrance, I caught sight of the corner where I had been momentarily nuzzled up to Lucas the night before. *The spot.* I quickly averted my eyes.

Lucas, professional game-face on, seemed to pay no mind. Clearly I was going in blind, with no plan and very little understanding, alongside a man completely oblivious to me. Or least entirely indifferent to our little . . . moment.

No, he was too busy focusing on pretending to be someone else. Someone who was, in turn, also a complete fake. *What a mess.*

Would I be able to keep it all straight? Maybe it *was* best that I was clueless. For everyone's sake.

As we neared the door my hand brushed against a lump on my side and I felt an instant zap of panic. I had handed my cell over, but I'd forgotten to take Sloan's out of my pocket. And I'd dealt with these guys before. My chances of getting in and out with the phone, undisputed, were pretty much nil. We were supposed to be going in incommunicado.

I quickly scanned for options. Next to the service door ahead was a metal planter bucket filled with dirty sand, cigarette butts poking in the air. I paused next to it and, after checking that no one was watching, yanked up on the edge. My other hand felt for a void underneath. I was in luck. I quickly shoved the phone under the bin and sighed with relief when the bucket settled back to the concrete, even and undisturbed.

Lucas watched silently, stone-faced. His hand hovered at the door, ready to knock. He raised one eyebrow at me, questioning, but I said nothing. No need to fill him in on my mistake. *Maybe I planned it the whole time.*

He rapped confidently on the door and turned his head to mutter over his shoulder. "I'll do the talking."

Fine by me. I would have no idea what to say anyhow. My mouth stayed firmly clamped shut.

The door swung open and we were ushered in silently through the empty kitchen by a restaurant employee. The elderly man kept his head down as he limped down the hall, leading us to a small private dining room. The long table was surrounded by suited men with serious faces. In front of them lay a large spread of food covering the center of the table. Italian dishes, waiting to be served. Everyone looked up expectantly when we entered.

Men approached from either side of the doorway, tossing our arms in the air involuntarily. I recognized them from my bathroom encounter. Goon number one patted me down gently. Goon number two was a little rougher with my companion, eyeing him with contempt but saying nothing.

The little wand signalled at my ears, but this time the man ignored it and backed away. When Lucas's search came up empty they retreated to their corners and we were waved toward two chairs at the head of the table. No one filled the seat of honor.

The silence was disturbing. I sat obediently across from Lucas and tried to avoid staring at the men surrounding us. I immediately recognized many of the faces from the news. These men were newly released from prison. All thanks to me.

But the eyes at the table were far less interested in me than with my companion. And I quickly realized it wasn't just curiosity—they were studying their supposed long-lost co-conspirator. Their presumed-dead colleague, now in the flesh. Expressions in the room ranged from amused fascination to bald hostility. I couldn't help but squirm with discomfort.

Lucas was somehow completely unaffected by the scrutiny. Or just a very good actor. He leaned forward, elbows on the table, and gazed back confidently at the gathering. As he met each pair of eyes, one by one, an inscrutable half-smile played on his face.

Awkward silence hung in the air, thick and heavy, the tension palpable. Everyone seemed to be in holding mode, just waiting. *But for what?* I glanced at the empty seat beside us, wondering who would fill it.

Finally the silence was too much. I couldn't wait any longer. I was here for one reason. Despite my best instincts, I found myself suddenly speaking up, however timid my voice. "So where is Sloan?"

The gray-haired man at the other end of the table chuckled lightly. "Patience, my dear," he said slowly, his accent only slight. "Just relax, she'll be along shortly. But first we must break bread." He gazed intently at Lucas. "It's a long-awaited family reunion, you know."

The only reunion I care about is with my friend. I held my tongue and returned my gaze to the table, forcing the patience he instructed. My thoughts resumed their downward spiral, now toward the motivations of this forced gathering. I refused to believe this was about reminiscing old times. So what, then? What did they want with Dominic?

They wanted answers.

"So," the man finally continued, "before we get into this delicious meal they've prepared, why don't you tell us what you've been up to, *ol' buddy?*" His mild demeanor belied an undercurrent of hostility that further electrified the tension in the room. Somehow the quiet got even louder.

Lucas flashed a confident grin. "I bet you're pretty curious. I don't blame you one bit. But I thought I was here to see Vinny." He shrugged and sat back in his seat. "I'll be happy to talk, all day if you want. Once he gets here." His voice hardened a bit. "Not before."

"Oh, he'll be along shortly, I assure you. In the meantime we can at least make pleasant conversation, no?" He leaned forward, elbows on the table. "We're all very interested to hear of what must be a fascinating adventure, you disappearing like that. You must forgive us for assuming you were dead." His smile was thin. "Even in retrospect it does seem a little convenient."

Convenient?

"Dear, wise Uncle Frank. You always were the most *polite* brutally-impatient man I'd ever known. But I told you. Not until the man himself gets here." He added a quick wink to his smug grin. "Rather not have to tell my tales twice, you know?"

"So you do remember me, after all this time." The man nodded. "That's nice, that's good to hear. And how about the rest of this merry band?" He spread his hands toward the crowded table. "You still recognize all of my family gathered here?"

"Of course I recognize them. They were my family too, remember?"

262

"Right, right. Certainly." A slow grin creeped onto the man's face. "But you know, it's funny. Because there should be—"

"Except for *that* guy." Lucas pointed at the man two seats down from me, the youngest at the table by a decade. He narrowed his eyes at him. "Pretty sure I don't remember you."

The young man returned the stare for a long moment, impassive, before turning toward the far end of the table with a sigh. "I guess I'm satisfied."

The older man nodded. "As am I."

I let out a silent breath. *We were almost blown.* Good thing Lucas had been in on the case from the beginning. He might just know enough to get us out alive after all.

But the man's hand shot up. "Or at least I will be," he continued, his eyes boring into an unruffled Lucas. The fake smile returned. "One more little check before we waste the boss's time, if you would be so kind." He tipped his head at the door goons. One of them quickly disappeared.

"He'll just be along shortly with your friend," he finished lightly, glancing at me. "I'm sure you'll be pleased."

THIRTY-SIX

I stiffened. *Is this a trick?* Hope that the whole ordeal was almost over began to mingle with the tingle of fear already circulating rapidly in my system. I had trouble breathing as my pulsed kicked up a notch, preparing to be disappointed once again.

Only this time they weren't lying.

Sloan appeared in the doorway, handler by her side. She looked wary as she entered the room, timid for the first time since I'd known her. But healthy and visually unharmed.

I let out a deep sigh of relief at the sight. Her eyes immediately flew to mine and I rushed toward her. We held in a long, lingering hug while the men looked on. *My friend is safe.*

Finally someone cleared their throat to interrupt, bringing us back to the present.

I whispered in Sloan's ear just as she pulled away. "Did you get our message?"

Her eyes shot to mine, then immediately began scanning the room. They froze when they reached Lucas, standing silently only feet away. Their gaze locked. The room was utterly silent once again as everyone watched.

Lucas's jaw flexed as he visibly gulped, his face tense but still unreadable.

Sloan's breath quickly became ragged as she stared, her eyes never leaving his. A multitude of emotions crossed her face as we watched. Confusion. Disbelief. Joy. Maybe a touch of anger. A single tear appeared and began to slide down her check. She swiped it away with the back of her hand.

Clearly she got the message. I watched the Oscar-worthy performance in awe. She really was a phenomenal actress.

She took a hesitant first step, then another. When she reached Lucas they stood staring, unmoving. Studying each other. They were entirely oblivious to their audience.

Finally Sloan reached a hand up, moving carefully to touch his cheek while their eyes continued to converse in secret. Lucas's typical stoicism dropped away. His face hardened as he held back the tears welling in his eyes. Suddenly he pulled her toward him and their lips met, hard and fast.

Were they even acting anymore? Doubt began to grow as I watched. *Danger brought out their true feelings.* I felt a growing discomfort.

The embrace rapidly intensified. Their arms wrapped around one another, pulling as if afraid of drowning. They held tight, their faces close. Lucas cradled the back of her head as he deepened the kiss.

No, their passion felt way too real. I had suspected but hadn't wanted to face the truth.

Sloan loves Lucas. And Lucas loves her right back.

None of my business, really.

I would have to process the petty feelings I didn't have later.

Finally the lovebirds pulled apart and Lucas straightened.

She gazed up at him a moment, studying his face once again. Then suddenly her arm swung back and up, delivering a powerful slap across his right cheek.

The loud whap echoed across the otherwise still room, snapping everyone to attention.

Lucas looked stunned as Sloan stepped back, pulling away.

"Do you think I'm a fool?" she hissed.

The men watched intently, leaning in a bit with curiosity. Lucas eyed her, quizzical, but still said nothing. Just waited for explanation.

Should I intervene? I hesitated, unsure what was happening.

Sloan finally filled everyone in as she glared at Lucas, seething. "You've always wanted to be him, I know. But you're not."

She never got my message after all. Lucas could fool the men, sure. But he obviously couldn't fool his brother's fiancé, up close and personal.

And *that* was going to ruin everything.

The man called Uncle Frank stepped closer. "What are you saying, *cara*?" He eyed Lucas suspiciously. "Is this man not your fiancé?"

Panicked, I had to step in. "Of course he is." I shoved my way closer, trying desperately to catch Sloan's gaze. I had to make her understand. "She's just in shock, after everything."

"No." She shook her head, resolute. Her gaze stayed firmly on Lucas's deadpan face, her voice icy. "He's a fraud. That's his *brother.*"

I watched, horrified, as all the men stiffened. They exchanged looks, reassessing the situation. Panic began to creep up my spine.

A deep voice boomed from behind. "So you think you can trick us, eh?"

Our heads turned to find the man from Sloan's bathroom, now filling the doorway. The real boss. *Vinny.*

Everyone froze at the sight. Even the men seemed to be waiting, deferential. Following his lead. I held my breath, unsure how to get us out of the situation. *Keep up the lie, or try to play into it?* What would keep us from being killed for the ruse?

Vinny remained in the doorway, watching, eyeing each of us. Taking his time as his gaze lingered on each face. Just as the tension in the room was about to boil over, his voice burst forth again. But this time as a gruff chuckle.

Everyone exchanged uneasy glances, unsure. Vinny's face broke into a wide smile and his chuckle continued again, louder and with gusto. He seemed genuinely amused.

He stepped closer. "I'll admit, I wasn't sure about this guy from the beginning. I had my doubts. And now we know the truth." He reached a hand out to clap Lucas hard on the shoulder. "Welcome home, Dominic. We've been waiting quite a long time for this."

I froze. Sloan finally met my gaze again, her obvious confusion mirroring my own.

The man took us in and laughed again. "You two don't think you fooled us with your little act, do you?" He flashed a condescending smile at Sloan. "My dear, only true love would try that hard to make us think that's *not* really him. So I thank you for making it easier on us. My concerns are *vamoosed.*"

What just happened? Apparently we had achieved our goal, in spite of Sloan not playing along. They believed he was Dominic. And Vinny was here in the flesh. I took a breath for the first time in what felt like hours. Days.

"And now I think you two have served your purpose," Vinny continued, waving at the men guarding the door. "Let's show these ladies out so we can finally have our chat, shall we?"

The dimmest goon moved forward to grab both of our arms, gripping them tightly. Neither of us put up a fight as he led us back the way we came, stone-faced and silent.

We did it. I was on my way out the door with Sloan, safe and sound. I was practically beaming as we entered the kitchen. The exit was only steps away. The end of the horrific adventure. The nightmare.

But what did that mean for Lucas?

"Say Quinn . . . " Sloan's voice interrupted my conflicted elation. "You remember that thing I showed you the other day? In the mini-mart?"

"Quiet," her goon barked.

My mind raced as I held her gaze. Her eyes were trying to make me understand. Make me ready. As I watched her hand slide toward the man's arm, getting into position, suddenly I knew.

In a flash Sloan whirled, releasing the man's grasp with ease to pull his arm over her shoulder. Before he could realize what had happened, she had him twisted backwards, his arm pinned awkwardly behind his back. His attempt to fight it only made the position more untenable and he groaned with the effort.

Sloan read my wide-eyed expression and smiled. "Check his pocket. On the right."

Bewildered, I reached into his jacket pocket to retrieve a small black device.

Sloan grabbed it and turned to the man. "I believe you were kind enough to show this to me on multiple occasions," she said, appraising the object. "But I don't think you ever truly appreciated what it can do." She shoved the device into his back and squeezed the trigger. The goon's body began to jerk and twitch uncontrollably, his face panicked. A moment later Sloan dropped the lifeless man to the floor with a thud.

I stared at the man a moment, shock mixed with satisfaction. "I'm not gonna lie, that was pretty awesome." I looked up at my friend. "But I don't think that was necessary."

"Those men didn't believe me." She spoke quietly but her eyes shined with urgency. "So we have to find another way to change it around. We have to *fix* it."

"You don't understand." I moved closer and lowered my own voice. "They wanted *Joel*. We were giving them what they wanted."

"I know exactly what you were giving them. A *dead* man." Her face was serious. "He was a goner the second you guys walked in here."

I froze and watched Sloan for signs of her normal jokiness. She was not playing.

"I heard them," Sloan continued, her voice low but rapid. "They didn't always speak Italian around me, sometimes they forgot. And what was crystal clear in what I could pick up is that they want to ask him some questions, get the real story . . . before they make him disappear again. For good this time."

They'll kill Lucas.

"No," I said, stubbornly shaking my head. "Obviously he doesn't think so. Or he wouldn't have gone in."

I realized the naivete of the words the moment they left my mouth.

She stepped closer. "You don't know him like I do. He knew full well how this would go. Me—us—walking out of here is all he cared about."

I knew deep down she was right.

"Then let's go get help," I pleaded. "Everyone's all waiting out there, a whole bunch of agents. I don't know what in the world they're waiting for."

"They're waiting for us to walk out. Don't you see? They're here to round everybody up when it's all over." She shook her head sadly. "And they come raiding in here, he's the first to go. Those mobsters'll get rid of him so he can't talk. You know I'm right."

I gulped. "But . . . then why would those guys just let *us* walk out of here?"

"Maybe they wouldn't." She let the words hang a moment as she met my eyes. "We don't know for sure he was actually leading us out the back door. We know too much." She gave a quick smile. "Luckily they underestimated us. As usual."

Despite her sudden levity, the seriousness of our situation finally hit me. *I was so naive.* This was not some little manipulation game as I had originally thought. It was real. And there was no secret plan to save the day.

I steeled my resolve with the realization. "Listen Sloan, my job's done. I came here to get you out. The door's right here. Let's just go and let the professionals handle it." My eyes pleaded urgently. "Please."

Sloan ignored me as she opened a door in the corner and peered inside. Then she turned back and gave me her full attention. "I hear you, I really do. But the problem is I *am* a professional. So are you. And pros never leave a man behind. I can't trust his life to anyone else."

She pulled the door wider, allowing me to see the dark staircase beyond, leading down. "Time to choose your door, Quinn. In or out. Either way, we've gotta go."

***

I chose both. Sort of.

Out of breath and nearly out of my mind, I convinced Sloan we could proceed her way—but only with help. After slipping out the back door to retrieve the stashed cell phone, I helped Sloan drag the unconscious goon into the walk-in cooler, locked him in with a broom, and retreated into the basement, following blindly.

"Hopefully he'll be wise enough to keep them talking," Sloan said. She flipped a lightswitch, dimly illuminating a storage cellar. "Buying us time."

"Time for what? What are we doing?" I took in the room. It was a half-finished space, with shelf after shelf of restaurant supply reaching to the ceiling. "And what are we doing *here*?"

Sloan reached to the closest shelf. "If I understood correctly," she said, her hand sliding over giant cans of tomato sauce, "we are here for . . . this." Her face lit up as her hand emerged from between the cans with a large pistol. She held it up proudly.

My stomach began to boil with frustration. "This is your big plan? Guns?"

"Reinforcements," she said with a shrug. "I heard they're stashed everywhere down here. Now we can talk our way out." She wiggled the gun in the air. "With a little help."

I sighed. "Not gonna work for me. How about we get some *real* help?" I raised the cell phone, grateful to have one back in my possession. But I immediately paused. *Who to call?*

"Fine, we'll play it your way." Sloan grabbed the phone from my hand and stabbed at Lucas' name on her contacts list. "For now. But I wouldn't hold my breath that whoever's out there will have a better idea."

Someone picked up immediately. "Listen, they've got our guy," Sloan said into the phone. "But we're hiding out in the basement with a boatload of weapons, nice and safe for now. I'm sure you all were told to hang back . . . but whatever your extraction plan for him was—now's the time."

Sloan's face hardened as she listened. She opened her mouth to retort, then thought better of it. Finally she sighed. "Ok," she said through gritted teeth before hanging up.

"Well?" I practically shouted, my nerves on overdrive. "What do we do?"

"They said to sit tight. They'll be making their way in."

I practically squealed with delight. *Almost out of here.* And the grownups were in charge again. It would be any minute now.

Sloan tucked the gun in the back of her jeans and began moving toward the stairs.

"Where are you going?" I shrieked, following at her heels. "They said to stay put."

"I'll stay back, but I can't *not* help." She took the first couple steps up but then froze, staring up at the door. A second later she twirled and flew past, grabbing to pull me with her as she fled past the aisles of dry goods and into a small dark room at the back.

She met my wide eyes as we slipped behind the heavy open door. "They're coming." She peeked out through the crack. "Someone's coming down."

The first clomp of footsteps on the stairs echoed through the slightly damp space. Then they multiplied, picking up pace. More and more. They just kept coming.

I shivered with fear as we both huddled behind the door, trying to hide. We had been at the exit, free and clear. *Now we're stuck in a basement with the mob.*

And I had been too stubborn to grab a gun.

THIRTY-SEVEN

The room quickly filled with dark suits. I suppressed a gasp when I got a glance of Lucas amongst the crowd. The left side of his face was distorted, the skin around his eye beginning to swell. *They hurt him.* My stomach churned with rage and I had to look away.

Suddenly a loud boom shook the building, then another. I peeked through the crack of the door to watch as the men instinctively grabbed for their weapons. Handguns of every variety appeared, gripped by men on heightened alert. They stared suspiciously at the ceiling, guns ablaze.

All except Vinny. He held court in the middle, unarmed and protected by his men at all sides. His eyes narrowed as he gazed up, anger simmering.

Footsteps began to pound on the floor above. They proceeded methodically, with slamming doors followed by feet racing through, clearing the restaurant room by room. Muffled shouts neared. They would soon be at the basement door.

Sloan's eyes were wide as she looked at me. "Everyone thought we were safe down here, away from everything," she whispered. "Now we're trapped in the middle."

Maybe we should've just left when we had the chance then, huh?

But now was not the time for regrets. She was right. We would be caught in the crossfire. And we needed to find a plan.

Unfortunately, the plan found us.

"In the back, boss," someone shouted. "Let's get moving. You, too. Time to go."

The rest of the men took up defensive postures, focused on the stairs, as both Vinny and Lucas were shoved toward our hiding spot. The men stumbled through the doorway into the dark. Vinny immediately reached at the wall, searching for a switch.

My eyes met Sloan's only for a second. That's all it took. We both threw ourselves against the door, slamming it shut in the face of the hefty armed mobster at their heels. I twisted the lock on the handle and was surprised to find a deadbolt just above. I secured it with a satisfying clunk.

The man on the other side yanked at the handle and cursed when he realized he was locked out. The door shook as he slammed his shoulder into it. It wouldn't budge. The heavy metal door would hold them off for a bit. Panicked voices immediately began to yell at each other on the other side.

Vinny's hand found the lightswitch. The room illuminated and he was faced with Sloan, feet away, pointing the gun at his chest with a smirk. He took her in and glanced to me in surprise.

"Good to see you again there, Vinny," I said.

Vinny's hands shot into the air. "Easy now," he said, holding his arms steady. He took a slow step back. "No need to do anything impulsive, darlin'."

"Name's not *darlin'*, I can assure you," Sloan replied with an icy smile. "But yours might be soon. I expect there's a market for all types where you're going."

A soft chuckle sounded to our left. We finally took notice of Lucas in the corner, just watching. His arms were pulled unnaturally behind his back. "Cute," he said with a hint of a smile. He twitched his shoulder. "But perhaps you could give me a hand?"

Sloan kept the weapon trained on our new captive while I inspected the situation. His hands were tied with some sort of thick twine. The wrappings went far up his forearms, over and over. A hasty but effective binding.

I glanced around the space in search of something sharp. Nothing but bare shelves at the far end. An otherwise empty room.

I tried tugging at the twisted strands at his wrists. For the first time, I felt no spark when my hands touched his skin. I was too focused on freeing him. But with no tools, I had no way to do it. "Sorry," I said, giving up. "You'll just have to wait. But we've got this."

"Yes. We. Do." Sloan continued staring down Vinny. I got the feeling she was willing him to make a move. To give her an excuse to fire the weapon. He kept his arms in the air, barely moving to breathe. His eyes bore into her right back.

I heard another burst of activity outside the door and pulled out the phone. We needed to let someone know where we were. I dialed Lucas's number, copying Sloan's move. An unfamiliar voice answered curtly.

"Everyone's in the basement," I said, trying to speak calmly despite our circumstances. "We have Vinny and Lucas, safe in this back room with us, alone. For now."

"Standby." There was a long pause. "Ok, block off the air under the door all you can. Tight. Best we can do. We'll be down momentarily."

I hung up and scanned the room, anxiety immediately escalating to borderline frantic as I took in the space. "They said to block under the door? I don't know what that means."

"Tear gas." Lucas moved toward the door, studying it. "Now that we're out of the way, they can roll in. But we need to keep the gas out." He turned his focus on our captive and eyed the man's wardrobe. "We could use a little help there, buddy. Mind if we borrow your nice outfit?"

Vinny narrowed his eyes at him and looked to the weapon-holder in charge, questioning.

Sloan shrugged. "We can use your *clothes* as a doorstop . . . or you. Makes no difference to me." She lifted the weapon a little higher. "But we won't ask twice."

Vinny eyed the crack under the door, pondering. Then he yanked at his jacket, stripping it off to throw it to the floor with a sigh, and began hastily unbuttoning his shirt. He added his dingy white undershirt to the pile and paused with his hands on his belt buckle.

I stepped closer, hands on hips. "We don't have all day."

He groaned and finished disrobing with minimal objection. *How do I always end up watching unattractive middle-aged men take their clothes off?*

We all watched with one eye on the door as it jumped and shook, the men outside trying their turn at getting it open. Vinny spread his arms when he was down to his sweat-stained white boxers. Sloan waved him back with the gun. He took a step back and I gathered the garments, tucking them tightly under the bottom edge of the door. It seemed a decent barrier for now.

Sloan threw a faint smile at me as I returned to standing. "Guess there's nothing to do now but wait." She turned her gaze back to Vinny. "Enjoy your last few minutes of freedom."

He scoffed in response, putting on a show of indifference. But you could see the panic boiling underneath. He was trying to think of a way out. He knew what was next.

Finally he spoke. "You know that might not hold *all* the chemicals, darlin'. It could get pretty messy. So why don't we all just get ourselves to safety, and then we can handle the police business. You want, I'll even turn myself in. Just get us out of here for now, would you?"

"Sure," I said, sarcastic. "Why not. And how do you propose we do that?"

Vinny returned a cocky half-grin. "Why do you think they sent us in here? To trap themselves in a shoot-out with the feds? Go down in a blaze of glory for their beloved boss?" He chuckled harshly. "Trust me, they ain't that loyal."

I glanced at Sloan. She was just as unsure.

"What does that mean, exactly?" I said.

"It means there's a way out, kiddo. Our own personal path to salvation." Hands still in the air, he used his head to nod at the back. "Just behind that cabinet."

We all turned toward the back wall. A tall shelving unit took up the middle. Lucas moved closer to inspect. With no hands available, he kicked and pushed at the bottom with his foot. It moved forward a crack.

"Impossible," he murmured to himself. He turned to face Vinny, brow furrowed. "What is it, a tunnel?"

Vinny grinned. "Our business has expanded since you've been away, Dommy boy. Why don't you let me show you our newest innovation?"

The fake Dominic ignored the comment and turned his focus back to the wall. I moved to give him a hand. I slipped my hand around the edge of the unit and pulled, my fingers stinging with the effort. The shelves scraped the floor to slide forward a few inches, revealing endless darkness beyond.

"See, man of my word," Vinny continued. "That tunnel's worked out pretty well. Helps avoid all the prying eyes. So I could reward you all pretty nice for getting us out of here, keeping us safe. Just name your price."

I pondered the blackness beyond before looking back at Lucas. "What do you think? Should we take it?"

Vinny's lips pursed with satisfaction. "Wise girl." He tried to take a step toward us but Sloan flicked the gun in warning.

I scoffed. "Not the money, fool. The tunnel." Emboldened, I turned to Lucas again. "Stay or leave?" My mouth quirked in an unexpected smile as my words struck me. "Hey, it's another song title. Not sure Dave's content applies here either, though."

His eyes narrowed at me curiously, confused by my inappropriately-timed attempt at an inside joke. *I'm such a moron.* Clearly he had better things to worry about. I felt my cheeks flame with embarrassment.

He shook off the comment and focused on the opening again. "It's tempting. But too risky. We don't know what kind of trick he has waiting down there. Should probably just wait it out." He nodded to Sloan with the gun still steady on our captive. "I think we have it under control."

A sudden increase in the clamor outside the door returned our attention to the situation beyond. The yelling and door-pounding was intensifying. Thin streams of smoke were beginning to seep in around the fabric. It was really happening. My heart rate increased further as I stared at the suit stuffed in the crack. *What if it's not enough?* We wouldn't be able to keep control of the room if we were hit with the gas, too.

I shrugged off my jacket and bent to stuff it in with the rest of the pile, just for good measure. Vinny watched carefully, staring me down when I straightened.

"So I guess that's it, then," he said to himself, wistful with a touch of bitter. "*You* two will be the heroes walking out of here with the FBI's most wanted." He scoffed to himself. "Never thought it would be a couple 'a chicks. No offense."

Sloan and I glanced at each other, then back at the door. More leaks had sprung. *Forget the glory.* I just wanted out in one piece.

"But what I can't figure," he continued musing out loud, "is how you planned it. How'd you end up the hero, work it out so I'm stuck in here with you at gunpoint? That's some real conniving, there. Call me impressed, I'll admit it."

Sloan shrugged, her focus on the wisps streaming in, growing thicker. "We're actually only down here because your guys like to brag about the weapons hidden all over. But to be honest, we had no idea you guys would end up here, too." She dragged her attention away to flash him a broad smile. "Just our lucky day, I guess."

Vinny narrowed his eyes. "Yeah, mine too." He shook his head. "Clearly I'm a lucky, lucky man. So you found the gun down here, huh?"

"Maybe." Sloan's smile was icy. "The irony's nice. How's it feel to have your own weapon be turned against you?"

He chuckled softly in response. "Serves me right, I guess." He licked his lips and took a step closer. "But you know what's really funny? You two'll get a kick out of this, I think."

"Stay back," Sloan ordered.

Vinny held his hands at his chest, palms out, but stayed put. He chuckled again. "See, all those guns down here?

They're in storage, tucked away for a rainy day. Not the best environment, I admit. But we tend to run out of space. I have a bit of a thing for handguns. Especially those." He nodded his head at Sloan's weapon. "Just so versatile, you know?"

Sloan shrugged. "Good to have a hobby, I guess." She glanced to me and back at Vinny, suspicious. "So what's the joke, then?"

He stepped forward again and leaned toward Sloan just a hair. He lowered his voice.

"Well, with those guns in storage and all . . . it wouldn't make much sense to keep them loaded, now would it?"

THIRTY-EIGHT

Everyone froze.

All eyes shot to Vinny, watching as his face twisted in a sinister grin. No one made a move as we processed, coming to the same dark realization. *Mayday.*

Sloan instinctively glanced down at the gun and Vinny lunged forward, grabbing at her hands. Her finger immediately pulled the trigger and an empty pop echoed through the space.

Her eyes went wide. Vinny capitalized on her surprise to yank her hands upward and swing hard, flinging her into the door. Her head hit the metal of the deadbolt with a sickening thud and her eyes closed in pain. She slumped toward the floor, the gun clattering uselessly to the ground.

Lucas let out an agonized cry. Vinny turned toward him, sizing up his next adversary. I felt the weight of my own empty hands as I watched. I had no weapon and Lucas had no hands.

The two men exchanged a stare, daring the other to move. When Lucas broke his gaze to glance at Sloan, beginning to stir on the ground, Vinny charged. He plowed his large frame into Lucas, using the force of his entire body weight to slam him against the back wall with a sickening thump.

Lucas grunted and fell to the floor in a heap. With no limbs to help him move, he laid still, winded and trying to catch his breath. Vinny straightened and stood over him, watching.

Satisfied his rival was incapacitated, he turned toward me. My blood ran cold as Vinny weighed his options. We were both unarmed, but he was double my size and cornered, fueled by an instinct to fight for his life by any means necessary. I was the only thing standing between him and freedom, just beyond that secret threshold.

After a long moment, one side of his mouth turned up as he decided I was no foe to fear. He took several heavy steps toward me as my heart pounded. I gulped, keeping my eyes on his. There was nowhere to go.

Suddenly he smiled. "Let's get out of here, doll."

The statement caught me completely off guard. *A trick?*

Before I could respond, Vinny reached out to grab a hunk of my hair. He yanked at my scalp, pulling my head toward him.

"You're gonna be my ticket out," he muttered in my ear, "should anything else happen to get in our way."

I shrieked in pain and fear as he dragged me, head first, toward the tunnel opening. He used his free hand to shove the cabinet fully out of the way and then push me into the darkness.

"You first, sweetheart." A moment later a beam of light appeared as he held up his phone, directing the way. "I'll be right behind you."

I hesitated, gazing ahead at the darkness of the narrow dirt path. Another shove at my back sent me moving forward, one timid step visible at a time. I felt the weight of the earth surrounding me as we walked, and had to fight a growing sense of claustrophobia. Vinny's panting breath at my heels kept me in the moment. Deeper and deeper we went.

"Watch out up here," he finally said, his voice startling me. "Some steps at the end."

The end.

A tingle ran up my spine as the first hint of incline appeared. Then a weathered hunk of wood packed into the ground as a makeshift step. I began to feel a growing sense of panic, not knowing what the end would mean for us. He would be slipping away, undoubtedly into hiding again for who knew how long, possibly for good. *But how long would he have use for me?*

As we started up the crude stairway, I could see the outline of a trapdoor ahead. My mind racing, focused on the opening, my foot caught on the edge of a step and I almost stumbled. Immediately Vinny's hand was on my arm, steadying me. He grunted with displeasure.

I righted myself and continued forward, carefully stepping. His grasp remained tight on my arm. And an idea began to brew.

I took a deep breath as I hastily reviewed my lesson. Only a few steps from the exit, I caught my foot again, this time intentionally and hard. As I pitched forward, throwing Vinny off balance as he moved with me, I twisted to grab his gripping hand in both of mine and yanked backward.

His phone fell to the floor and we were plunged into utter darkness. Taking advantage of his surprise, I moved by feel as I wrenched his arm painfully around his body and in the wrong direction. He dropped hard to his knees, trying to gain leverage. But his position was awkward and I felt the power of my hold. I shoved him into the dirt.

Pinned to the ground, Vinny struggled against me. His breathing became loud and ragged as his large frame weighed him down. I pushed harder on his twisted arm and he cried out in pain. I felt a rush of satisfaction as he became still, momentarily dropping the fight.

Then reason flooded in. *Now what?*

The darkness surrounding us became heavy. My stomach clenched as I realized my victory would not be able to last. I could not hold the man off forever; maybe not even minutes. It was a temporary move. Strictly a subduer.

As if reading my thoughts, Vinny's entire body suddenly lurched, testing my hold. I held steady but on his second attempt felt him rising up against me, regaining strength little by little. He twisted toward me, loosening my grip. Suddenly his hand slipped out of mine and I felt his weight shift, moving quickly toward me. My panic went into overdrive. He was back in control and I was a goner.

BOOM!

We both froze as the tunnel shook. The sound of dirt trickling down the walls beside us followed the impact. Then suddenly a bright light filled the space, blinding me. I lost all sense of reality as everything stopped, my only perception that of the overwhelming glare filling my vision.

Until the most beautiful sound I'd ever heard appeared.

"Hands up," the voice boomed.

I became aware of Vinny's face, only inches from mine, just in time to see the shock register. Then the contempt. His features cast sinister shadows in the light as he returned my gaze, pondering a last-ditch move. A quick retaliation.

Suddenly his head jerked forward with a thump.

"I *said*," the deep voice broke in again. "Hands. Up."

Vinny let out a groan as he grabbed the back of his head

and hunched over, rolling away from me. The light shifted away toward the floor and a man moved forward to crouch in front of me. It took a moment for my eyes to adjust to the dim light again.

"You okay?" he said, concern etching his face.

My eyes clearly hadn't adjusted properly. Because gazing back at me, with a seriously furrowed brow, was Lucas. Not the Dominic-clad Lucas with a buzzed head I had just left behind. But the scruffy-faced, chestnut-haired Lucas I tried so hard not to dream about.

How is that possible? Last I saw him he was wearing a tight black t-shirt and dark glasses, gasping at the head of the tunnel. Now he was at the other end, wearing an olive henley with perfect floppy hair intact. It was just impossible.

Unless I was a fool.

Realization hit me hard and fast. *Played again.* Always the one out of the loop. A step behind.

I took a deep breath and gazed back at the real Lucas, reprocessing my reality. I was only vaguely aware of the swirl of activity surrounding us as the space lit up with yelling, swarming agents. They pinned down Vinny and hauled him out in handcuffs. Uniformed men and women began to fill every inch of the tunnel. Lucas held my gaze, never wavering. Just watching the understanding flood in.

He hadn't changed his look. He was never in disguise. In fact, he was never here with us at all. His brother was. That was the real Dominic. The real *Joel.* On the other end of the tunnel, with his real fiancé.

And Sloan was neither acting nor in love with Lucas. She was reuniting with her true love, long gone. It was real. It had all been real.

"So he's not . . . dead?" I muttered, in a daze. It was all I could get out.

Lucas's emerald eyes twinkled in the light as he took a deep breath, relieved, and flashed me a reluctant smile. "We'll talk about it later." He grabbed my hand, the sudden voltage zapping my dulled senses. "Let's get you out of here."

THIRTY-NINE

"Alright, folks," Sloan announced as she carefully placed an armful of drinks on the table, one at a time. "And by folks, I of course mean you two." She eyed the guys. "No more goofing around. Time to spill it."

Joel gave one final sophomoric elbow-shove to his brother and gazed innocently back at his fiancé as she settled across from him. He rightly read her expression in an instant and straightened with a sigh. "What do you need to know?"

"I *want* to know everything," she replied. "And no more putting it off with the excuse that we're not alone. Just start talking."

It had been less than twenty-four hours since we had all stumbled out of the tunnel, dazed and relieved. Sloan and I were given only the vaguest briefing and shipped off to yet another safe house to wait out the remaining chaos. Meanwhile the boys had joined the effort to right all the wrongs. With Sloan safely back and the real top bad guy now in custody, there was no reason to continue allowing freedom to all his men. The rounding back up of the crew was almost complete.

So we were finally sitting down, all together and in

public for the first time. The boys had chosen a newish downtown microbrewery for our first outing. I could feel my breathing lighten by the minute, the taste of freedom sweet. But I too needed answers.

Joel's head lowered as he licked his lips, thinking. "Where should I begin?"

"How about explaining how you're here, for starters?" I said, kicking things off. "I knew you were helping on the mobster case. But I was told you were killed on the job."

Sloan's head whipped toward me, suspicion creeping into her gaze. "You *knew* he was helping?"

"Calm down," Lucas jumped in. "I filled her in once you were taken. The part about the case, anyway." He lowered his gaze and his voice, sensing the bumpy road ahead. "Not about the whole . . . not dead thing."

Sloan's eyes narrowed as she became laser-focused on Lucas. "But *you* did know, then. That he had not only been investigating them, without telling me—but he was not, in fact, *killed* while doing so?"

He held his hands up in surrender. "Look, I'm really sorry I had to lie to you. It wasn't easy, trust me. I was just following orders." He nodded his head across the table at Joel. "But I'm not sure I should get all the blame here, huh?"

Joel scoffed and glared at his brother. "Thanks man."

"Oh, don't worry," Sloan replied, shifting her focus to her fiancé. "We definitely have plenty of blame to go around, I think." She settled back in her seat with a sigh. "So, got anything to say for yourself?"

Joel took a deep breath, watching Sloan closely. A slight smile creeped onto his face. "I throw myself at your mercy? Look, all I can say is that it wasn't my choice, none of it was my decision." He paused a second, thinking. "Well, getting involved in the first place was, I'll give you that.

It sounded like fun. I was asked to infiltrate the mafia and gather evidence for the FBI, undercover." He grinned. "You know me, when could I ever say no to that?" He held Sloan's steady gaze. "I *also* couldn't say anything to you. Their rules, not mine."

Sloan nibbled on her lip, thinking. "Okay, so you pretend to me you're doing normal investigative work while you're out doing god knows what, masquerading as some bad guy. For years, apparently. Fine. So, why stop? And, most importantly, why *fake* your own death?"

"It wasn't planned." Joel shrugged. "But something went wrong. They were starting to get suspicious. Asking funny questions, making strange comments. We were just about to pull the plug on my involvement when they cornered me. And right then I knew I was made."

"Cornered?" I leaned in. "So how did you get out?"

"We got lucky." Joel picked absently at the label of his beer as he talked. "My guys got a last-minute tip there was going to be an assassination. The turf wars were getting pretty heated, fighting amongst themselves for control of certain sectors. But things took a turn and someone who wanted to move up was going to blow up a room full of their adversaries. Or so we heard."

Sloan's eyebrow went up. "So that part was real? There really was an explosion?"

Joel nodded. "And I came *this* close to being toasted in it. Fortunately we had another guy under, who barged in with a lame excuse and got me out of there. His quick thinking saved my life."

I tried not to watch as Joel and Sloan exchanged a long look. A slight smile creeped onto her face as she gazed. She really *had* almost lost him. Her eyes twinkled with gratitude.

Finally Joel broke the stare. "Anyway, we hustled out of there just in time and the explosion got covered up as an accident, caused by a gas leak. And we did nothing to stop it. Too many questions would just lead to me and all of our undercover involvement. And the victims were all serious criminals, capable of some pretty heinous stuff. So nobody cried too hard about it, on our end anyway."

"So then Dominic died in the explosion, I guess?" I said.

He nodded. "We figured everyone who knew otherwise was in that room. So it was a perfect out. The questionable cover no longer existed. But that would only work if he *stayed* non-existent."

"But *you* weren't your cover," Sloan retorted. "Why couldn't Dominic have disappeared, and Joel stayed put?"

"My cover was good, but not that good." Joel rubbed his shorn head absently. "I still looked like me. It was risky enough before I was dead. But if I had been spotted in town *after* the explosion, it could mean all sorts of trouble. I'd get blamed for all of it. They would follow me and find you. *Use* you." He lowered his head. "As we saw."

His comment left an awkward pause. Everyone sat back and nursed their drinks a moment, the relief of having the kidnapping drama ended safely palpable at the table.

"Anyway," Joel finally continued, "I just couldn't take that chance." He took a deep breath, his eyes doleful as he gazed at Sloan. "Everyone agreed. I had to stay out of sight until they wrapped everything up, finally got them behind bars. *All* of them."

Sloan shook her head, not buying it. "But you could've told me. I would've hated if you had to stay away, but it's certainly better than the alternative. You could've trusted me to keep it secret."

"Wasn't up to me." Joel slid his hand gently over hers.

290

"That's just how they do things. One slip of the tongue and it could mean everything is in jeopardy, lots of people are in danger. Stinks, but it's just how it is. I really am sorry. I can't imagine."

Sloan gulped, her eyes misting momentarily before she shook it off and forced a smile. "Well, you're back now, so I guess I'll get over it."

Joel sighed, his shoulders seeming to relax a little for the first time since I'd met him.

Sloan flashed a sly grin. "Eventually."

He rolled his eyes, beaming back.

I met Lucas's gaze briefly. He had stayed very quiet throughout, calmly sipping his beer and watching without reaction. He took another swig and cleared his throat.

"Okay, so we've got all that unpleasantness out of the way, right?" he called out. "Who wants to play a game? Think we've had enough truth for tonight, but I could be convinced to go for a nice dare."

I wasn't finished. "Hold on, now," I said, turning to Joel. "If you were so dead, why did they kidnap Sloan to get to you? How would they even know you were alive?"

"It wasn't Joel they wanted," Lucas jumped in. "It was Dominic. Which is who they thought was in the photo they found at Sloan's apartment." He turned toward her. "Remember, when they ransacked the place?"

Sloan's face turned white. She looked suddenly ill as she gazed down at the table, brows furrowed. Her mind was far, far away.

"Ah, I see now," Joel said, watching her just as closely. "*That's* why all of that went down?"

She looked up and the two shared another long, silent look. I glanced to Lucas, hoping for an explanation. He took another swig, calmly holding my gaze.

"Turns out," Joel finally continued, "Vinny had never suspected I was working with the feds after all. They thought I was cheating them, working for someone else to skim. We're pretty sure the large sums of money they were missing was taken by the guy behind the assassination attempt. And I—Dominic—was being set up for it."

"So when they used you guys to bring 'Dominic' back out of hiding," Lucas said, "they were just looking to get their stolen funds back."

"And render some harsh punishment, no doubt," Joel added.

"No doubt." Lucas nodded. "They were pretty excited about that part. And all thanks to your girl here breaking the rules."

Sloan groaned, eyes averted. The brothers shared an evil grin. Clearly they were trying to get under her skin.

"Will someone please fill me in?" I finally said, exasperated. I looked to Sloan. "What rules?"

She took a deep breath, still looking away. "I wasn't supposed to have any personal photos, not out in our apartment. I had to keep them in the safe."

"I warned her," Lucas offered. "Until we had all the answers, she needed to keep her connection quiet from snoops. Nothing out in public view. Can't be too careful."

"It wasn't public," she retorted. "It was my home. And there was no real explanation for it, far as I knew. It made no sense." Sloan shrugged. "So I got weak, sue me. You couldn't really expect me to obey that rule all that time. Not after what happened."

"Guess not." Lucas leaned across the table toward me. "Bottom line, our culprits seem to have made the connection to Sloan—and decided that her boy Dominic must still be alive and behind much of their problems—when they broke into her apartment looking for dirt. And found their cute little framed engagement photo, out in plain sight. So, in fact, our bride-to-be here is behind her *own* kidnapping." He grinned mockingly at Sloan.

"That's enough," she snapped back, only half-serious. "I will not be held responsible for the actions of those thugs." She turned to Joel. "Besides, that mistake is also the reason you're *here* right now. Without me you'd still be . . . actually, we haven't heard that part yet, now have we?"

"Here, here," Lucas jumped in quickly, raising his bottle in salute. "Glad to give credit where credit's due. Our man is back." He leaned forward a little, gazing curiously at both of us. "Actually, I have a feeling you two are going to end up the heroes of this whole thing. Putting *all* the bad guys in prison. How's that feel?"

I stiffened. My breath caught as the truth of his words began to sink in. We may not have put in the years of investigating but, regardless of our intent, we *were* sort of the reason the entire case had finally come together. Including their most important catch of all. It was a delightful and unsettling realization.

I glanced to Sloan, wondering if she was having the same reaction. But her focus was locked on Joel, who was intently working on removing the last of the label on his bottle. He seemed to be purposefully avoiding her eyes.

"Seriously?" she said. "I know you, Joel. I know both of you." She looked accusingly at the two men. "And I know you're still keeping something from me. So where were you all that time? What's the big secret?"

"What do you mean?" Joel shrugged, leaning back in his chair. His attempt to hide a grin failed. "I was around."

"Do you see what I'm dealing with?" She huffed to me and took a sip of her drink. "They're maddening."

I watched as Joel and Lucas's eyes met across the table. Joel's eyebrow shot up as he held the gaze, the brothers holding a detailed silent conversation. Lucas finally broke the stare by casually leaning back in his chair, mimicking his older brother.

"It's okay, Joe-Joe." Lucas flicked his eyes to me momentarily before continuing. "She's been smack in the middle of everything, really. And you have to admit, she was pretty crucial in getting Sloan out of there. In fact, she's part of the reason *you're* even back with us now." He grinned at his brother. "Whether that's good or bad, now that's a different story."

Talking about me like I'm not here. I squirmed, uncomfortable.

Lucas turned to me, his gaze now direct. Searing. "I'd say she's good as family now."

My stomach flipped a little. I held his eyes for a moment, unsure what to make of his intensity. Then I averted my gaze, suddenly aware of the other occupants of the table watching us, curious.

Joel turned back to Sloan for confirmation of his words. She raised her eyebrows defiantly. "Got that right."

He licked his lips as he studied her face a moment, considering. "Okay, fine. I'll talk. But really, it's not that big a deal." He sat forward in his chair, cradling his beer. "They hooked me up with some new training, is all. Since I was out of commission for a while. Picked up a few new tricks here and there, you know how it is."

"Okay." Sloan did not look satisfied. "You were training. Where?"

Joel shrugged. "All over. Few different headquarters. And a little out in the field with some guys."

Sloan nodded, pondering. "Okay." She picked up her drink, lost in thought. "Still a little vague . . ."

Joel smiled and raised his own drink. "The details are pretty boring, really. And if it makes you feel any better, I never went that far anyway. Just right up the road, couple towns over for most of it. Practically down the street." He brought the beer to his lips. "Spent the bulk of it on a farm, actually," he mumbled just before taking a sip.

Sloan's glass paused on the way to her lips, hovering in the air a long moment. Then she carefully lowered it back to the table, watching Joel intently. "A farm?" she said calmly. "You're telling me you spent time on *a farm*?"

Joel's smile wavered. They locked eyes for a long moment, entire conversations passing between them without words. I tried to look away and make sense of it.

Finally Joel broke the standoff by shoving his chair back, the legs scraping the floor with a loud groan. Before standing, he tipped back the last of his beer and gulped. Bottle emptied, he stood and gazed down at the table. "Whelp, looks like we need another round. Any requests?"

I glanced to Sloan. Her eyes were fixed in the distance. She was far, far away again.

"I think we're good," I replied.

Lucas's chair scraped even louder as he pushed it back, slowly and with purpose. "I'll help," he called out. "Let's just leave the hens to gossip and giggle a minute." He flashed me a quick wink before he turned away and caught up with his brother.

My face flamed at the word. *He remembers.*

I watched as they disappeared into the crowd, then leaned in to Sloan. "I don't understand. A farm? What's wrong with that?"

Her voice was monotone, robotic. "He wasn't at *a farm*. He was at THE Farm." She took a deep breath and let it out. "As in, the not-so-secret secret training facility, about 40 miles from here. Used for new recruits." She looked up, the faraway look replaced with a mix of anger and disbelief. "To the CIA."

FORTY

"The boys'll be here in a bit," Sloan began as we settled into our booth at Joe's, facing each other. "So if you want any food they won't devour, I suggest you go ahead and order."

"Coffee's fine," I said. I was thrilled to be back in our own haunt, without the disguises or fear of mobsters chasing us around town. Life, getting back to normal. Sort of, anyway.

"Two hot ones, Dottie," Sloan called out.

An unseen voice rasped back. "Roger that."

Sloan sighed. "A little peace and quiet." She sat back in her seat. "I wanted us to have a few minutes to ourselves, without all the chaos. Just us girls."

"Uh huh." I smirked. "And you're sure wanting that has *nothing* to do with the revelation about your fiancé's new career path?"

"Nah." A reluctant grin broke through. "Well, maybe a little. Honestly, I probably should've always known that was coming. I'll get over it. One day." Her smile widened as she rolled her eyes. "It is a bit of an adjustment getting used to him back, though. Having them *both* around all the time. It's a lot of energy when they're together. You'll see. And here I thought *I* was the exhausting one."

I suppressed a smile, saying nothing. I could no longer imagine my life without my fun, adventurous . . . and incredibly exhausting friend. *Not sure it could get much worse.*

Dottie appeared with our coffee. We thanked her for the mugs and carafe. Only, instead of trudging away silently, as usual, she stayed put. Hands on hips, she stared down at us, a funny look on her face. She eyed us carefully.

Sloan and I exchanged a glance.

"Everything okay, Dottie?" I ventured.

"Oh, it's fine alright," she said. "Right fine indeed. Place is runnin' like clockwork, now that I got my kitchen help back. No more callin' out and strollin' in looking like a crazy chicken, I'm happy to say."

"Oh, so Sayid's having an easier time with the fraternity?" I said. Sloan flashed me a look. "Guess he finished all that hazing stuff, huh?"

"Nope." Dottie looked smug. "Quit. Turns out his silly frat was nothin' but a buncha jerks, just like I told him."

"Hardly shocking, you're right," Sloan said with a sigh. "But good to hear he walked away."

"Yep," Dottie continued. "Seems kinda relieved, too, now that he's got loose. And apparently those guys are in a whole heap 'a trouble. School's shuttin' the whole frat down for a while, on account of some investigations. Looks like he dodged a bullet there." Her eyes narrowed. "You two haven't *heard* anything about that?"

We shared a thoughtful look and turned back to Dottie, shrugging innocently.

"We've been pretty out of the loop," I said.

"Uh huh," Dottie grunted as she eyed us again. "Okay then. Well, glad you girls are back anyway. You *and* your troublemakin' boy. We'll leave *that* story for another day. I gotta get back to work."

CARRIE ANN KNOX

She trudged away, muttering to herself. We focused our attention on fixing our coffees, sharing only the briefest secret smile of acknowledgement.

Black coffee in hand, Sloan looked over my shoulder and perked up. "Oh, looks like my surprise is here. There's someone that wants to see you." She put her mug back down and slid from her seat. "Think I'll just run to the restroom a sec."

She headed for the back before I could respond. Confused, I turned to see a young man approaching. Out of his uniform, it took me a second to recognize. Levi wore ripped jeans, black Chucks, and a faded black band t-shirt. I didn't recognize the name. Only his dark glasses gave him away.

My stomach dropped with guilt as I remembered the last time I saw him. And what I'd been informed of since. *Poor guy.*

He flashed an uncertain little wave, his eyes narrowing with curiosity as he moved closer. "Umm, Daisy?" he said.

"Actually . . . it's Quinn." I felt sheepish as I waved him into Sloan's vacated spot. "No one told you?"

"Oh, right. They did, yes. You were . . . undercover, sort of." He flinched. "But I wasn't clear on just how *much* of it was an act?"

I took a deep breath. "Unfortunately, all of it. And I'm so sorry you got caught up in our mess. I hear you were clean. You were never working for the other side at all." My gaze was sympathetic. "The mobsters somehow used you?"

He shrugged and sat back in his seat. "All I know is a neighbor . . . well, some guy anyway. He told me you were a part of some kind of investigation. Said it was an interesting story, and I should ask you about it. Now I know he was clearly just setting me up. I really had no idea what I was talking about when I asked. Honest."

I felt my face heat with embarrassment. "I'm sure you were just being nice. And here I come along and send a SWAT team after you." I shook my head, annoyed with myself. "I hope they didn't hurt you."

Levi bowed his head. "Just shook me up pretty good, is all. We eventually got it cleared up." He spread his hands on the table. "But I hear it all turned out pretty good in the end?" He met my eyes and smirked good-naturedly. "Glad I could do my part to narrow down the suspects, anyway."

I held his gaze and nodded my head sagely, smiling. "You definitely played a pivotal part." I leaned in. "But I really am sorry."

He shrugged again, playing nonchalant. "Gives me a nice story to tell, anyway." He chuckled to himself. "Although I'll definitely be watching my back the next time I try to ask someone out."

Right. We had made a date. And I had ruined our plans with my misdirected panic. *Should I help him out?*

"You know, there's no reason we couldn't still hang out," I offered. He still wasn't really my type, but he seemed like a nice enough guy. "Wanna give it another shot?"

Levi froze a moment, just looking at me.

I leaned my chin into my hand and gazed at him with an encouraging smile. He studied my face a moment, thinking. Finally his eyes crinkled into a shy smile.

"This is kinda awkward," he said.

"Doesn't have to be." Despite my lack of immediate attraction, I wanted to at least give it a chance. I could use some normal in my life. I smirked, trying to break his shyness. "Don't tell me you're afraid of men jumping out of the shadows again. I promise you're safe this time."

"It's not that," he said, hesitating. "The thing is," he trailed off a moment, then sighed and looked up at me, brow furrowed. "I was sort of asking out . . . *Daisy*. You know, the girl with the funky black hair and the nose ring, working on a movie set?"

I looked down at my conservative graduation dress, suddenly self-conscious. He was totally right. I had looked like someone else entirely. I had been pretending. And he had no idea who I really was when he asked. *Why would he still want to go out with me?*

"I mean, I'm sure you're a cool girl and all," he mumbled, "but you're not really my type, you know?" He scrunched up his face awkwardly. "Does that make sense?"

I chuckled quietly to myself. "You wouldn't believe how much." I took a deep breath and faced him, ignoring my flushing face. "Well, I'm sorry there was no Daisy. I do hope you find her." I extended my hand. "It was nice to meet you anyway, Levi."

His sweaty hand grabbed mine for a brief moment before he flashed me a quick smile and rushed toward the door. I grinned as I watched him go, trying to hold back laughter.

Sloan was back in her seat in seconds. Clearly she had been monitoring the situation. Probably heard the whole thing from around the corner, knowing her.

"Everything's all sorted out, I see," she said, eyebrows raised. "And I like the looks of that smile. Guess you've got a hot date?"

"Nah," I replied, shrugging. "Wasn't feeling it. Not really my type."

"Indeed." Sloan flashed me a sly grin, enigmatic. "Good call. Besides, your 'type' will be here any minute." She wiggled her eyebrows mockingly.

My face flamed brighter but I refused to acknowledge her statement. I cleared my throat. "Anyway, I have news,"

I said, trying to change the subject. "I heard from my boss. Or ex-boss, rather. Since I've graduated and all." I grinned, happy to say the words out loud for the first time.

"And what did Dr. Me-Bore have to say?" Her eyes lit up. "Is she ruining Grant's *entire* life, or just his career? I can't wait to see him fry."

I sighed. "Actually, they still don't know about his evil plotting. Or any of his lies. I . . . haven't told them."

Sloan gaped. "You finished your last two weeks of internship. Why in the world didn't you say anything while you were there? You have his taped confession. It clears you completely."

"Not exactly," I sighed. "If I play that, yes, they will know he faked the first kidnapping." I cringed. "But then they will also learn that *I* was responsible for the second, *real* kidnapping. They don't know there was more than one. And it's better for me that we keep it that way."

"So he just walks away scot-free?" Sloan's face screwed up with disgust. "With everyone thinking he's some kind of *victim*?"

I shrugged. "It's mutually assured destruction. I can't say anything. He knows it and I know it. So I guess his secret's safe with me." I groaned. "The little weasel."

"Oh, no." Sloan looked up, realization hitting her. "I'm pretty sure he also walked away with his parents' ransom money. Half of it, anyway. Can we really let him get away with that?"

Disgusting. I spread my arms and touched my fingertips to my thumbs in a meditation pose, taking a dramatically deep breath. "I'm trying to focus on minding my *own* business for a while. And he is most definitely no longer my problem."

"Hmmm." Sloan's face hardened. "We'll see."

"But anyway," I said quickly, trying to redirect the beginnings of a plot forming behind her eyes. "There was something else interesting. She re-offered me a position at the clinic. Now that the truth is out—the truth they know, anyway—they have officially rescinded my rescinding. I can have my permanent job back."

"So now that you're a hero and all, they no longer want to kick you to the curb? My, that's generous of them."

"Actually, it is." I ignored her sarcasm. "I dreamed of working there after graduation. So it means a lot to me they would admit they were wrong and take me back. She knows she misjudged me."

Sloan's face genuinely lit up. "Then congratulations, really. I'm so happy you finally get exactly what you want." Her voice lowered to a mumble. "Even if they don't deserve you."

"Thanks." I met Sloan's coffee mug with my own in a cheers motion. "Their only requirement was that I give up the sleuthing business, for good. They feel all the lying and mixing with shady characters is not exactly a good look for the practice. Can't say that I blame them, really."

I raised the coffee to my lips for a sip, slowly, keeping an eye on Sloan. She said nothing immediately, but I could've sworn I saw her begin to turn white. She bit her lip, thinking hard.

A long moment went by. Finally Sloan couldn't seem to keep it in any longer. Her voice burst forth in a mix of outrage and disappointment. "You *agreed* to quit investigating?"

My reply was simple. "No."

"Oh." She stopped, confused. "So they gave in, then?"

"I didn't try to argue." I shrugged. "No point."

"I don't understand." Her brow furrowed. "Then what are you telling me?"

I sat back, secretly pleased to watch her squirm for once. "I said they *offered* me the job. I never said I took it." I took another sip, letting her stew a moment before continuing. "Look, as much as I thought I wanted to stay there, I just couldn't do it. Someday—*not today*—I know I'll want to help you with another case. With *something*. There's no doubt. And even if I could get them to agree to let me do some snooping on the side . . . they would *always* be watching. Judging, somehow. They would never accept me or what I want to do, not really. And I don't believe I would ever truly be free." I shrugged. "So I turned them down."

"Good for you." Sloan grinned. "And me, I have to admit." She picked up her coffee, finally relaxing again. "Freedom to live your life your own way. Invaluable. So now you just have to find another opening, I guess. Someplace that will mind its *own* business."

"Yes, hopefully," I said, my voice cheerful. "Although I'm honestly not sure where that is, at the last second." I lowered my gaze, confidence beginning to wane. "And the money's running out pretty quickly. Not to mention I'm about to be homeless." Panic quickly pierced my optimism. "Oh gosh, who's going to rent to me now?"

"I wouldn't worry about that." She brushed off my concerns with a wave of her hand. "So then, why don't you forget all that and just open your own practice? Trust me, working for other people is *highly* overrated."

"Ha!" I couldn't help but laugh out loud. "I just told you I'm broke. Are you crazy?"

She was undeterred. "You don't think you'd like that?"

"It's a great thought, sure." I shook my head, wistful. "That's the dream, but it would be about a hundred years before I could afford something like that, if ever. My education was pretty much all on credit, so private practice is not exactly an option for someone like me. Besides, I'm not sure I'm quite ready to call my own shots."

"I think despite all your hesitations, you are more than capable of making your own decisions. You made it just fine without your boss's intervention." She raised her eyebrows. "And mine, for a while there."

I took a deep breath, thinking back on our adventure. Nothing had gone as planned, but I had been forced to make plenty of moves without anyone looking over my shoulder. I shrugged, trying to hide my grin. "Maybe."

Sloan pursed her lips. "But just curious, how much are we talking here? What do you think it would take?"

"To open my own place?" I gazed back, suspicious. "Why?"

She shrugged. "Gotta have goals, right? And knowing is the first step."

"Okay, I'll play along. But I'm not sure exactly. All I know is it would be a lot of dough. Like, more than I've ever seen before, that's for sure. Except maybe on my student loans."

Sloan cringed. "Gotcha." She slouched back in her seat. "Well, don't worry. You'll find something. It'll just take time."

We sat quiet a moment, sipping our coffee and listening to the din of the late lunch crowd. I tried to keep my thoughts on the possibilities just ahead. Despite all the recent obstacles, I was officially an audiologist. My career was about to really begin. And a fresh start was definitely in order.

Sloan suddenly sat bolt upright, as if startled. "Oh, right. I have a graduation gift for you." She reached a hand to her bag next to her and returned with a long, thin white envelope. She slid it across the table. "Maybe this could help."

I gazed skeptically at the envelope, then at her. *What is she up to?* Her deadpan face gave no clues.

Finally curiosity got the best of me and I took it. I opened it carefully and confirmed my suspicions. A check.

But not just any check. I stared at the amount, my eyes focusing and refocusing as I tried to process. It was a normal number, followed by zeros. Only it was many, many zeros. And the check was made out to me.

Oh, the things I could do.

I nearly choked as I tried to talk again. "Yes, I think that would go a long way toward a *lot* of things." I stared down at the amount another moment, mentally saying goodbye. It was a good dream for a few glorious seconds. "But I'm certainly not taking your money, Sloan. That's insane."

"You're right. That *would* be crazy." She reached a finger to the top of the check. "But check the payer. It's not *from* me. That's your reward money."

Could it be? My heart started pounding as the numbers on the check began to come alive. Becoming real. The zeros danced before my eyes, throwing a party of possibility.

My voice croaked as I looked back up. "Reward?"

"Vinny. The top guy you found and put away—"

"We," I interrupted. "*We* put away. And it wasn't even on purpose. It was all just to get you back."

She threw her hands in the air. "They don't care about intentions. He's been wanted for years. That's why he faked his own death, he was about to go down." She grinned, her face beaming with delight. "And there happened to be a very large reward for his capture. This is your share."

I finally let out the breath I didn't realize I was holding. I moved my trembling hands off the table. "I . . . I don't know what to say."

Sloan shrugged. "*Say* you'll consider using it to set up

your own shop. Sounds like it's just what you need. And now there's *nothing* stopping you." She cocked an eyebrow. "Unless you're still scared."

I was, no doubt about it. But exhilarated as well. I took another deep breath and shook my head. I couldn't give up an opportunity like that for fear. I wouldn't.

"Excellent, it's settled then," Sloan said, her sly grin making a reappearance. "You'll be calling your own shots now. So I guess then there's *also* nothing stopping you from embracing your other passion, too." She wiggled her eyebrows, teasing. "Snooping with me."

I raised a single eyebrow back at her, but I really couldn't argue. My smile was in the way.

"On the side, of course," she continued. "After hours. Ears, then snooping." Her eyes brightened with an idea. "The sonic sleuth."

"I don't think so." I shook my head. "That's just not gonna work." I picked up the carafe and began carefully refilling our mugs, avoiding her eyes. Letting her squirm once more.

Finally I met her impatient stare. "It would have to be the sonic *sleuths*, silly." I grinned back and affected my snooty voice. "Obviously."

Sloan picked up her steaming cup and raised her chin, sticking her nose in the air. "Mmmm, true, true," she concurred, feigning pretension. "Obviously, *dahling*."

ABOUT THE AUTHOR

 **C**arrie Ann Knox is an audiologist, writer, and longtime mystery lover. After finishing a clinical doctorate and opening her own practice, she began to indulge her other passion, crafting stories that appeal to those with a thirst for adventure, technology and mystery. She also enjoys curling up with her family, two Boston Terriers Gizmo and Zelda, and a good book in their home in southeast Virginia.

***

WANT TO CONTINUE THE SONIC SLEUTHS ADVENTURES?

Sign up for updates & Connect with Carrie Ann!

K   www.CarrieAnnKnox.com

f   @CarrieAnnKnoxAuthor

🐦   @CarrieAnnAuthor

📷   @CarrieAnnBooks

Made in the USA
Middletown, DE
11 April 2023

28515632R00187